Kaytek the Wizard

JANUSZ KORCZAK

KAYTEK THE WIZARD

Illustrated by AVI KATZ

Translated by ANTONIA LLOYD-JONES

Penlight

Kaytek the Wizard
by Janusz Korczak

Translated by Antonia Lloyd-Jones
Originally published in Polish as Kajtuś Czarodziej in 1933
Illustrations by Avi Katz

This publication has been subsidized by The Polish Book Institute – the ©POLAND Translation Programme.

Typesetting by Ariel Walden. Cover design by the Virtual Paintbrush.
Cover illustration by Avi Katz.

First Edition. Printed in Israel.
Library of Congress Control Number: 2012938698

ISBN 978-098-386-850-7

Penlight Publications
527 Empire Blvd., Brooklyn, New York 11225 U.S.A.
Tel: 718-288-8300 Fax: 718-972-6307

Distributed by IPG

www.PenlightPublications.com

Author's Dedication

This is a difficult book.
I dedicate it to all the restless children,
those who find it hard to change and improve.
You have to want to change, very much and very deeply.
You need to strengthen your will power.
You need to play a useful role in life.

Life is strange and mysterious.
Life is like an extraordinary dream.
Whoever has the will power and a strong desire to serve others,
his life will be like a beautiful dream,
even if the path to his goal was difficult,
and his thoughts were restless.

Maybe one day I will write the ending to this book.

—Janusz Korczak

Kaytek the Wizard

Chapter One

KAYTEK LIKES TO MAKE BETS – KAYTEK GOES INTO STORES AND PRETENDS HE WANTS TO BUY SOMETHING, THOUGH HE DOESN'T HAVE A PENNY

"And so what?"
"So nothing."
"Don't you believe me?"
"No, I don't."
"Then make a bet."
Kaytek likes to make bets with his friends.
"If I win, you'll pay for us to go see a movie."
"All right, it's a bet."
"Let's shake on it. Don't forget: a movie on Sunday."
"But wait a minute . . ."
"See, you're chickening out already."
"No I'm not, I just want to know how it's going to work."
Kaytek repeats: "I'm going to go into ten stores. I'm going to pretend I want to buy something even though I haven't a cent in my pocket."
"You said twelve stores . . ."
"All right, twelve."
They make the bet.
So he'll go into each store, as if to buy something.
It's the final class of the day.
And here's the final bell.
They've packed their schoolbags.
Caps on their heads.
"So we're off?"
"We're off."

Down the stairs and into the schoolyard.
Then through the gate.
And they're in the street.
"I'm going to stand outside the store."
"Whatever you like. Just don't laugh in the window or they'll guess it's a joke."

The first store is a pharmacy.
Kaytek goes inside.
The pharmacist is dispensing the medicine very slowly so he won't make a mistake. Kaytek patiently waits his turn.
"What'll it be, little guy?"
"Two exercise books please, one checkered, and one blank for drawing."
"I haven't any for drawing – they all have a checkered career," jokes the pharmacist.
"Oh well, sorry."
Kaytek bows politely.
A gentleman feels sorry for him and says: "Go to the right, next door. You'll find them in there."
"Thank you."
He bows again and leaves.
He tells his pal what happened.

Next to the pharmacy there's a store selling stationery and teaching aids.
Kaytek goes in.
He looks around.
"A cream cake, please."
"What?"
"I want a chocolate cake with cream."
"Are you blind? Can't you see?"
"Sure I can see."
Kaytek stands there, looking as if he can't think what the problem is.
"Do you go to school?"
"Yes."

"Don't you know where to buy cakes?"

"They haven't taught us that yet," he replies, shrugging his shoulders, as if he doesn't know what to do.

The man loses his temper.

"What are you waiting for?"

"Nothing."

And he leaves.

"Well?" asks his pal.

"He got riled up. A grouchy kind of guy."

"He's always like that," says the pal. "I know this store. I never buy anything here."

"You should have said."

"I thought you'd do all right."

"And I did. He didn't kill me, did he?"

They walk on.

Kaytek boldly enters a third store.

It's a food store. They have cheese, butter, sugar, herring, and whitefish.

"Good day."

"Good day."

"Can I have some whale?"

"Whale?"

"Yes. Four ounces. Pickled."

"So who sent you?"

"A friend. He's waiting outside."

"Tell your friend he's a rascal, and you're a dope!"

"So you don't have any?"

"No, we have not. We'll have it later."

"When will that be?"

"When it gets warmer. That's enough now, beat it! And shut the door."

He carefully closes the door and tells his pal what happened.

"Aren't you afraid he'll recognize you in the street?"

"So what? They sell sea salmon. Herrings are from the sea too. What's wrong with asking about whales?"

"Just you wait. That's only three stores. You can still lose."
"We'll see."

The fourth is a tiny little store.
It's a shoemaker's shop.
The shoemaker doesn't have any work right now.
It's already the dinner hour and he's only sold a pair of laces and a can of shoe polish today.
He's waiting for someone to buy something.
In comes Kaytek.
"I'd like some cream cheese, please."
Either guessing it's a joke or because he's angry at being disturbed, the shoemaker reaches for his belt.
"I'll give you cheese, you clown!"
He takes a swing.
This time it hasn't quite worked – Kaytek has had to make a quick escape.

Kaytek passes by several small stores.
He stops outside the barbershop and does some thinking.
"But you keep doing the same thing," says his pal. "There's nothing smart about that."
"No, not if you don't find it amusing. But you go in and try thinking up something different yourself."
"All right then. What will you say in here?"
"Don't be in such a rush. Just wait a bit. You'll see."
Kaytek goes into the barbershop.
It's nice in there, clean and fragrant.
There are perfumes in lots of different bottles, as well as colored soaps, combs, hair oil, and powder.
The girl behind the cash register is reading a book.
"What would you like, young man?" asks the barber.
He's young and chirpy.
"Some hair oil to grow a king's moustache, please."
"Who is it for?"
"It's for me."
The girl stops reading and looks up.
The man opens his eyes wide.

"What do you want a moustache for?"

Kaytek puts on an innocent look and says:

"For a show at school."

"So who are you going to be?"

"King John Sobieski."*

"I can paint a moustache on you."

"I'd prefer a real one."

"But what'll you do after the show?"

"I'll shave it off."

They laugh.

They've fallen for it.

"Give him some Eau de Cologne."

"I don't want any," says Kaytek, flinching.

"Why not? It'll make you smell good."

"I don't want any. The boys will laugh at me. They'll say I want to get married."

"Don't you want to get married?"

"No way. What the heck for?"

The young people in the store are bored, so they're happy to joke around.

But a lady comes in to buy something and interrupts the conversation.

"Come here and I'll paint you a moustache. It'll be just like a real one," says the barber.

"But you will invite us to the show, won't you? Don't forget," says the girl.

Kaytek's friend is getting impatient.

"What took you so long?"

"They wanted to spray me with perfume."

"For free?"

"I guess so."

"Why didn't you let them?"

"Why should they waste their stuff? It's all right to have a joke, but I'm not a jerk. I don't like cheats."

"Well, sure."

---

* King John Sobieski (1629–1696) was the Polish king who defeated the Turks at the Battle of Vienna in 1683. *(All notes have been added by the translator.)*

Kaytek goes into a store selling cleaning products. He asks for flea killer.

The lady gives it to him.

"That's for fleas, bedbugs, and roaches."

"We don't have any bedbugs or roaches at home. My mom said just get it for fleas."

"Doesn't matter. That's good powder, everyone buys it. Show me how much cash you have."

Kaytek tightly clenches his empty fist.

"No . . . I have to ask . . . I have to do what my mom says."

"Well, go ask her. And tell her it costs a zloty.* Do you live far from here?"

"Just round the corner."

"If you buy things here often, you'll get candy . . . See this?"

"Yes."

She shows him a jar full of candy. Kaytek leaves.

"Thinks she's so smart – as if I'd give her a zloty right away!" he tells his pal. "She thinks I'll be tempted by candy. It's been dyed those colors for sure. How many stores is that now?"

"Six."

"Exactly half."

"OK, let's go on."

"What's your rush? Let me take a rest. My head's already spinning."

But it's nothing. Kaytek is okay. He goes into the seventh store.

It's a garden center.

"Can I get a coconut palm here?" asks Kaytek.

"We haven't any," says the lady.

"Please would you look, miss? The nature teacher told me to get one."

"So you tell the nature teacher he's got bats in his belfry."

"No he hasn't. Our teacher knows what he's talking about.

---

* The zloty is the Polish currency.

It's not nice to talk to children like that. You're not allowed to insult the teacher."

"Get out of here, you little brat! Trying to preach morals at me!"

"Sure it's about morals, because you shouldn't talk like that."

In the doorway he sticks out his tongue at her.

"Pity I didn't tell her to get stuffed and wallpapered too."

"Why are you so annoyed?"

"Because I'm getting bored with all this traipsing about."

"Tough, you made a bet."

"I know that without you telling me. I started it so I'll finish it."

Outside the store there's a stall selling soda water.

"A glass of gas, please," says Kaytek.

The lady fills a glass with water and hands it to him.

And Kaytek says: "I don't want the water, just the gas."

He makes another innocent face. But she doesn't even look.

She takes a swing and flings the water at him.

Kaytek dodges just in time.

She misses.

"Go break an arm and a leg, you thief!"

But Kaytek isn't a jerk or a thief. He could have drunk the water and run away. And he is feeling thirsty.

"You're the cheat, lady."

He's mad at her, and at himself.

And at his pal.

"Hey, listen," he asks his pal. "What does 'he's got bats in his belfry' mean?"

"It must mean he talks garbage. You could have figured that out for yourself."

They stop outside a photography studio.

"I'm coming in with you."

"As you wish."

They go inside.

"How much do half a dozen pigeons cost?"
"What sort of pigeons?" says the lady.
"Carrier pigeons, for the office. We're going to keep them on our laps."
"Do you have any money?"
"Not yet. But we're trying to get some."
"First go try, then come back."
"What are you telling them?" a man in glasses butts in. "Here we only take pictures of people. And jackasses."
They leave.

Kaytek says nothing.
Then he remembers:
"That guy called me a jackass, the other one called me a little brat. That lady threw water at me, and that other guy wanted to thrash me."
But why?
"Because I don't have any money."
If he had a zloty, everyone would be polite to him.
They'd let him in the movie theater too. And give him water – not just plain, but with juice.
"How many stores is that?"
"Eight."
"You're wrong, that's nine."
"Maybe I made a mistake."
They start counting: including the stallholder, it is nine.
"OK, off we go!"

They go into the next store together.
"Please show me a belt," says Kaytek.
He looks at it, picks it up, and tries it on. He examines the buckle. He counts the holes. He breathes on it, and gives it a rub. He makes a face.
This belt is too thin, this one's too dark, and that one's too wide.
As the young lady fetches each one, she puts the last one straight back in the box.
"She's afraid I'll steal it," thinks Kaytek.

And no surprise. All kinds of people hang around in stores. They come along because they're bored, but they don't buy anything. And they really do try to steal.

Kaytek knows that, but he's mad at being suspected.

And he thinks about his pal: "How bold he is now. He comes in with me, but he still can't open his trap."

Finally he chooses a belt – a nice one for scouts.

"How much is it?"

"Two zlotys and fifty groshys."*

"Too expensive."

"How much did you think it would be, young man?"

"My friend bought one like this for forty groshys."

"So go to the place where your friend bought his."

"All right, we will."

"What a pair of wise guys. One of you does the choosing, while the other cases the joint. I know your type."

"And I know yours."

She shouts abuse and chases them out of the store.

"What would you have done if she'd called the cops?"

"You're dumb."

Kaytek knows what he'd have done. He'd have searched his pockets, as if he'd lost his money.

But he doesn't want to talk – his pal will just have to guess.

"So tomorrow you're paying for a movie."

He stops and waits for the answer.

His friend hesitates.

"I'll ask my dad – I'm sure he'll give it to me."

"And what if he doesn't?"

"Then next Sunday for sure."

Kaytek makes a face and waves a hand in an annoyed way. He's thinking: *That's what you get if you make a bet with a squirt like him . . .*

In the tobacco store they feel sorry for Kaytek.

He stands timidly in the corner, chewing his cap.

---

* A groshy is a Polish coin – 100 groshys equals one zloty.

"What do you want, little guy?"
"I'm shy."
"Come on, tell me, I won't hurt you."
"My master told me to buy three cigarettes."
"What kind?"
"They've got an ugly name."
"Out with it boldly."
"He said he'll kill me if I don't get them."
"So say it."
"They're called 'Dogsnout'."
And he covers his eyes with his cap.
"Your master's been drinking. Let him sleep it off."
"But he's only just woken up."
"Are you from the countryside?" asks the lady.
"Yes, ma'am."
"You can tell at once – so timid. And they send a little kid like that wandering off to town."
"I'd better go now," says Kaytek.
"You must be hungry, aren't you?"
"No, I'm not."
"Here's a bread roll. Take it, you poor little orphan boy."
And whether out of regret or tiredness, Kaytek's eyes fill with tears.
"Don't be shy, take it."
"No, I can't."
He hightails it out of there in a hurry.
"Why are you crying?"
"Oh . . . there's a fly in my eye or something."

Finally they reach the last store, number twelve. It's a laundry.
He doesn't want to go in because he prefers classier stores. But his pal insists.
"Go on in. Don't be afraid. It's the last one."
He isn't afraid. And he isn't being cautious.

"Excuse me, can you press a cat for me?"
"A cat?" says the young lady in amazement.

"Yes. A dead one. With a tail."

But he hasn't noticed the young lady's fiancé sitting by the door, who up and grabs him by the scruff of the neck.

"Just you wait. We'll press you. Pass me a hot iron, Frania."

He's strong. He has a firm grip. He lays Kaytek across the ironing board.

"Is this what you want? I'll give you a stuffed cat all right!"

Kaytek doesn't try to break free, he just begs the man: "Please let me go."

Frania, the girl, takes pity on him.

"Let him go, he's just stupid."

"He's not stupid, he's a con artist – he's just acting dumb."

"And I say you're wrong. He looks like a good kid."

"I can explain," groans Kaytek.

"All right, so what's with the dead cat?"

Kaytek sees the door is open.

Luckily he gave his schoolbag to his pal – that makes it easier to escape.

"Just you wait! We'll meet again," the man shouts after him. "I'll recognize you. You'll get what's coming to you."

His friend catches up with him.

"Why did you run off like that?"

"It was pretty clear I had to."

"Aren't you going to tell me what happened?"

"You never said I had to tell you. Give me my schoolbag. And go to the movie by yourself. Just be glad you didn't come in there with me – you'd have been thrashed, you dope!"

They go off separately, feeling riled up. It's not Kaytek's first fight.

And not his first bet. Because Kaytek loves to make bets.

One time at school they were talking about a soccer game.

What's better, a game of soccer or a movie? Swimming or boating? Riding a bike or skating?

Kaytek says grown-up movies always end with kissing.

"Come on, I'll show you how they kiss," says one of the boys.

"Kissing a boy isn't hard – you have to kiss a young lady," says Kaytek.

"What a wise guy – just you try and do that."

"You think I won't? All right – I bet you an ice cream."

"OK, shake on it."

So along comes the final lesson.

And the final bell. They pack up their books.

Here's the schoolyard, and the gate, and the street.

"You guys follow me," Kaytek tells the other two.

And he goes off in front.

But now he's sorry he made the bet.

He doesn't want to pick on a little girl. It'd be a shame to do that because he'll frighten her. Anyway, he said "young lady," and that means a big one.

How's he going to do it? He walks along, looking around.

He walks along, looks, thinks, looks, and waits.

"Not that one. Or that one."

Never mind the ice cream, it's just that it's embarrassing to lose. He has to stick to his guns.

Until finally, there they are.

Two of them. Schoolgirls. And they're older than he is. They're laughing and chatting. They're not in a hurry. One of them calls the other one Zofia.

She says: "Listen, Zofia, next time you come over . . ."

Kaytek doesn't hear more than that. But now he has a plan.

He signals to tell the boys he's about to start. He crosses to the other side, gets ahead of the girls, turns around and walks straight toward them.

He lets his head droop, as if he's deep in thought.

Just as he's passing them, suddenly he stops and looks at them.

"Oh! Zofia! When did you get here?"

She stops and stares at him in amazement.

And hop! he throws his arms around her neck and smack! he kisses her.

Silly girl – she even leans forward. That's how superbly it worked.

Only then does she wake up.

"Who the heck are you?"
"Me? I'm Kaytek."
"Kaytek who?"
"Kaytek no one, just a boy."
He licks his lips, as if the kiss was tasty.
And runs for it.
The girls stare in surprise, until finally they guess what's going on.
"Just you wait, you little scamp!"
"What an impudent boy!"
"How did he know my name?"
That time Kaytek won with honors.
He won with honors and got twenty groshys.
They shared the ice cream equally.
The third boy got some too, even though he didn't deserve it.

So that's what Kaytek is like.
Impatient. Bold. Head full of ideas.
He was like that before he ever went to school.
He was like that before he became a wizard.

Chapter Two

COMPLAINTS ABOUT KAYTEK – SCARS – ANTEK OR KAYTEK? – HE SMOKES CIGARETTES – A MOUSE BY THE STOVE

There are endless complaints about Kaytek.

"What a bothersome boy," his mother sighs.

"I'd never hit him, but if I lose my patience . . ." threatens his father.

"He has a kind look in his eyes," his grandma smiles.

"He has a good head," says his father.

"He's curious about everything," adds his mom.

"He takes after his grandpa," his grandma smiles.

But the complaints keep coming in.

The building watchman says he threw a herring out the window onto the landlord's head.

"Did you do that?"

"It's not true."

Firstly, it wasn't a herring, just a herring's tail.

Secondly, it wasn't the landlord's head, it was his hat.

Thirdly, it wasn't out the window, it was through the stair rail.

Fourthly, it wasn't Kaytek, it was another boy.

And on top of that he missed – the klutz.

The watchman says Kaytek put out the lights in all the stairwells.

"That's not true. Not in all of them, just in one hallway. How does he know it was me? What if it was someone else? What if a girl did it, not a boy? Maybe it was a firefighter? There are firemen in Warsaw, after all."

The watchman says Kaytek rings the doorbell and runs away.

"I do, yes, but at other gates. Never at ours. I once rang it, a long time ago."

"Why do you do that?"

"Just because."

Because he wants to know if the bell is working. Sometimes because he's bored. Sometimes because he's annoyed that he has to go to school, while the stupid bell just sits there like a prince and doesn't have to do anything.

The watchman says: "He pried out a rock and dented the drainpipe."

That is a total lie.

Kaytek even knows who did that.

"I nailed together a sled, but I did it with a hammer, not a rock. And I leaned the board against the store cupboard, not the drainpipe."

He has a witness. He can go fetch the boy who lent him the hammer and held the board.

Yet again they come and complain.

"He broke a window. He threw a stone."

"I saw him running away. He threw it at a dog."

"It wasn't a dog, it was a cat! It wasn't a stone, it was a piece of brick! A completely different boy broke the window." They had just run away together.

Kaytek knows who did it, but he won't tell.

"Why can't that lady look properly?"

And even so, she still comes and complains, and says he has to pay for the window!

It looks as if no one else ever does anything bad, as if it's only Kaytek who does all those things.

But there are worse kids than him!

The people say: "If he didn't do it, it was one of his pals."

So what? Is he responsible for all of them, or just for himself?

One time, when he was little, before he went to school, he went for a swim in the river, leaving his clothes on the sand.

He had his swim, and then he got out of the water. And in the distance he saw some rascals running away.

They'd taken everything: pants, shoes, cap, even his shirt.

A man took pity on him, wrapped him in his jacket, and took him home.

And there was quite a fuss.

So little boys can be thieves too.

But Kaytek never touches other people's stuff. He can't stand thieves.

He's just had lots of adventures.

When Helenka was alive, they used to jump down the stairs; from one step up, from two, from three, from four, and from five.

He wanted to prove he could jump without holding the banister.

And he did it – he jumped from five steps up. He'd have been fine, but he was wearing new shoes . . . with slippery soles . . .

He had to stay in bed for a long time after that.

Now the hair in that spot on his head never grows.

Because of the scar.

Kaytek has another scar on his leg where the butcher's dog bit him.

Because the boys said no one could pet that dog.

"He's a bad dog."

"I'll try, I'll be really careful. It might work."

He had tried being really careful. And it hadn't worked.

He once made a bet he could dash across the road in front of a tramcar.

"You might trip. Better skip it."

"Why should I trip?"

"You won't make it."

"All right then, I bet you."

But the bet never happened. The tram driver slammed on the brakes and stopped in time, and Kaytek was escorted home by a policeman.

He was forbidden to go outside for a whole week.

Once he was left alone in the apartment.

He wanted to surprise everyone by chopping firewood with an ax.

That didn't work either.

That was how Kaytek got his third scar, on a finger on his left hand.

But it could have been much worse. Next time he was left at home, he tried to light the gas-lamp in front of the holy icon,* but the curtain caught fire. Luckily, just then Grandma came home and put out the fire.

Kaytek just has that sort of nature – he has to see and know, and then try for himself.

Mom told him a fairy tale about Ali Baba.

Ali Baba was the leader of the thieves.

He was an Arabian bandit. There were forty of them. Ali Baba was the chief – the ringleader.

The thieves had an underground cave in the forest. They called their cave Sesame.

That was where they hid the treasure they had stolen. There were sacks full of ducats and gold and precious jewels and diamonds.

There was a magic doorway into the cave.

If you said: "Open, Sesame," the door opened by itself.

The fairy tale was very interesting.

So that night Kaytek was lying in bed, thinking about hidden treasure.

And then he asked his dad: "Is there really treasure?"

Not in a fairy tale, but for real.

Because when Mom and Grandma don't explain things properly, he checks with his dad.

"Yes, there is," said his dad. "There were wars fought on our lands. The enemy went around burning and robbing the houses,

---

* Some Polish homes used to have holy pictures with a light or a candle burning in front of them.

so people buried anything valuable. Not so long ago it said in the newspaper they'd found a pot full of coins in a field."

His father said the government minister prints paper money because gold is too heavy to carry, so gold bars are kept hidden in cellars.

Kaytek didn't understand this very well, because it was too hard. Or maybe he was sleepy at the time.

Well, I had better give it a try, he thought.

All right. So that day he went into the cellar of the apartment building with Grandma to fetch some coal.

You have to go downstairs, under the ground. And there's a door and a long corridor. And there are various small doors, each leading into a separate cellar.

Grandma lights a candle. Along they go, and there in the corner of the corridor stands a barrel.

Kaytek hides behind the barrel.

Grandma has put some coal in the bucket and she's leaving. But Kaytek has vanished.

"Antek! Antek!" calls Grandma.

Where has the boy got to?

But he's crouched down behind the barrel, waiting quietly.

Grandma thinks he must have gone outside already. So she padlocks the cellar shut.

Kaytek is left in the dark corridor. But he's not afraid. He wonders if he'll be strong enough to lift a heavy gold bar.

He looks in the barrel – it's empty.

He feels his way to the first door and says: "Open, Sesame!"

Nothing happens. He feels his way to the second door and says: "Open, Sesame!"

Again nothing happens.

He walks up and down. It's dark in there.

He wanders about, searching. He doesn't even know where he is any more. He just blunders about in the dark, in silence.

"Open, Sesame!"

But then he starts to cry. Suddenly he's feeling scared.

Because what if there are ghosts or rats in there?

He was little then. It was before he went to school.

He shouted, and banged his hand against the wall.

He thought he'd never get out of there.

"Momma, Grandma!"

And he might really have sat there for a long time, because Grandma wasn't looking for him. It wasn't exactly the first time Kaytek had been out in the street or at a neighbor's house.

He was starting to lose his voice.

"Grandma, Dad, Momma!"

But the people on the stairs couldn't hear him for the clatter of their shoes. And Kaytek wasn't standing by the door, but at the far end, somewhere near the barrel.

Then along comes the mailman. He stops in the hallway and sorts the letters in his bag. And he hears something. He listens. What's that? Someone's shut in the cellar.

Probably a kid.

And he calls out.

"Why didn't you respond when Grandma called you?" they asked afterward. "Why did you creep behind the barrel?"

He didn't answer, not because he was afraid of being punished, he just didn't want to. He had suffered enough already. But they were still laughing at him.

"Oh, Antek, Antek, always up to something!"

Kaytek's real name is Antek. That's what they call him at home.

He became Kaytek out in the yard with the boys.

Because one day he was standing by the gate smoking a cigarette.

He drags on it and puffs, drags and puffs.

And he's trying to make lots of smoke. Because he paid five groshys for the cigarette, so he wants it to look neat.

He could have bought chocolate, but a cigarette is more interesting.

And along the street comes a soldier.

He stops, looks and laughs.

"Well I never!" he says. "Look at little Kaytek puffing away like a steam train!"*

---

* See Translator's Afterword for more about Kaytek's name.

"So?"

Antek was embarrassed and offended.

And at once the boys were saying: "Kaytek! Kaytek!"

They were annoyed because he wouldn't let them have a drag. They were afraid to smoke themselves, but they envied him.

And so that's how it stayed: not Antek, but Kaytek.

That's how it is with nicknames. If you're not annoyed, they usually forget about it and stop. But if you get riled, they use it all the more. Because they love to tease.

At first Kaytek fought back – he wasn't going to let them change his name. But how can one guy alone beat everyone else?

What's more there were two Anteks in the yard, so it was more convenient for one of them to be Kaytek. They'd know who was being called. Eventually he got used to it, but not entirely. And on the whole he didn't like his playmates much anyway.

Kaytek is in his third year at school now, but he's never had a good friend for long. There are very few really decent ones. Because they just pretend to be. They're toadies.

And that's because they're afraid. They're quiet out of fear, because at home they get shouted at or beaten. That type tells the most lies.

Kaytek has learned to fib and pretend too. You can't admit to knowing too much. If the grown-ups understood better, things would be different.

Kaytek says: "I don't know what they want from me."

Although he knows perfectly well.

He says: "All lies, from beginning to end."

Although there is some truth in it.

They say: "He hit the boy so hard he couldn't move afterward."

"How come he couldn't move? I didn't kill him, did I?"

"He almost broke his arm."

So you're supposed to answer not just for what you really did, but also for what could have happened.

Of course, there are some serious boys, but they're stuck on themselves.

They're either the silent type, or the touchy kind.
At once they say:
"Lay off."
"Stop that."
"Get lost."

Kaytek's in the third grade at school.
But there are non-stop complaints here too.
When he joined the first grade, the teacher praised him.
"You can read already. Who taught you?" she asked.
"I taught myself."
"All by yourself?"
"It's not hard at all."
He sat in the front row.
And then it began:
"Sit up straight. Don't fidget. Don't talk."
And again:
"Don't fidget. Sit quietly. Don't play with your pencil. Pay attention."
The start of the class is easy. But then it gets harder and harder.
When will the bell finally go?
The teacher tells them something interesting. She gets awfully riled if they interrupt. She starts to get so mad you don't want to listen any more.
At home you're allowed to lean against the table while Dad is telling a story, you're allowed to lean against the bed while Mom is telling a fairy tale, and lean against a chest while Grandma is reminiscing about the past.
At home you're allowed to bend and stretch, and ask a question if you don't understand.
But at school if you want to say something you have to put two fingers in the air and wait.
Well, all right. There are lots of kids in the class and the teacher can't talk to you separately because the others will start to make a noise. And that's a terrible drag.
"Well, Antek?" asks his father. "How did you get on at school today?"

"Humph."
"What's up at school?"
"Nothing."
He doesn't even like talking about school much.

The teacher moved him to the fourth row by the window.
But you're not allowed to look out of the window.
In the front row his neighbor was quiet, but the kid in the fourth row keeps pestering him, tugging the back of his ear. It doesn't hurt, but what's his game?
Kaytek tries telling him to stop, and at once the teacher says: "Don't turn around."
"What if I have to?"
"Go stand in the corner."
"But you don't know the facts," mutters Kaytek.
"Leave the room."
Until finally they send for his father.

"What have you been up to?"
"I had a fight with a boy. He started spreading it around that I'm called Kaytek."
"Because it's true – that's what they call you."
"So what if it's true? The yard at home is one thing, school's quite another."
"You should have explained that to him."
"And how. Sure he'll listen next time."
"You mustn't fight."
"I know."
"Oh, Antek, you're making a bad start. Oh, Antek, I'm going to lose my patience . . ."

At the school office the teacher does a lot of complaining.
"He doesn't do as he's told. He behaves badly to his classmates. He asks for trouble. He bad-mouths the others."
His father is worried.
"You have to make an effort."
He does, but what of it?
It's all right for a few days, but then there's another fuss.

Someone sits in front of Kaytek and jogs him with their elbow; not him, but his exercise book.

"Get your arm off," says Kaytek.

"Why should I? It's not illegal," says the kid.

"Just you wait – I'll get you after the bell."

"Gee, I'm so afraid."

Kaytek just pushes him a little, but the boy knocks his elbow against the inkwell and spills the ink. And lies about it too.

But the teacher doesn't believe Kaytek.

The other guy gets away with it, but Kaytek doesn't.

Kaytek does make an effort.

All for nothing.

If he's quiet in class, he'll make trouble in the recess.

Until eventually his anger gets the better of him.

And then it's not worth making an effort any more.

And he can't always restrain himself when something tempts him or a joke occurs to him.

So one time Kaytek got bored during arithmetic.

Even the teacher was looking at his watch and waiting for the bell.

What can I do to make the lesson end sooner? thought Kaytek.

He jumps up on the bench.

"Eeek, sir, there's a mouse! In the hole by the stove.* You can still see its tail."

The teacher falls for it.

"You should be ashamed. A big boy like you, afraid of mice."

The whole class starts laughing. Just to suck up to the teacher.

"He's afraid of mice. He's yellow!"

Kaytek gets down from the bench and says:

"Phooey! There wasn't a mouse, I was just kidding."

"There was one too," they say.

"Then you look for it, in the hole by the stove."

They take a look; there really isn't one.

He thought the teacher was sad, so he was just trying to cheer him up.

* Buildings used to be heated by large stoves, even in classrooms.

But the teacher was annoyed.

At once he started writing a note to Kaytek's father.

Only the bell saved him.

They say he's a clown.

It's not true.

He reads a lot, and he does some serious thinking, and asks smart questions in class. But his classmates don't respect him for that at all, only for the nonsense.

Chapter Three

THE WORLD IS STRANGE AND MYSTERIOUS – A MAGICAL CLOCK – KAYTEK TAUGHT HIMSELF TO READ

Kaytek likes anything fun.

He likes things that are hard.

But most of all he likes things that are mysterious.

The first mysterious fairy tale his mom told him was about Little Red Riding Hood.

From this fairy tale he found out there are wolves. Wild animals.

He saw a wolf in a picture. It looked like a dog.

After that he saw a wolf in an iron cage.

He wanted to put his hand between the bars; he wanted to try. But his mom wouldn't let him.

Another fairy tale was about Sleeping Beauty.

This time he found out there are fairy godmothers.

The third one was about Cinderella.

The fairy godmother touched Cinderella with her wand and the poor little orphan girl changed into a princess.

Later on, Kaytek saw a real magician's wand.

It was at a show in the park.

The man struck the wand against some water, and the water changed into wine.

Then the man cut up a handkerchief and put the pieces in a hat. He tapped the hat with his wand and said: "Hocus pocus."

And the handkerchief was whole again.

Kaytek's dad says those are magic tricks.

"But how's it done?"

Kaytek is very curious to know.

"Mom, tell me a fairy tale," he asks.

It's the story of Puss in Boots.

In the one he heard earlier a wolf talks to Red Riding Hood, and in this one a cat talks to the miller's son.

"Can you really talk to a cat?"

Mom says it's just a fairy tale.

Grandma says hermits talk to animals.

Dad says there are talking birds. They're called parrots. And Grandpa used to have a talking magpie.

Then Kaytek heard a parrot speaking human phrases.

Kaytek thought golden fish were only in fairy tales, but all of a sudden he saw some in a store display.

Truth and fiction are all mixed up in fairytales.

So maybe there really is a magic lamp that can summon up a genie?

Kaytek wants to have a lamp like the one Aladdin had.

There are so many different wonders in the world.

The grown-ups know, but they refuse to explain.

Grandma says Helenka appeared to her after her death. But Dad doesn't believe in ghosts.

Grandma says you can read a person's future in their hand.

"When I was a young girl, a Gypsy told me everything that would happen."

"Gypsies tell lies," says Dad. "They fool people."

Kaytek wants to know what's going to happen. But his father doesn't like Kaytek to be told mysterious things because he has trouble falling asleep, and when at last he does, he has bad dreams and talks in his sleep.

That's strange.

How can you sleep and talk all at once?

And there are even people who actually walk in their sleep.

They actually walk!

That sort of person gets out of bed on a moonlit night, goes out the window and onto the roof. He has his eyes closed, but he can see, and he doesn't fall off the roof.

Kaytek has forgotten what the strange name for them is.

The world is strange and mysterious.

Why is that? His father was once a little boy, Grandma used to play with dolls, and Mom had a grandmother too.

Isn't it strange that Kaytek will grow up and be a dad as well?
It's hard to understand it all. One thing already happened, but long ago. Another thing has yet to happen in the future. And a third thing's going to come about one day, but far, far from now.
There are faraway countries where the people are black. The children are black, and so is the teacher at school.
Kaytek once saw a black man in the street, but he wasn't a cannibal.*

Grandma says there are eyes that can cast spells; if you cast the evil eye at someone, they fall ill.
Dad says that's not true. But Kaytek once saw a man who had a glass eye, a real eye made of glass.
Dad says there aren't any wizards, but there are Indian fakirs. You can bury them in the ground and they go on living. Dad read about the fakirs in a newspaper.
Sometimes even the newspaper tells lies.
If only Kaytek could know everything entirely for sure.

He thinks the world was more interesting in the past.
Where there are now houses and Warsaw, there used to be forests and marshes, and bears.
Robbers used to hide in the forests.
There were knights.
There were kings wearing crowns.
Six white horses pulled the king's golden coach.
There was something to look at.
The Tatars were always invading. They took people prisoner. They kidnapped children and sold them to the Turks as slaves.
There were magic clocks.

At Grandma's house there was a magic clock. It was big and

* See Translator's Afterword.

it hung above a bureau. Grandma's parents had that clock. They didn't live in Warsaw.

"Tell me about the clock, Grandma," asks Kaytek.

"Your father gets mad if I frighten you, and then you have bad dreams."

"Just this one time, please, Grandma. I know it already anyway. And I'm not scared, am I?"

"All right then, the clock was old, very old."

"It was gold," Kaytek prompted her.

"No, not gold, but gilded. Made of wood. And gilded. It was carved."

"And there was a hand on the clock, and under the hand there was a key," says Kaytek.

"Yes, that's right. The clock face with the numbers was below, and the hand and the key were above them."

"And the clock didn't work," says Kaytek.

"It didn't work and it didn't chime. No clockmaker knew how to repair it. It just hung on the wall, biding its time."

Kaytek moves up closer.

"Was it big?"

"As big as a picture. It hung above the bureau."

"And was the hand big?"

"As big as yours."

"So go on," says Kaytek impatiently.

"Well, so there hangs the clock, it doesn't go and it doesn't chime. But whenever some misfortune was going to happen in the family, the hand took hold of the key and the clock chimed, striking the hour."

"What time? Twelve o'clock?"

"No, I can't remember. I was young then, and your mom was little. She didn't have any teeth yet."

"And then what?"

"One time the hand took hold of the key and the clock struck the hour of Grandpa's death. One time it chimed just before a fire. And the last time, I saw it and heard it myself."

"Did it ring loud?"

"Just normally, like any clock."

"And did the hand hold the key for a long time?"

"What can I tell you? I can't remember."

"Did the fingers move?"

"I don't know, Antek."

Kaytek has forgotten a lot of things too – he can't remember when he himself was little.

"Grandma, please tell me how the robbers poisoned King."

"I've already told you so many times before. We had two dogs. King was a young dog, and Fido was old and wise."

"He was a good watchdog," adds Kaytek.

"He was a wise and faithful dog."

"And the robbers threw them some poisoned sausage," prompts Kaytek.

"That's right. But Fido knew at once. He sniffed the sausage, barked, and didn't move."

"Oh, Grandma. What about the doctor? That's a funny story."

"It is and it isn't. Your mother was sick. So Grandpa went to fetch the doctor."

"Fido was on his chain."

"That's right. He was a strong dog. He could have mauled a stranger."

"But he broke free of his chain."

"He did, and he jumped up at the doctor."

"Who opened his umbrella."

"Yes. He leaped onto the trash can and opened his umbrella."

"And Fido ran for it."

"Wait, don't be in such a hurry. So Fido tucked in his tail and jumped down. Then he stood there like an idiot whining for help."

"He must have thought the umbrella would start firing?"

"Who knows what a dog thinks."

Kaytek yawns. He's not sleepy, but he is getting tired.

"It was funny," says Grandma, "how that great big dog ate out of a wooden tub with a little kitten."

"With Kitty?"

"No, Kitty was before that."

"So please tell me the story, Grandma."

"All right then. We put some food into the tub for the dog, and the kitten was there in a flash. She wasn't hungry, she just came to tease. And Fido sat waiting for her to take what she wanted. But then he started getting impatient. He was annoyed and tried to push her away with his paw. And then she spat at him. How we laughed!"

Grandma is laughing now, although it all happened long ago.

Kaytek is laughing too, although he didn't see it happen.

"Tell me about the rats, Grandma."

"But then I'll stop."

"All right," Kaytek agrees.

"Well then, our cottage was old, but it was clean. There were no vermin, no mice. But we had a nasty neighbor. Our cottage was here, the fence was here, and his old shack was right next to it."

"He was a drunk," says Kaytek.

"A drunk and a troublemaker."

"He beat his wife."

"He did. So your grandpa and I were sitting there together. Grandpa was reading a book, and I was sewing. We were sitting on the small porch outside the house. It was like a little veranda."

"With a wild vine growing on it."

"That's right. Your momma and uncle were already asleep. In those days children went to bed earlier. So there we sat, each of us doing our own thing. It was quiet. When suddenly there was a shout: 'Help, someone, help!' Grandpa didn't do anything yet, he just listened. But then that man's wife, the neighbor's wife, shouted: 'Help! He's going to kill my child!'"

"And Grandpa jumped up."

"In a flash, Antek. Your Grandpa was made of strong stuff. He was good, but also fair."

"He grabbed a stick."

"A big stick, and jumped over the fence."

"And whacked the drunk on the head."

"What else could he do? He had to defend the child, didn't he?"

"The drunk got revenge," remembers Kaytek.

"He did indeed. He knew some secret way of getting the rats to invade our house. They didn't do much harm because Grandpa had his own special ways too. Until there was only one left – a great big monster of a rat."

"Was it as big as a cat?"

"Not quite. But it was impossible to catch, that rat."

It must have been enchanted, thinks Kaytek, but he doesn't say anything.

"Grandpa lured the rat into the kitchen. It was in there. Good. He shut all the doors and looked for it. It was gone. He looked here, there, and everywhere, but it had simply vanished."

"It was hiding under the step."

"No, it wasn't. You didn't listen carefully. There was a step from the kitchen into the hall, and Grandpa whacked the step with an ax, but the rat wasn't there. Come on, Antek, try to remember."

"I know. It was hiding in the pocket of your apron."

"No, that's not it either. The apron was hanging in the corner. But the rat was clinging on to it by its teeth. It had jumped up and was hanging by the teeth – it had bitten into the cloth. That's enough now."

"Grandma, tell me about the rainwater barrel."

"What's so interesting about that? The time I found a toad in there?"

"And what about the fire, Grandma?"

"No, no. It's late. Your father will be angry!"

"Then tell me about the hens who laid eggs in the woodshed."

"No. You're sleepy. You're yawning."

"I don't feel like sleeping at all."

But Kaytek can see Grandma doesn't want to go on, so he gets changed for bed.

Grandma told the most stories when Mom was in the hospital.

Kaytek is lying in bed.

His eyes are closed.

He's thinking: "What does it mean, Grandpa was made of strong stuff? Why does Grandma say you can't know what a dog thinks? Why was it a wild vine? Grandma said a wild vine has ordinary leaves, not poisonous ones, not even like a nettle, so what's wild about it?"

It's unpleasant to have to keep asking them to explain. Sometimes they're willing to tell him, sometimes they're not. And if they're not, they twist and tangle it all so you can't understand. It's maddening.

"I'll have to learn to read. Then I can find things out for myself from books. Why wait till I start going to school?"

Everything's written in books. Anyone who can read knows things. And can do everything himself. Doctors know how to cure illnesses from the things they read in books. That's what Dad says.

If Kaytek knew how to read, Mom would be well.

He'd only have to seek out a good remedy in a book.

Kaytek already knows four letters. He can write a one and a four.

"I'll give it a try!"

When Kaytek was small, his dad gave him a newspaper.

"Here you are, read that."

Kaytek looks at the paper and speaks gibberish, which makes saliva fill his mouth: "Etly, fetly, metly."

He doesn't understand what "to read" means.

And everyone's laughing.

Or he makes marks on a piece of paper with a pencil, and thinks he's writing.

Now he knows it was all a joke.

"Grandma!"

"Aren't you asleep yet?"

He jumps out of bed and fetches a book – it's Tom Thumb.

He looks. T-O-M. Three symbols. He counts them: three. There's an O in the middle. A circle is a letter. So where's Tom? How do you get Tom?

"Grandma, is it true there's a letter O in the middle of Tom?"

"Yes, that's right. Now go to sleep or your father will be angry."

Kaytek woke up early.

And went straight outside.

He asks a boy who goes to school: "Show me some letters."

"What do you want them for? You won't understand anyway."

Kaytek promises him a reward – a pineapple candy.

"So pay attention. Look."

He looks hard. He pays attention.

But he can't understand.

And the boy's laughing.

"You're too small. Too dumb."

Kaytek feels embarrassed.

He didn't ask any more boys after that. Because girls are more patient.

They explained a little bit.

And his dad did the rest.

"You see. Like that it's CAT, that's CAP, and that'll be CAN."

At last he knows.

He guessed for himself why you have TAP and TOP, why BAT and BUT.

In the street he read: BAR.

Then he read: MILK – EGGS – BEER. BARBER.

He reads the store signs, street names, tram tickets, and cigarette packets.

One time it's easy so he sings and whistles to himself. Another time he's riled because he can't do it.

"I'll buy a school book. Why should I keep having to ask?"

So he started saving money. He saved thirty groshys and lost it because he had a hole in his pocket.

Until his father took pity on him and bought him the book.

"Here you are. Now read. Maybe you won't go racing around the yard anymore."

His father guessed right. Kaytek sits and reads.

"He'll soon get bored."

His father guessed wrong. Kaytek doesn't get bored.

He wakes up in the morning and he's straight into his book. He goes to bed with the book under his pillow.

But best of all he likes reading by the River Vistula.*

He reads and reads until he gets tired and his eyes ache, then he looks at the water, at a cloud, at the boats. He has a rest, and then it's easy again.

* The River Vistula is the main river that runs through Warsaw, Poland's capital city.

He already kind of knows and can do it – here you read two letters together like a single one.

There are symbols you don't read at all.

There are big and little letters, handwritten and printed.

But suddenly alongside the easy phrases there's a tricky one.

Or a word written differently from how it's said.

Because you say ENUFF, but you write ENOUGH. Why?

Sometimes a word looks familiar, but you have to guess what it means.

There are also new words in books which Kaytek has never heard before.

Because grown-ups use harder words when they talk to each other.

Kaytek is already trying to read the titles at the movies.

Buuuut . . . it's too much all at once.

Mom came home from the hospital and was amazed.

"Antek can read. Well, well, what a surprise."

"The boy's got character," his father praised him.

"He's going to do well in life," said Grandma.

"Keep learning, son, so no one will mess with you."

His father didn't say: "Keep learning, Antek."

He didn't say Antek or Kaytek. He said: son.

That's fine, that's grand.

Son. Three letters. Ssss – o – nnn.

Now at school Kaytek doesn't just read fairy tales, but fat books with no pictures too.

He reads a lot. He has even forgotten he ever found reading difficult.

Chapter Four

A DRAGON, A WATER SPRITE, AND A MERMAID – OCCULT SCIENCE – KAYTEK WANTS TO BE A WIZARD – THIRTEEN SPELLS AT SCHOOL

Kaytek reads.

He reads about wars.

About fires.

He reads about countries and people. About animals and about the stars. And about what happens to other people in the world.

And so . . .

It looks as if everything's fine.

As if he's getting to know more and more. As if he's understanding better and better. He almost understands them by now. But not the way he wants to – not everything perfectly. There's always some mystery.

Until he had some luck. One day there was a lady substituting for the teacher who was sick. The lady was fun. She was happy to give answers. You could ask her precise questions.

Kaytek had been waiting ages for a lesson like this.

Somehow it began with the dragon on Wawel Hill, in the famous legend about Krakus,* the prince who killed it.

"Were there really dragons, or not? How many heads did they have? Did they belch fire? Were there really water sprites and mermaids?"

"There were winged creatures," explains the lady. "Antedilu-

* Wawel Hill is a real place in the Polish city of Krakow. Krakus was the legendary founder of the city.

vian birds. And there were mammoths. There are archeological excavations to prove it."

"What about a king?" asks Kaytek. "And a page, and a royal squire? Princes and knights? Did the jester have to be a hunchback? Why were there astrologers and alchemists, and Egyptian dream books?"

The lady gives an answer about predictions and fortune tellers.

"Astrologers read the future from the stars. Alchemists made gold, and medicines to cure old age and all diseases."

Kaytek hears her talk about things like: The philosopher's stone. Perpetual motion. Occult science.*

He's been waiting ages for a lesson like this.

"And what about magicians, please miss? And what's a hypnotist? What about ghosts? Do Gypsies really steal children and sell them to the circus?"

"Wait a minute, not all at once."

One of the children laughs, as if these are childish questions. But the teacher tells him off sharply and goes on: "So it was, so it is, so it may yet be. There are some things we know, and other things we don't know. But you shouldn't laugh."

After that, it's as if she's only talking to Kaytek. She explains so understandingly.

Did the strongmen Samson and Hercules really live? And Madey, the robber chief? And Master Twardowski, the legendary Polish nobleman? And Boruta the devil?** What's the difference between a wizard and a sorcerer?

Suddenly . . .

The wretched bell goes. The puppies are leaping to their feet. The bell makes a shrill insistent noise.

"We don't want a recess!" cries Kaytek. "Please go on talking."

The teacher smiles.

---

* The philosopher's stone was the legendary substance that alchemists tried to develop in order to turn base matter into gold, and also to produce an elixir of life. Perpetual motion describes a hypothetical mechanism that could go on working forever. Occult science is the mysterious science of magic and the supernatural.

** Madey the robber chief, Master Twardowski, and Boruta the devil are all characters from Polish folklore.

"Why are you so interested?"
"Because he's Kaytek, miss, and he smokes like a chimney."
"Because he wants to be a wizard."

Kaytek jumps up.
He leaps toward the kid. He aims. There's going to be a fuss.
No!
The teacher frowns. She has a strange look in her eyes.
And she just says: "Antek, please! Stop it! Out of the classroom, all of you."
Kaytek goes red and grits his teeth. He stops and waits.
The two of them are left behind.
"Thank you, Antek," says the teacher.
"Why do they tease me? Why did they keep interrupting?"
"Think about it. You're an intelligent person."
He was amazed that she said: "person."
Then she says: "You wanted to go on listening after the bell, and they didn't. They had the right not to want to. And don't you ever interrupt? You don't have to be so impulsive."
The teacher called him: "impulsive," not rude. Grandpa was impulsive too.
Then the teacher leaves, and Kaytek is alone in the classroom.
That's it! Now he knows. That boy was right!
Now he knows entirely for sure.
He wants to be a wizard!
Not a royal page, not a knight, not a circus performer, and not a cowboy. Not a magician, who does tricks. Or Ali Baba, or a detective.
But a sorcerer.
Now he knows definitely. And he sensed it ages ago.
Even when he was small, in the days when Mom used to read him fairy tales, when Dad went on about ancient history, and Grandma told him about the wild vine, the rats, and the old clock.
He doesn't even want to be a strongman like Hercules, or a movie star. Or a boxer, or a pilot.
He wants to, and has to, know every single spell.

He wants to be powerful . . .

That boy was right . . .

The teacher says there are no spells or charms, but it's not true. There have to be. There are. The teacher just doesn't know them. Because school books are one thing, and occult science is quite another.

The great Polish poet Mickiewicz wrote about Master Twardowski, who knew magic. And the kings believed in him. So it must be true.

An astrologer must have read the stars the same way Kaytek can read letters in books. There has to be an elixir to cure all diseases, it's just that the regular doctors don't know about it.

Kaytek was wrong when he thought he'd find everything out at school and that he'd discover it all by reading books.

No. He'll have to do it all by himself.

It's going to be hard. But never mind.

He just has to make a start. Once he gets started, he'll finish.

Yes!

He wants a Cap of Invisibility and a pair of seven-league boots. And a magic carpet, and a bag, and a lamp, and a hen that lays golden eggs. Not regular ones, golden ones. He'll be able to cast spells on whomever he wants, anyone who's disobedient. He'll be the most powerful ruler of all, so they'll have to obey him.

He must practice his magic gaze. Somehow he'll discover his first spell – just one magic phrase, in Indian or Greek.

He has made a decision. He has made a vow.

He has started, so he'll finish.

From then on Kaytek has two different lives.

One is regular: at home, at school, and in the street.

The other life is different: his private, secret, inner life.

It's as if nothing has changed.

He still plays games, chases about, makes bets, wins and loses them, teases, lives life, and clowns around.

But in fact he also thinks hard about magic spells and tries to make them work. He tries various ways, and waits to see what will happen.

He practices his magic gaze and thoughts. He tries issuing commands by thinking and staring.

He stares with all his might at the boy sitting on the bench in front of him. He looks hard at him, and commands: *I order you to turn around. Turn around.*

He says it with his eyes and thoughts, not his voice.

Or he stares at the teacher.

I want to go to the blackboard. I demand you to call me up. I want to give the answer!

Or at his father.

I want fifty groshys for the movies. I demand it. Please. I want to go to the movies!

One time it works, lots of times it doesn't.

That's no surprise. Spells are tricky, and he's only just starting.

Kaytek waits patiently.

Until finally . . . he does it.

His first spell was like this.

The teacher wants to give a bad mark. Not to Kaytek, or even to his good friend, but to some other boy.

Kaytek thinks very hard: *Make his pen go missing.*

And at once the teacher asks: "Where's my pen? It was here a moment ago."

The boys and the teacher look for it.

"It's not here. Who took it?"

"Not I . . . And not I."

Meanwhile the bell rings. The teacher leaves, and there's his pen, lying on the table, as if it had never been lost.

His second spell was like this.

The teacher is writing on the blackboard, and Kaytek thinks: *Make the chalk turn into soap.*

The teacher tries to go on writing – but he can't. He examines the chalk. He's riled, muttering something to himself.

"What's up?" the students wonder. "What is it? What do you need, sir?"

At once the teacher gives the chalk a hard squeeze and goes on writing. But he's making an awful face.

And it was the same in geography.

The teacher was standing in front of the map, explaining something. It was a boring lesson.

And Kaytek just thought briefly and quickly: *Make the map turn upside down.*

The teacher blinked. He frowned. He rubbed his eyes. The boys didn't even notice, because a moment later the map was the right way up again.

Afterward, when Kaytek counted how many of his spells had worked, he didn't even know whether or not to count them as real spells.

Because what had happened?

He could have imagined it.

He could have fallen asleep for a while out of boredom and just dreamed it. Sometimes it's hard to tell the difference between dreams and reality.

What about the pen that vanished? That often happens. Something gets lost, you search and search, but it's definitely not there. Then you look again, and there it is. It's enough to make you wonder. It's enough to make you lose your temper.

Kaytek wanted to be sure it wasn't just a coincidence, or a dream, or a mistake, and that it really was a spell and not something else.

So he only counted the things that couldn't possibly have happened without a magic spell.

So in the class there was a klutz. He was so clumsy that they teased him and made fun of him.

He was worst of all in gym. And the thing he did worst was jumping over a rope.

They say: "What are you afraid of? If you trip on the rope, it won't kill you."

Kaytek feels sorry for him. What do they want from him? He's a good, quiet kid.

So he gives a command the magic way.

And it works. The klutz jumps the rope. A huge long way. So easily – about twenty yards.

"Well done!"

The boys open their mouths wide in amazement. The klutz cringes in terror.

"Again. Do it again!" they shout.

But he's crying. He refuses, he won't jump a second time. He doesn't know what helped him over it.

Kaytek is smiling. "What a silly crowd," he thinks. Because it feels good to know something no one else knows, to understand what no one else can understand, and to be able to do what others can't.

Yes! That was a magic spell.

But so what? What if it wasn't Kaytek's command that made the boy jump the rope?

He did have some stronger proof.

The teacher gives them an exercise. Kaytek isn't in the mood, so he doesn't write it down. He'll copy it off a pal in recess.

But he doesn't like to ask.

Maybe the teacher won't check?

The teacher calls a boy up to give the answer, then another one. Finally she tells Kaytek to show her his exercise book.

It's a nasty moment. He had actually decided he'd always do her lessons, because he likes her, and he knows she likes him.

What will be, will be, he thinks. *I want – I demand – I command. Let it be written.*

He goes up to her boldly. He hasn't even opened the exercise book. But he has a feeling it's bound to work.

The exercise book feels hot, then cold, then normal. He hands it over.

The teacher opens it and reads.

"Very good. To your place."

Kaytek goes back and sits down.

He looks in the book, and the exercise is right there on the page.

The writing is black, normal, then it goes pale – he can hardly see it – and it's gone.

He sighs. He feels tired. His head is spinning.

Then came the spell with the bicycles.

It's recess.

The boys are chasing about, shouting, crowding and pushing. It's boring. Total chaos.

Kaytek's annoyed, so he thinks: *Make everyone ride a bike.*

He's horrified by what he sees next.

That's enough!

If it had gone on longer, they'd have been injured, they would have broken their arms and legs.

Because they don't know how to ride bikes, and anyway, how can they all fit in the schoolyard, when they're going fast as well?

Silence reigns.

An ominous silence.

Kaytek is pale and in a sweat.

Make them forget, he orders.

And so it ends happily.

Only one of them is lying on the ground, holding his head. He doesn't know if someone pushed him, or if he just fell over.

Only that one had fallen off his bike and gotten a bump.

All the boys have forgotten, and only the janitor is looking around uneasily. Maybe because he's old. But he obviously suspects something.

Then Kaytek sits on a bench and thinks what would have happened, how it would have ended if he hadn't immediately said that was enough.

It looks as if spells that last a long time are harder.

Why do some of them work at once, and others not at all?

Maybe sometimes real wizards also want to do something, but can't? Maybe sometimes it comes out differently from how they wanted? In fairy tales they talk about spells that didn't work.

Kaytek is only a student so far. He's studying, learning, and experimenting.

The next spell was like this:

There's an arithmetic test.

The teacher dictates the problem.

"Too hard," cry the boys. "We don't know! We can't do it!"

And Kaytek thinks: *Make the ink change into water.*

And at once someone says: "Please, sir, the ink won't write. It's water."

So the teacher sends for the janitor.

"I filled the inkwells yesterday," says the janitor. "With just the same ink as in the whole school. The boys must have sprinkled something into them."

The monitor doesn't know, he hasn't seen anything. There was ink. No one touched the inkwells. How could he not have noticed?

The teacher licks his finger to taste the water once, twice, then spits it out and shrugs his shoulders. He's pretending to understand what's going on.

"Just wait. I'm going to tell the headmaster. The whole class will answer for this. Enough of this hooliganism. You won't get away with it. You can write with pencils."

But they don't have any pencils. So there was no test.

Kaytek's ninth spell caused even greater confusion.

They were having a handicraft lesson.

In fact, handicraft can be fun if the teacher makes an effort and the boys do what he says. But if not, handicraft is even more tedious than a regular lesson.

Kaytek sees there's a long time to go till the end of the lesson.

For a week now every single spell has worked. So he thinks: *I'll give it a try.*

I want. I command. Make the bell go now.

And it does. But it's different from usual. The sound seems to come from above, as if the bell were flying through the air and ringing.

The boys pile out of the classroom wondering why the lesson's over so soon, and feeling thrilled by the surprise.

The headmaster comes out of his office in a fury.

"What's going on here? Why? Who?"

"I didn't ring it," says the janitor.

"So who did?"

"I don't know."

The old man stands there with tears in his eyes.

"Headmaster, either believe me, or don't. I am not drunk. It's not the first year I've been working at this school. I know what kind of tricks the boys get up to. And I tell you: there are ghosts or something in charge at this school."

"All right, all right. Ghosts! Please come to my office. Boys, back to your classrooms!"

Kaytek stretched and yawned, feeling discouraged.

It was never going to be possible to do something really interesting. It always seemed to end a bit stupidly somehow.

So he was a wizard – and what of it?

He felt sorry for the janitor. What had the old fellow done wrong? And the headmaster had taken him into his office and was probably telling him off.

Kaytek really didn't want to upset anyone.

Then two serious spells worked for Kaytek – one straight after the other.

One of his classmates is a rich boy.

He brings various goodies for breakfast. He's greedy and sly – he never offers any of it to anyone else. He brings in cream cakes, then licks the paper with his great big tongue.

First thing in the morning Kaytek sees the glutton getting out his package. Kaytek stares hard, takes a deep breath of air, and thinks: *Make him have a frog instead of breakfast.*

At once there's a scream.

"Frogs in the classroom!"

The greedy boy is goggle-eyed, frozen to the spot as if paralyzed. The frog hops off, and the rest of the boys are laughing.

"Look at that! He's brought a frog for his breakfast."

"It's sure to be a foreign one!"

"With cream on top!"

"If he brought it, let him eat it."

Just then the teacher comes into the classroom.

She makes a long speech.

"That's not a clever joke. But what's worse is that someone has stolen two ham rolls, a cake, and an orange."

Kaytek can see he has upset the teacher, so he wants to console her.

Make a rose appear on the table in front of the teacher.

Then he's sorry he said that, because something stabs at his heart and something yanks painfully inside him – it's like an electric shock, or like a tooth being pulled, as if that rose has been torn from his chest.

And there it is, lying on the table.

That other time the teacher asked: "Who took my pen? It was here a moment ago."

This time the lady teacher asks: "Who put this rose here? I don't want it. You boys take too many liberties."

Then the boys ask her: "Please smell the rose, miss. Please take it. We'll pay for his breakfast."

Some of them are asking for real, others are just clowning. Because they're pleased when something like this happens.

After the lesson they took up a collection.

"Put a penny in the cap for the hungry glutton."

They bought twelve rolls, a dozen – a whole bagful.

"There you are. Eat these as a snack, after your frog."

Kaytek has grown proud, stand-offish and impatient.

Whatever happens, at once he says: "Do you want a smack in the face? You dope! Just look at him: the jackass is playing the wise guy."

No one likes him anymore because he keeps asking for trouble. Now he's even started provoking the older boys.

One day he has a quarrel with a boy in the sixth grade. He's really getting into hot water.

They've surrounded him in a circle. They're all staring, expecting to see a fight.

"Are you going to call me a jackass too?" says the older boy.

"Sure I will. And I'll give you ears like a jackass as well."

Kaytek has a small mirror in his pocket, which he uses to reflect sunbeams on the wall, even in class during lessons.

He hands the boy the mirror and says: "You've got them. Take a look."

He focuses his mind, bending his wizard's will like a bow. He demands and he commands.

The boy looks in the mirror: his ears have grown longer and sprung upward. And then they're gone.

What the heck? Was that real or was it just an illusion?

"Where did you get this mirror? Sell it to me. Teach me how that's done."

They've forgotten about the quarrel. They think it's some kind of trick.

"Give it back," says Kaytek, with an effort.

Now the other boys are scared. They can see he's gone pale, and his lips have turned blue. He's leaning against a wall.

They run off, and Kaytek is left alone.

"The spell for changing people into animals must be really tough if just the ears have worn me out so badly."

He feels weak and lonely.

He imagined it all quite differently in the days when he so badly longed to be a wizard

Until he did his thirteenth spell, the last one in a month: the flies.

The teacher is explaining something. Kaytek isn't listening. He's thinking about this and that. He doesn't even know where he is and what's happening around him.

"Did the rose I gave the lady teacher disappear at once too? Maybe quite the opposite – maybe it won't ever wilt or dry up, because it's magical, it's enchanted."

He gazes at the stove, at the ceiling, at the walls.

He notices a fly on the stove.

The fly is moving upward, quickly, as if it's in a hurry and is worried about being late. Then it stops, as if it has just remembered something, and goes back down again. And so on, three times over: up and down, up and down the stove. Then it flies away and disappears.

What was it looking for on the stove, and what made it take off like that?

Kaytek looks around, and sees a fly sitting on the wall. And

the same thing happens: it goes up three times, then down three times. Maybe it's the same one?

And then he sees four flies on the ceiling: two big ones and two little ones. They're marching funnily in pairs. Then a fifth one flies up.

The teacher has turned around and is staring at the class.

"Did you understand that?"

Then Kaytek gets a fright because the teacher tells him to repeat what he's just said.

At once Kaytek thinks: *Make a fly sit on the teacher's nose.*

And the fly is there, waiting for further orders.

Make it three flies . . . he thinks. *Make it five!*

All five flies come and sit on the teacher's nose.

The teacher waves his hands about, but the flies keep coming back, because flies are persistent.

That should have been the end of it, but as if someone else were giving the orders for him, involuntarily Kaytek thinks: *Make it a thousand flies. Ten thousand – on his nose.*

At once, a huge swarm of flies comes crashing through the open window, a whole pack of them.

Kaytek hides under the bench, pretending he's dropped his pen and is busy picking it up.

The teacher says something or shouts. There's no sound, just *bzzzzz* – buzzing.

Then the teacher rushes out and slams the door.

There's laughter. And stamping. The boys are banging on their desks with delight.

Kaytek crawls from under the bench, and the flies fly out the window in clusters.

"What's all that screaming?"

In comes the headmaster – and at once there's an investigation.

"It wasn't us. The teacher saw: they came in through the window."

"Maybe they're forming a new swarm?"

"They were flies, not bees."

"I thought they were locusts."

"Maybe they've gone crazy?"

The lady teacher took the class for the rest of the lesson.

Then all the boys went home, while the teachers held an official meeting.

They closed the school for two days and had a big clean-up. They even wanted to repaint the walls.

A notice was hung on the gate saying: "No classes until Thursday because of renovations."

Chapter Five

KAYTEK'S SPELLS AT HOME AND IN THE STREET – SONOLO, KASOLO, SYMBOLO – THE FIRST PERMANENT SPELL – DANGER

They say money doesn't bring happiness.

"Health matters more," says Mom. "So what if someone's rich if he's also sick?"

Mom is sure to think like that, because she's had operations. She's been in the hospital twice, once for quite a long time.

"Knowledge matters more," says Dad. "You can lose all your money, but knowledge stays with you forever. A scholar does well in life."

And his dad asks Kaytek to apply himself to his books and be hard-working and obedient at school.

"The greatest treasure a man can have is a good heart and a clear conscience," says Grandma. "A good man is never troubled. He gets on with other people, he'll never offend anyone, he'll be forgiving, and he'll always find friends who will help him in need. And his life will go by peacefully without harm to anyone."

But Kaytek reckons wealth is important too.

If his dad had money, Mom could go to the countryside and she'd be sure to get well.

If his dad had money, he could set up his own workshop – he'd have a place of his own and wouldn't have to put up with other people's griping.

And, if he has a fortune, a good man can share it with a poor one.

So Kaytek wants to be rich.

He wants to have a hen that lays golden eggs.

One evening he went into the attic and tried to do some spells.

Please, I demand, I want to have a hen that lays golden eggs.

Sonolo-kasolo-symbolo . . .

Pramara-rumkara. I want, I command.

Lorem, ipsum, karakorum ...

Nomen, omen, sesame, simile. Let me have a magic hen!

He doesn't know what language he's speaking or what the spells mean. They're words he has never heard, or familiar ones he's twisted . . .

He looks through a small window at the stars, he looks hard at his cap, where the hen is supposed to appear, then shuts his eyes again.

He holds his breath, then breathes deeply and slowly, then rapidly again.

He locks his fingers together, then spreads them wide, then clenches them into a fist.

He raises his head, then lets it droop.

He talks loudly, then tries a whisper.

Nothing at all happens.

There's no hen, and not a single egg, not even a tiny one – as if to spite him.

As golden eggs haven't worked, he tries silver. That doesn't work either. "Maybe it has happened for the best?" he tries to console himself. Because where would he hide the hen, and how would he sell its eggs?

What would he say if they asked where he got it?

He went up to the attic three times.

And came back down very tired.

No. Better learn how to find money the usual way – in the street.

He'd start from a small amount, that'd be easier. A zloty to begin with.

It was a shame to be a wizard but not know how to do anything. He didn't have any spells of his own – he didn't know what or how or when. As if it wasn't he, but someone else who was doing the magic for him.

Why did the spells work at school, but not in the street?
So he starts with a small one: *I want to find a zloty!*
On his way back from school he searches.
Or rather he doesn't search, he just looks around. Because if you have magical powers, you find things without searching.
He's walking along at a normal pace, not fast and not slow. He walks straight, then in a zig-zag. At first calmly, but then he starts to have doubts.
It hasn't worked.
Maybe try in the evening?
There are spells that only work at midnight. Before the rooster crows thrice.
He's done his homework assignments. He reaches for his cap.
"Antek, where are you going? It's late. Your dad's on his way home from work."
"I'll be back in a minute. I'll be just a moment."
Outside, the street lamps are already on.
It's muddy.
A tram goes by. A car lights up the street and rushes past.
I want to find one.
Let me find one.
I order. I command.
One little zloty, be found!
And he found one, in a very strange way.
He was on his way back, so they wouldn't be too upset at home.
It was so strange, when he'd already given up hope.
He's on his way back, thinking: tough. If not today, then tomorrow. If not tomorrow, then next week.
Suddenly a car comes along, and he sees something shining in the mud. He bends down, and it's a coin – next to the street lamp, on the very edge of the sidewalk, almost hanging over it.
Fifty groshys – that's half a zloty.
"Good for us!"
He breathes on it for good luck.
"That'll do."
And he rushes home as fast as his legs can carry him.

Then came his second try.

He wanted to find money in the street, but he found it on the stairs, but only five groshys – you need twenty of those to make a zloty.

It was only a five-groshy coin, but it was a new one, shiny, just like gold.

Even before now Kaytek had occasionally found something or other. He'd lose an eraser, then he'd find a pencil, he'd lose a pen, and he'd find a pencil sharpener.

Kaytek loses things, and so do others. Because things can fall out of your pocket while you're running, or slip out of your schoolbag.

Or the grown-ups throw things out. They throw out things that might come in handy: a piece of string, a box, a small bottle, or a movie theater program.

But that's quite another matter.

The third time, it was different.

By now he was feeling discouraged and wasn't looking at all. He was hurrying to get to school, thinking: "No means no, I won't find any more money."

When suddenly . . .

I want to find a hundred zlotys! he thinks.

Because what does he have to lose?

And straight away, at the next corner store, right by the steps, he picks up a whole zloty, and next to it there are two fifty-groshy coins. So altogether that's two zlotys.

"So maybe I should demand more?" he thinks. "Maybe there's a chief wizard who's bargaining with me?"

Then it occurs to him for the first time that even a wizard has his own bosses and authorities. He is not independent. There are some secret commands.

Well, then? He has two zlotys. He goes to school feeling happy.

He meets up with his pals. He proudly tells them about the money and shows it to them.

He doesn't sense any trouble brewing.

Because lately various things have started disappearing at

school: breakfasts, books, some gloves, and a scarf have all gone missing.

Kaytek has even tried to expose the culprit using magic, because it's a nasty business. But nothing came of it.

And now suspicion has fallen on Kaytek himself, as if he'd taken the money from another boy.

That day the teacher is collecting the outstanding contributions to pay for the missing breakfast. And one boy is crying because he had two zlotys but they're gone – someone has stolen them.

"Where did you have them?"

"In my schoolbag. No, not in my bag, in my pocket."

"Maybe you lost them in the street?"

No. They were here. He had them in the cloakroom. He put them on the windowsill.

"Which of you has some money?"

The boys take out their money and show the teacher. One boy has ten groshys, another has thirty, yet another has two foreign coins.

Kaytek immediately comes clean.

Where did you get two zlotys?" asks the teacher.

"I found it in the street."

The teacher gives Kaytek a nasty look.

She takes the two zlotys and asks the other boy: "Is this yours?"

And he says: "Yes, it's mine."

Then the other boys cut in, saying: "He's lying, miss. It's not his at all. He didn't have any money. He was just pretending to cry."

Kaytek calmly looks the teacher in the eye. The other boy is red and confused. Until he stammers: "Mine was a whole two-zloty coin, two zlotys in total. Not separate."

"I can give it to him," says Kaytek. "He can have it."

The teacher doesn't know what to do, and the boys are urging Kaytek: "Don't give it to him, you dope. Look at him, the cheat. He says he had it on the windowsill, in his pocket, and in his schoolbag. He had different coins, but he says it's his. He's been found out, the wise guy! He's lying. He never had it at all.

He's always cheating. Kaytek showed us outside that he'd found that money."

Kaytek shrugs.

The teacher thinks for a while.

"Tell me, where did you find it?" she says.

He tells her what happened. He doesn't say anything about the spells, of course.

"So you'll give it to him?"

"He can have it, if he says he lost it. It's not mine, after all."

And the other boy takes it. His hands are shaking. And now he's crying for real.

Once again, it's all so strangely complicated.

"Maybe magic power gives to one and takes away from another?"

Because it was like that before, too.

He wants to try it a different way.

He wants to do a test, to see if he can transfer his magic spell to someone else.

So he gives a command for Mom to find a zloty.

And Mom comes back from town and tells a weird story:

"I found five zlotys. So I looked around to see who lost it. And I saw an old guy looking for something. So I asked him. He was overjoyed, the poor old boy. It was his."

It came out so weird.

It's all in such a pickle you can't get your head around it.

Kaytek found a pocket knife and some crayons.

The pocket knife was lying in the middle of the street. It was lying there so obviously, but no one had seen it and picked it up.

It was just as if it was waiting for Kaytek.

It was the same with the crayons – a whole new box of them, and just when the teacher warned he'd give them a bad grade for the semester if they didn't have crayons.

Even if it wasn't magic, no one loses a whole new box of crayons, do they?

Then the pocket knife went missing. He left it on the bench, and after the recess, it had gone. Maybe someone took it, though he asked the janitor and the other boys.

Or maybe it just disappeared on its own?

Once again, who knows?

Two more of Kaytek's spells worked out in the street. One time he pushed some little girls into the mud.

It was like this:

He's walking along, on his way home from school, lost in thought.

"Maybe it doesn't work in the street because there's so much noise. Maybe there are too many people – something's definitely getting in the way."

There was a good reason why wizards used to live in isolated towers or in the last cottage at the very edge of the village. Maybe they hide in the forest, or at the bottom of the sea?

Kaytek himself can tell that his thoughts take shape most easily when he's down by the River Vistula, far from the city, among peace and quiet; or in the silence of night, when he's lying in bed.

So on his way home from school he's thinking about it all, turning it over in his mind. And suddenly, there in front of him, are three little girls.

They're taking up the entire width of the sidewalk, laughing, pushing, and fooling around. They won't let him get past. If they were boys, maybe he wouldn't have noticed, but girls! That makes him even wilder.

It's raining.

Go splash in the mud! he thinks.

And at once they're lying in it. All three of them. They're filthy dirty, covered in mud.

"Serves them right," he thinks. "That'll teach them to cause a scene!"

The second time, he spilled a saleslady's apples.

He knows her from way back – she's always sold her apples here. Sometimes he used to buy from her.

He doesn't like her because she's rude to kids. She never lets them take a look, or choose, or haggle.

At once she says: "Are you going to buy it or not? All right, go to the Jew instead.* Go somewhere else – don't buy anything here."

True, sometimes the boys are annoying too.

Kaytek comes by with a pal. He looks and sees the woman is dozing.

Make her do a cartwheel, he thinks

And in an instant, she does!

She grabs at her big basket of apples to stop herself, but she and the basket end up on the ground.

The rascals are laughing.

"The old girl's drunk!"

She isn't even bruised, but she is embarrassed.

"That's the first time that has ever happened to me. Like some drunk! People are laughing. It's so embarrassing! Twenty years I've been trading. Year in, year out, spring, summer, fall, and winter. That's the first time – such a disgrace!"

She very nearly bursts into tears.

Kaytek feels sorry. He pities the old woman.

He tells his pal to keep watch and make sure no one touches any of the spilled apples while he picks them up for her.

"Thank you, boy, thank you, my dear. Here, take a nice big apple for your kindness."

And she thrusts an apple into his hand, but it's a wormy one.

His pal makes a joke of it, but Kaytek is upset.

"Did I really have to start it up with the old woman?" he thinks.

Until one day he managed a spell that was permanent. Every evening it kept repeating. Once again, it wasn't of any great use, but it was important proof that Kaytek really did have magic powers.

It started late one night.

At home.

---

* See Translator's Afterword.

In silence.

Kaytek is lying in bed and he can't get to sleep.

He can hear his parents and Grandma breathing in their sleep.

He's not afraid, but it's unpleasant being the only one who's not asleep. A person feels all alone in the darkness.

Suddenly the floor creaks, as if someone were walking around. There's a knocking sound in the wardrobe, or behind it, as if someone were prowling about.

Until finally he feels like having a bite to eat.

If only there was something under my pillow, a bar of chocolate or something else.

That's all he thinks. If he added any other words, he must have forgotten them.

And at once he hears a rustling noise, as if a mouse were scratching under his pillow.

He reaches under the pillow – and there it is!

A little bag. He doesn't open it at once. Why be in a hurry? He just feels it with his fingers and tries to guess what's inside.

Until he boldly opens the bag.

He tips the contents onto his hand – nine chocolate candies with fillings, nine big raisins, and nine almonds.

He counts them. Should he eat them or not?

He tries one.

It's sweet and tasty. They're just the same as the regular ones they sell in the stores.

"Why nine?"

He eats up eight of each kind, and keeps the rest to examine in the morning. The paper that the bag is made from seems stiff.

He wants to store them in his pocket because the chocolate will melt under his pillow. So he sits up and reaches for his pants. And makes the chair rattle.

"Is that you, Antek?" says Grandma, who has woken up.

"Yes, it's me."

"Why aren't you asleep?"

"I was."

But in the morning, his pocket is empty.

And after that it's the same every evening: chocolate candies, raisins and almonds.

He has tried them out and knows they're not poison. He wants to offer them around. He leaves three, and says: *Let them remain. Don't let them disappear.*

And next morning they're still there. They haven't gone. So he offers them around.

"Where did you get them?" asks Mom.

"My pal gave them to me."

"Eat them yourself."

"I've had some. I have a toothache."

He doesn't like fibbing, but what could he do?

Another spell kind of worked, and kind of didn't.

He really wants to have a watch.

He's often thought it would be good to have something useful instead of the little bag. But he's afraid to spoil things by being in a hurry.

Until one day he managed it.

Once again, everyone else is asleep.

He says some phrases in Egyptian or Arabic. He says the spell and . . .

Instead of candy let there be . . . .

At once there's the familiar rustle under his pillow, and the low ticking of a watch.

He hears it, reaches under the pillow, and starts laughing.

"Oh, how generous."

There's a watch, and also the little bag.

"Antek, is that you laughing?" says Grandma.

"Yes. I had such a funny dream."

Grandma's pleased he's not moaning in his sleep or gnashing his teeth. She doesn't ask any more questions.

But in the morning the watch was gone.

He tried this way and that way for several evenings in a row, but only the candy appeared.

Maybe it was better like that.

Because now he could see that it wouldn't work, so he calmed down and could get to sleep quicker.

And he was very, very tired by now.

At home they have noticed that Kaytek has grown sad and is looking haggard.

He's lost his appetite. He doesn't play in the yard much. And he's not sleeping well.

He used to wolf his food down like anything. Bread, cheese, dumplings, potatoes or ravioli – you name it, he ate it.

"Where does all the food go in the boy? He eats well but he's thin as a rail."

He used to read the paper to his grandma and play checkers with his dad. Now he's not eating and he keeps excusing himself from everything, saying he has a headache.

"He must be sick. We must go to the doctor."

Kaytek was worried.

What if the doctor realized he was a wizard? Doctors know Latin. Maybe they teach them Latin so they can make spells to cure illnesses and remove enchantments in a dead language?

Well, off to the doctor they went.

The doctor tapped. He listened. He examined Kaytek's throat. He told him to have his teeth treated by a dentist. He examined his eyes. He weighed up the facts. He said he was pale and prescribed some drops. He said Kaytek was growing.

He was wrong – he didn't realize.

These tricky thoughts won't let Kaytek rest – they're stopping him from eating or sleeping.

Because he is a wizard.

For a long time he didn't believe it. Now he's certain. His dream has come true.

But it's a tricky profession. A tough line of work.

A dangerous occupation.

Because if you make a mistake doing something ordinary, it's no big deal: you can put it straight. But if you make a mistake doing a magic spell, you could lose your life.

Kaytek became sure of this after a terrible spell involving a tram.

Kaytek is walking down the street. Nothing's up, he's just walking along.

He's looking at the numbers on the trams. That number is

even, that one is odd; that one divides by five, that one doesn't.

He's looking at the people and the stores. There's a dog sitting by the gate. Kaytek stops, calls the dog over, and strokes it.

Another tram goes by at full speed.

He turns around to see the number.

And suddenly he thinks: *Make me turn a somersault in the air and stand on the roof of the tram.*

There's a wind – a force – a power, something that throws him upward. Now he's in the air, head down. He straightens up, and he's standing on the roof of the tram.

A woman screams. Someone on a balcony raises their arms in the air. The dog starts to howl. A driver cries out: "Hold on or you'll fall off!"

Kaytek sways, and is about to grab onto the wire. And at the very last moment he remembers there's a high-voltage electric current running through it.

It's like lightning. That's how they kill prisoners on death row in America.

Kaytek falls over. He rolls. There's a roaring noise in his ears. He's going to fall off. Just in time he thinks: *Make me somersault to the ground!*

Once again he spins in the air. And he's standing on the sidewalk.

The rubberneckers crowd around him. A policeman is approaching.

Kaytek runs for it.

Panting for breath, he only stops three streets away.

He straightens his clothes and wipes the blood off his grazed hands with a handkerchief.

He stands up straight, takes a deep breath, and, feeling wild and rebellious, he quietly but distinctly says: *I command that no spell should work for me for a month.*

He takes out his pocket mirror and scowls at himself.

And hisses at himself: "You dope!"

Chapter Six

LIFE IS FINER WITHOUT SPELLS – THE MONTH IS OVER – KAYTEK GETS LOST IN THE FOREST – A STORM – FEVER AND DELIRIUM – IN THE HOSPITAL

Kaytek is walking along, whistling merrily.

He hasn't felt so relaxed for ages.

"I've rid myself of trouble for a whole month, and meanwhile I'll do some thinking and make sure I don't do anything stupid again."

Because the magic has to be done differently somehow.

He runs into the apartment and kisses his mom. Not just once, but over and over.

"That's enough, Antek. What's with all the loving?"

He skips over to Grandma.

"Dance with me, Grandma."

"What's gotten into your head this time?"

"Nothing. I feel like having something to eat."

"If you want to eat, then don't start dancing, but speak up. Here, eat, bon appétit! Did you take the medicine the doctor prescribed?"

"I don't want to. Why should I? It's a waste of time."

"Don't whine, Antek. After all, you can see it helps – you've cheered up and your appetite has come back."

So he eats up. There isn't much homework, so he runs out into the yard.

"We thought you were all proud these days," say the boys.

"No way."

"So why haven't you been coming out here?"

"There were holes in my shoes."

And at once he thinks: "From now on I'm going to tell the truth more."

Their games are a total success. He doesn't spoil them once.

That evening he chats at tea time. Then he plays checkers with his dad.

Late that night they go to bed.

Out of habit he reaches under his pillow. The little bag isn't there, but something pricks his finger.

"Maybe it's a spindle?" he thinks, as he sucks the blood from his finger, remembering the fairy tale about the Sleeping Princess.

But he didn't fall asleep for a hundred years, just for the usual number of hours. He woke up feeling refreshed. He couldn't find any marks on his finger.

On the way to school he decides to check if he has even a little bit of magic power.

Make that smart guy's buttons come off and his pants fall down, he thinks.

At once a button comes off and rolls across the cobblestones.

Make the policeman's cap fly off, he thinks.

The cap bounces on the policeman's head, but it doesn't fall off.

"My power is still there and will be back in a month."

That evening he added up on a piece of paper how many of his magic spells had worked – at home, at school, and in the street. He also made separate lists of the major and minor ones. He rejected the dubious spells.

"It's not even worth counting those. Maybe I just imagined them?"

Because he'd forgotten which ones came earlier and which later. He couldn't remember exactly what had happened.

"Maybe a wizard has the right to do nine spells a month, or maybe seven, or is it thirteen?"

"Maybe magic spells only work on Mondays and Fridays."

It was a pity he hadn't noted them down with secret signs, so no one could understand even if they found the piece of paper.

It says in the fairy tales that wizards have students. Sure it must be easier like that.

But Kaytek will manage by himself.

Anyone who wants things to be easy is a dope.

Things that are hard are interesting!

"Rome wasn't built in a day, as the saying goes."

Even to be a carpenter or an engineer you have to study for a long time, and the art of magic is harder than anything else.

He'd had plenty of success, even though he was young and inexperienced, even though he was on his own, with no one to guide him.

Yes. All on his own!

Because whom could he ask for advice?

Could he let a pal in on the secret?

His pal would be sure to blab. He'd tell Kaytek to do something, and if it didn't work, he'd laugh at him and say he was lying. Or start to pester him, saying: "Show me. Teach me how . . ."

Maybe tell the teacher?

But she wouldn't believe him; she'd say there's no such thing as magic spells. She doesn't know she sniffed a magic rose.

Tell them at home?

Not them either. Either they wouldn't believe him, or they'd forbid him, or start dictating what was allowed. Anyway, how could they help him if they don't know any magic themselves?

No.

He mustn't betray the secret.

He has time. A whole month. He'll check each spell separately and learn a lesson from it for the future.

Kaytek had a dream.

He dreamed he was sitting in a deep armchair, covered in oilcloth. He dreamed he was wearing a pointed alchemist's hat and a red tie with green spots. He dreamed he was sitting at a desk. On the desk there was a black cat, an owl, a skull, and the round thing the statue of Copernicus is holding.*

---

* Copernicus (1473–1543) was the founder of modern astronomy who first discovered that

And some large books. Big, fat, heavy volumes.

Because Kaytek once saw a large old book in a store front display – it had a yellow leather cover and a clasp that locked.

He went into the store to take a look and ask the price. But they refused to remove it from the display and show it to him.

"It's very expensive. It's not for you."

His great-grandfather and grandfather must have had books like that.

Then Kaytek saw some mysterious books in a bookstore: the *Egyptian Dream Book*, the *Kabbalah*,* *The Power of the Will*, and *The Divine Sorcerer*.

That's not interesting. It's just to swindle money out of people. Just to bamboozle people.

What sort of an art would sorcery be if anyone could buy a book, read it, and know all about it?

He has to learn how to do clever spells. Sensible, useful ones – purposeful spells.

Otherwise what's the point? All that trouble for so little effect.

They'd taken away his pocket knife. The watch had vanished and never showed up again.

Those two zlotys had almost made him into a thief: the teacher had given him such a nasty look, so mistrustful, so suspicious.

One time he had been to the movies using conjured-up money, but the picture was boring. It was a pity to leave before the end, so there he sat in the dark stinky auditorium, feeling pretty dumb.

Out of the whole sorry mess, the crayons are the only thing he has left.

From now on things are going to be different.

Maybe Kaytek shouldn't wait a month, but a whole year. Maybe he's even too young, and that's why he doesn't know what rights he has, what will work, or what will happen.

---

the Earth revolves around the sun. There is a famous statue of him in Warsaw holding a round device called an astrolabe, which is a model showing the relative positions of the planets in the sky.

* The Egyptian Dream Book is an ancient Egyptian text containing the interpretations of dreams. The Kabbalah is a philosophy concerned with the mystical side of Judaism.

Last year the teacher told them to sow peas and beans, and then note down the changes that happened to the plants. Kaytek was impatient at having to wait a long time for each change to occur. Because he wanted shoots, buds, leaves, roots, and stems all at once.

After that he'd sown some just for himself. And it was nice to know ahead of time what would happen tomorrow.

In the same way he has to investigate and note down his spells. And not just the spells.

He buys a small diary.

He writes on it: *Journal.*

He makes a note: *Tuesday. There was an arithmetic test. It went well. I did it.*

He was one of the first to solve the problem. And without the help of a spell.

That way is actually nicer.

He makes another note: *Saturday. I earned forty groshys.*

It was like this:

Kaytek is walking through the market, and there's a lady behind him with a basket.

"Please help me," she asks. "Please carry it home for me, if you can manage."

"Phooey," boasts Kaytek. "I've carried bigger baskets than that before."

But the basket is heavy.

He picks it up. And carries it. Soon his arms are going numb.

"Is it still far to go?"

"No. It's just around the corner."

Just around the corner or not, without the basket it might be near enough, but with a weight it's a long way.

He stops. He shifts the basket from one arm to the other.

"Here, let me help," says the lady.

"No need," he mutters reluctantly.

He has often carried Grandma's basket for her, and he'll manage this time too.

At last they get there. He's just about to leave – he thinks it was a regular favor. But the lady says: "Have some candy for your trouble."

"No need," says Kaytek.

"Then take this or I'll be offended. You deserve it. Thank you for helping me."

"Ah!" She gives him forty groshys.

"I won't spend it. I earned it. I'll keep it as a souvenir."

And he's pleased it's his own money, and he knows what he got it for, and who gave it to him.

He wrote in the journal: *R. to my h. T.s.i.d.b.*

No one will understand it, even if they read it. Only he knows what it means . . .

Because Kaytek wants to have a hideout. He has to find an isolated place where he can do his spells far away from other people.

He'll have jars with healing ointment and bottles filled with the elixir of life.

Instead of a skull, for now, he'll put a bone in there – a horse's jawbone with white teeth.

He found the bone in the sand by the River Vistula and took it home.

"What do you want those bottles and that bone for?" says Grandma. "You have enough trash already."

"It'll come in handy," says Kaytek grudgingly.

Grown-ups think everything they don't care about is dumb, and everything you can't buy or sell is trash.

Two weeks went by. Then Kaytek started to get impatient. Because if we all look forward to a holiday or a birthday, how might a wizard on vacation feel?

What's more, things had started to go wrong at home and at school.

Until Kaytek got mad – not just with himself and his stupid joke with the tram, but most of all with school. It was like this:

He's the class monitor. He refuses to let the boys into the classroom. They're pulling the door handle down, and he's pushing it up.

A whole gang of them have gathered outside the door.

It's a metal handle. Who could have seen it coming? But meanwhile – crrrrack! It's broken.

At once the teacher says to him: "Are you up to your old tricks again? Spoiling and breaking everything? Look – the walls are spattered and the benches are scored. Do you want to study in a pigsty?"

It's always true that as soon as a hooligan settles down, the moment one single thing goes wrong for him, absolutely everything collapses around him.

So his father will have to pay for the handle, in the third recess he has a fight with another boy, and in class he gets an unfair grade.

On top of everything else, that really riled him up. What has good conduct got to do with his studies? If he knows the lesson, he should get a good grade. A hooligan can be a good student, and a quiet kid can be a lazybones or a dimwit. Why bother to study if they don't respect you for it?

That day the lady teacher was sick, and the other teacher sent for his father.

His father had his own worries then, because Grandma was sick and he was only working three days a week, so his income was low and they were late paying their bills.

"Just you wait," thought Kaytek. "The month will soon be over. Just let me get into some magic spells and the whole school will fly off to the cannibals. I'll change that teacher into a rat and feed him on F grades. I'll fill his bowl with Fs and he'll have to eat them – bon appétit!"

He thought his father would be really mad.

But he wasn't; he hugged Kaytek, kissed him on the head, and just said sadly: "Make an effort, Antek. I know it's hard for you."

Straightaway Kaytek wrote in his journal:

My resolutions:

1. *No joking. No clowning around.*
2. *No fighting.*
3. *No chasing about with the boys.*
4. *Do my homework.*
5. *Read a lot.*

Kaytek reads. At home there's trouble. Now Grandma, now Mom are getting weaker by turns.

Until along came the last day of the month.

So unexpectedly.

Tomorrow his power will be back. What should he start with? Apart from the bottles and jars, he hasn't made any preparations at all.

After five classes he went home. He didn't eat dinner: there'd be more left for his dad.

So he goes out by the river. He crosses a bridge.

It's a muggy day.

He'll go out of the city.

He hangs onto the back of a tram. He goes five stops. Then the conductor chases him off.

He walks along, then does the same thing again, on a different tram. Then he goes on foot along the highway – then a dirt road and into a birch forest.

There are birches, more birches, then oak trees, pines and more oaks.

He never thinks about when he'll get home. He just goes deeper and deeper into the forest. As if he were being lured.

Until he feels tired. And hungry. He sits down. Then he lies down on the grass. He stares at the sky through the branches. He has unbuttoned his jacket.

Silence.

He's fallen asleep.

He's having a bad dream: they're chasing him – he runs away, but they release poison gas after him. Until he's suffocating. His head aches.

It's cold!

He opens his eyes.

He looks around, amazed. Aha – he's in the forest. He looks upward: the crowns of the trees are swaying violently. There's an ominous roaring sound – it's the wind.

It's dark.

There's a shot. Not a shot, but thunder. And at once it starts to rain. Big, heavy drops.

Once again there's thunder and lightning.

It's a storm. A storm in the forest.

He must get to the highway. To the tram.

But which way?

He doesn't know.

He's lost.

That's bad.

He runs. But where should he run to? It makes no difference. There's more thunder.

His cap is soaked through, and there's water streaming off its peak. His clothes feel heavy. There's water sloshing in his shoes.

But maybe it's a trap? That was just how the legendary robber chief Madey lost his way, signed his pact, and sold his soul to the devil.

He thinks there's someone lurking behind a tree.

He stops. No – it's just a bush. He rushes onward.

The forest has kind of ended, but there's no highway, and no ditch by the highway. Just the sad-looking stumps of cut-down trees.

He slips and falls. He has trouble getting up. He turns left.

A small light looms in the distance.

Maybe it's a cottage, or maybe it's the eyes of a wolf? Or maybe it's the hideout of the wizard who has lured him into the forest, made him fall asleep, caused the storm, and is now tempting him with that light?

A spark lights up and goes out – now there's one, now two – they come closer, then move away.

At last he's found the road. There are wheel tracks.

Now the mud is sticky and his feet are getting bogged down.

He hears someone calling. It's Grandma's voice: "Antek, Antek!"

He stops. He listens hard. No, he was just imagining it.

He passes a small wooden bridge. Maybe it'll break? Kaytek will fall into the water and the ghost of a drowned woman will drag him to the bottom.

The moon has floated into the sky – and Kaytek sees the drowned woman. He shuts his eyes and runs away.

But he has no strength left.

He leans against a post. His knees give way. He lies there and waits.

He hears the whirr of wheels. Friend or foe? Will he help him or kill him?

It's all the same. It was cold, and now it's hot. He starts coughing. It hurts.

"Momma!"

He groans.

"Hello, who's there? Where have you come from? Who are you?"

"Don't kill me," begs Kaytek. "I'll give you a sheep with a golden fleece."

Kaytek hears another question, but he doesn't answer. He feels strong arms picking him up. Now he's lying on something soft. He doesn't open his eyes. He's rocking.

"Gee up!"

He wakes and dozes by turns.

He shouts. He leaps up.

"Don't get up or you'll fall off the cart."

Kaytek has woken up in a strange room. He's lying on a bench.

"Here you are. Drink this."

He eagerly swallows the good, warm liquid.

There are people saying something, asking questions. Kaytek can hear, but he doesn't answer. He's too tired.

He hears a woman's voice:

"What will we do with him, with the boy?"

"I'll take him to the hospital. Maybe he'll say something in the morning."

"What if he dies in the night?"

"Don't talk nonsense."

"What a bother."

"So what was I meant to do? Leave him in the field, stupid?"

"That's not what I'm saying."

When Kaytek wakes up again, he can feel them dressing him. The clothes feel unpleasant, hard. Kaytek tries to defend himself, pushing them away. He just wants to lie in peace.

"Come along now. You're going back to your dad."

"Ow, my head. Stop. That's enough."

They carry him outside. He's on the move again.

At last he opens his eyes. He recognizes some tall houses. He recognizes a policeman.

"Where do you live? What's your name?"

He tries to smile but he can't.

They pick him up again. They fetch him off the cart. They carry him. Put him down. Undress and dress him again. That's how these wizards torment you.

He has opened his eyes again. This time he can't see a policeman or any houses, just a white room and a lady dressed in white.

"A witch?" wonders Kaytek.

"Yes, a witch."

"White. Clean."

"Yes. White. Clean. Go to sleep."

"And are there dwarves?"

"Yes, there are. What's your name?"

"I don't know."

He's not called anything at all. It's all the same to him. He's lying in a white bed. It's warm, it's hot – and it's all right.

He coughs.

"It hurts!"

"He's more conscious now," says the hospital nurse.

"So tell us, why did you run away from home?" asks the doctor.

Kaytek turns his back on them and covers his head with the quilt. He doesn't like this man who keeps tapping him and listening through tubes.

"Tell us, what were you doing in a ditch at night? Did some wizard take you there?"

The doctor forces Kaytek to sit up.

And then suddenly his father comes into the room.

"Antek, what happened to you?"

Kaytek doesn't know if he can really see his father, or if he's just imagining it.

He doesn't listen to their conversation. Thank goodness they've left him in peace.

"I'd rather take him home," says his father. "He's my only child. Is he seriously sick?"

And then he says: "I'll take a cab and carry him carefully. I would be extremely grateful."

The doctor says: "You say you take good care of him, but he ran away from home. He must have been up to mischief and was going to get a beating."

"No, I never hit the child. Perhaps the other boys persuaded him. Did you run away, son?"

With a trembling hand, Kaytek strokes his father's face.

"Water!"

He has a drink.

"Do you want to stay here?"

He doesn't know how to answer. All he can think is why hasn't his father shaved?

"Three days," thinks Kaytek in amazement, and repeats in a whisper: "three days, three days."

What does it all mean?

Who was found in a ditch? And who found him?

Chapter Seven

KAYTEK IS WELL – A FAILED SPELL – A MIRACLE – SOME BIG SPELLS – A FUSS – THE FOREIGN GUESTS – A SPECIAL SUPPLEMENT

Kaytek is home now. He's well. He's already walking around the room. He has even been outside once by now.

His father is at work, his mom is doing the housework, and his grandma has gone to visit his uncle.

"Why has she gone? When will she be back?"

"She's not coming back, Antek," says Mom.

She hasn't told him the truth – they didn't want to upset him because he was weak after his illness.

Grandma has died.

"How, why did she die? What'll happen now? Why did the doctor let her die?"

Kaytek has guessed that when they spent the whole night looking for him, and it was raining – that was when Grandma caught a bad cold.

"So it was because of me . . ."

"No. She'd been feeling ill for ages. She'd been in bed for a whole week. Don't you remember, Antek?"

Mom is trying to console him. He remembers, now he remembers everything. He knows.

"It was because of me."

He knows. He has remembered that he is a wizard. The month was over long ago.

He goes to stand by the window; why should Mom have to see his tears?

I demand . . . Lilliput . . . I demand: make Grandma appear to me.

At once he sees Grandma's face on the window pane.

She's smiling at Kaytek. She always used to smile like that whenever his dad got mad at him, whenever he got up to some major mischief. She's smiling on the window pane, gazing at him gently with her gray eyes, and then she vanishes.

"I'll bring Grandma back to life. Yes. This spell has to work."

He'll go to her grave, wake her up, and bring her home with him. They'll be amazed. It'll be a big surprise.

After all, there are cases where someone is asleep, and they think they're dead. He's just forgotten what that kind of deep sleep is called.

Sometimes miners survive being buried in a coal mine if they're dug out in time. He read about it in the paper.

"Mommaaaa . . ."

"What?"

"I'm going to the cemetery."

"All right. Don't cry, Antek."

"But I'm going now, right away."

"That's impossible. It's too far. I haven't the time now."

"Well, exactly – I'm going by myself!"

"You don't know where it is. And it's too cold today."

"I do know where it is. And it's warm!"

"You can't. I won't let you. Tomorrow."

"I'll go without your permission! Today!"

And then Mom agrees because she knows Kaytek well. He's not stubborn, he can be persuaded or begged not to do something. But sometimes, though rarely, you have to give in to him. Because that's the way he is: he takes after his grandpa. There's no alternative.

So – she gives him money for two trams and a scarf to go around his neck, and does up all his coat buttons.

She tells him where Grandma's grave is. She does try again to stop him:

"You won't find it. Better wait until tomorrow."

"I'm off now."

"Just come back quickly."

He goes to the cemetery. There are graves and crosses.

Kaytek walks at a confident pace. He's absolutely sure this is the right way. He passes some old avenues, and then he stops in the right place among the fresh graves.

He reads out the inscription on his grandma's grave.

He stands there for a long time, staring with a penetrating gaze, reaching deep under the ground with his sight, all the way down to the coffin.

He takes a deep breath; he has felt a pain in his chest. Then it happens a second time, and a third, and there's a roaring noise in his head. Then a fourth and a fifth time – he's gasping for air and his heart is aching.

I want and I demand! I demand and I command: make Grandma wake up and come out of the grave!

Silence.

A butterfly settles on a small flower, fanning its wings. The grass begins to ripple.

I demand by my wizardly power. I, Antek, Antek. I, Kaytek the Wizard.

Silence.

A cloud shields the sun, casting a shadow on the grave.

With a fierce thought he cries:

Make Grandma wake up!

Suddenly . . .

Suddenly an invisible hand slaps him twice in the face, on the right and left cheeks.

He's swaying on the spot.

The butterfly has flown away.

There are red spots and circles before his eyes.

No one has ever hit Kaytek in the face before. It's the first time.

He stands there feeling rebellious. He's clenching his fists. That's what usually happens when he starts fighting with some boy.

"Just you wait, I'll pay you back for that!"

An old timer comes up to Kaytek.

"I can see you're upset, my boy. You're upset. Here, have a drink: this will give you strength."

Kaytek reaches out, takes the silver cup the man is offering, and drinks from it.

It tastes good. The liquid is cool and sweet.

The old man fills the cup again.

"Have some more."

He drinks it.

"Thank you. Here you are, Granddad."

And he gives the old man a gold coin; he doesn't even wonder how it ended up in his hand.

He doesn't even look at the stranger's face.

He bows his head toward the ground and walks fast, as if he's in a hurry.

As he speeds along, his rage and rebellion are receding.

He feels a cheering warmth and a strange lightness inside him, as if he has risen into the air. And his heart is beating fast.

He passes the cemetery gate.

He starts walking home – he doesn't take the tram.

He goes down the first, second, and then the third street.

It's a narrow street.

There are two ladies walking in front of him. One has a case under her arm, and the other is wearing perfume. She's holding a handkerchief to her face. Does she have a toothache, or what?

Kaytek wants to pass them, but one of them keeps pushing and obstructing him.

He grows impatient. He thinks: *Make them go backward.*

He barely has time to get out of the way, because instead of walking forward, now they're going backward. Just like crabs. They haven't turned around, they're just moving their feet backward.

People are staring in amazement, but the women are chatting as if nothing has happened.

Have those dames gone crazy, or what?

"It's the latest fashion. In Paris all the rich ladies walk like that," jokes a cyclist.

But when they bump into a baker's boy who's carrying a tray of cakes on his head, he instantly hurls abuse at them: "You freaks, you oafs, you broads!"

Terrified, they flee for their lives – backward – to the other side of the street.

But there's a car dashing down the middle of the road.

The driver tries to brake, but it's too late.

"He'll run them over!"

Kaytek thinks calmly: *Change into an airplane . . .*

He says it to the car.

And at once it flies into the air because it has grown wings.

The two ladies, the one with the case and the one holding the handkerchief to her face, have crashed into the wall of an apartment house and stopped. No one is looking at them now – they can stay there.

Everyone is craning their necks upward. The people in the car are screaming with fear like madmen.

But now the flying car has vanished behind the roof tops.

At once a policeman appears. And a man from the newspaper.

"What happened here? Who was run over?"

"No one was run over, it's just some new American trick."

Each person tells it differently. The man from the newspaper has taken out his pen and is writing.

"How did it start?"

"Oooh, it was those two ladies standing over there. They were walking backward. Over there, by the wall."

There are more and more rubberneckers. They're pushing and shoving. The policeman is trying to break it up, but he can't cope.

"What a stupid crowd," thinks Kaytek.

And walks on.

He stops at an advertising pillar* because he wants to see what is playing at the movies. And on the pillar there's a big yellow poster saying a professor's going to give a lecture.

"A lecture on politics and economics."

"What's that?"

Kaytek doesn't know that a group of foreign visitors has come on a special trip to Warsaw. They're rich guys, and they're

---

* A big cylindrical post in the street, on which advertisements are pasted.

going to found a bank. They're going to lend Poland some money.

The professor is going to talk in French especially for the foreign guests, so they won't be afraid to lend the cash; there's a financial crisis,* but Poland is rich and will pay back the loan one day.

"A lecture. What a waste of time. Politics and economics."

Sometimes Kaytek likes words he doesn't understand, and sometimes they annoy him.

"A lecture." What a waste of time. Make it say:

Professor Pootle
Is going to tootle
On his flootle.
He'll turn a cartwheel,
Swallow a sword,
Crow like a cockerel,
And dance the polka.

And it's exactly as Kaytek has ordered – on all the advertising pillars in the whole city, all over Warsaw.

Kaytek feels like having something to eat.

He takes a cab to a fancy street. He gets out at a restaurant.

It's an expensive restaurant, top class. Through the large shiny windows he can see tables covered with white cloths; there are flowers on the tables.

"Should I go in or not? How much does dinner here cost?" he thinks.

He reaches into his pocket – he has a hundred zlotys.

Good. He goes in.

By the door there's a doorman in a red coat with gold buttons. And he won't let him past.

"What do you want? What are you doing here?" he says.

"I'm hungry," says Kaytek.

"You can't beg in here."

"I'm going to pay."

---

* This a reference to the Great Depression, the economic crisis that hit the USA in 1929 and spread to Europe.

"Get out, I tell you."

"Why?"

"Because I say so. Or I'll grab you by the scruff of the neck and throw you out."

"All right, just you try to move," says Kaytek.

The doorman tries to stretch out his hand – but he can't. He tries to shout – but he can't. He just rolls his eyes, as if he were choking. And Kaytek walks across the carpet into the dining room and sits at a table.

There are two gentlemen and a lady sitting at one of the tables. There is an officer at another one, and a lady and a boy in a sailor suit at a third. Finally, there is a jolly group of actors and actresses who perform at the theater.

Kaytek has sat down on his own and is looking at the actors, and they're looking at him.

"What does that little scruff want in here?" one of them says.

"Wait, we'll see in a moment," says another.

"Look, he has muddy shoes."

"And a dirty collar."

"His nails haven't been trimmed."

Well, yes. Kaytek is poorly dressed, like a carpenter's son. He got muddy at the cemetery. He doesn't like cutting his nails.

He tucks his feet further under the chair; he doesn't know what to do with his hands.

"Waiter," calls the actor, "there's a new guest wanting to be served."

"What kind of a guy is that? Who let him in? Get out of here at once."

Everyone has stopped eating and they're all staring in curiosity.

The doorman rushes up.

"I told him he wasn't allowed in here," he says to the waiter.

"But he still came inside. Can't you deal with a small kid, you idiot?"

Then the boss arrives, the owner of the restaurant in person. He's as fat as a barrel.

He bows to the officer: "Hello."

He bows to the gentleman: "Good day, Your Excellency."

Suddenly . . . he growls at Kaytek: "What do you think you're doing?!"

"I'm having some dinner, please, that's what. I have a hundred zlotys and I'll pay for it."

"Bravo! Well done, boy! He has a hundred zlotys. Don't give in," the actors egg him on.

"You bet I won't."

There's going to be a fuss.

"Momma, let's go. I'm scared," says the little boy in the sailor suit, and starts to cry.

Kaytek sticks to his guns. "I want to eat," he says. "I'll pay. How much will it be?"

"You stole that money. Get out of here."

"I stole it? Just you wait."

"Call a policeman."

Kaytek gets up. He mutters something. He stares.

Suddenly the windows open wide, and plates, knives, bottles, roast chickens, bowls, and tablecloths all start to fly away.

The waiters start reaching out to grab Kaytek.

Buuuuut . . .

Instead they fly up to the ceiling. Now they're stuck to the ceiling by the hair and are waving their legs about as if they were dancing. So is the fat owner.

The actors have started to applaud in delight.

Kaytek commands: *Make them stay there until I've gone.*

Kaytek thinks bitterly:

"The saying 'It's not the clothes that make the man' is a lie."

He touches his clothes with a single finger, and at once there's an elegant young fellow walking along the street.

He goes into a café. He drinks a cup of chocolate and eats four cakes.

He pays. He adds a tip.

He gets in another cab.

"To the Royal Park, please."

And in a flash, he's at the Royal Park.

He sits on a bench by the pond.

There are people walking by and children playing.

Everything would have been all right. He would have just had a rest and gone home.

But just then the group of rich foreign bankers was visiting the King's Palace at the Royal Park.

Just then the bankers come out of the palace and stop in front of a statue. The statue is of a Greek goddess with a garland on her head, holding a mandolin.

There's a man showing the guests around who keeps bowing and smiling in a phony way. Just like the restaurant owner.

Kaytek just has to cause trouble.

Make the roses in the garland change into wieners and the mandolin into a big sausage.

And that's just what happens: there stands the statue with a garland of wieners on its head, playing a big sausage.

A white-haired man, one of the foreign visitors, is shocked – he starts saying something in a loud voice and waving his cane about. Another one explains that there's no need to get mad, because each country has its own different customs.

But Kaytek hasn't finished. *Make seven elephants, five camels, and three giraffes walk down the center of the main avenue*, he thinks.

And they're there. The hump-backed camels are plodding along, the solemn elephants are uncurling their trunks, and the giraffes are nodding their small heads on their long necks.

Some of the children are pleased, others are scared; and the grown-ups think it's all to welcome the foreigners.

But not even that is enough for Kaytek.

Make all the gentlemen be in dresses, and all the ladies in men's pants, he thinks.

Now the fun really gets going.

There's a student with his girlfriend, and they're looking at the elephants.

Suddenly he says: "What have you done?"

"I haven't done anything, but what the heck are you playing at?"

He's staring at her, and she at him. He's in a dress and a lady's blouse, and she's in pants.

"What the . . . ?"

One poor old dear has screamed and fainted as soon as she's noticed she's wearing pants and a man's hat.

And here comes a girls' convent school outing. There are twenty pairs of schoolgirls, with their teacher lady behind them. She's making sure there's order and good conduct. And all of a sudden, like a thunderbolt, she and the girls are all in men's pants. What will people think? What will she tell the Mother Superior?

"Home, let's go home at once!" she cries.

She covers her eyes with a glove and they run off, as fast as their legs can carry them.

Afterward people including the Court Prosecutor, the Deputy Minister of Communications, a senator, a literary critic, and a professor of hygiene all told how they had fled from the Royal Park wearing ladies' silk dresses.

But what amused Kaytek the most was the policemen who kept falling over as they tried to run along in high-heeled shoes, silk stockings, and lacy dresses.

And they had to work fast to protect the millionaires from an unfortunate accident.

Because as a grand finale Kaytek does one more spell.

Make the trees stand upside down.

The ancient trees – the pride and joy of the park – shuddered, leaped up, turned a cartwheel, and came to a standstill, but with their branches down and their roots up.

He's hell-bent on creating the ultimate chaos.

And he's done it.

That's what the world is like nowadays.

It's enough for a wizard to give a few orders, and at once nobody knows what sort of world they're in.

It's enough for a wizard to twist something for a joke, and at once everybody starts to worry and think it's the end of the world.

What a stupid crowd.

Kaytek gets up from his bench. He's had enough of this by now.

Put it all back in order again, he thinks.

And off he goes, home.
That's enough fun.

The news vendors are selling a special supplement.
They're yelling like crazy.
"Attack on the bankers! Special supplement!"
"Extra, extra! Bomb in restaurant!"
"Gang of spies arrested! Mysterious flying car!"
People are buying the papers. They're gathering in groups.
They're standing in the street, reading.
They're all buying them, so Kaytek buys one too.
He reads it.
Kaytek's spells are described, but they're so twisted he can hardly understand it.
The paper says:
The police successfully eliminated a gang of spies who were planning an attack on our guests. Enemy forces do not want Poland to receive a loan for investments.
What the heck: "eliminate" and "investments"? What kind of things are those?
He reads on: *The plan to kidnap the bankers was frustrated.*
"Frustrated – that means it didn't succeed."
The attackers decided to blow up the restaurant where a banquet was going to be held.
"Banquet – that must mean a dinner."
Their infernal machine exploded prematurely and threw into the air . . .
"What sort of machine?" wonders Kaytek.
Further on, he discovers that the firefighters were called, and had removed from the ceiling "*waiters thrown there by the force of the blast.*"
Luckily no one had been hurt.
An unknown kind of airplane appeared. When the police tried to check the ID of the suspicious passengers, the car flew into the air and glided toward the foreign border.
They tore down posters announcing a talk.
"Aha. That's my Professor Pootle. What was it? Economics?"

Kaytek hasn't even read to the end when the news vendors start shouting again: "Second special supplement."

"Extraordinary events at the King's Palace! Extra, extra!"

"Greek goddess, sausage and wieners!"

"Lions and tigers in the Royal Park!"

"Hurricane overturns trees!"

"Numerous casualties!"

Kaytek knows there weren't any casualties. They just wrote that to sell more papers.

"Let them say what they like. What do I care?"

There are crowds of people outside the restaurant.

There are crowds of people rushing to the Royal Park.

Kaytek squeezes through and plods home step by step, exhausted.

He taps his finger, and in his old coat with the scarf around his neck, he goes in the gate.

He's anxious what his parents will say about him staying out for so long.

Chapter Eight

SCENES THE WORLD HAS NEVER SEEN – PEOPLE, CLOCKS, STORE SIGNS, DOGS AND CATS ALL MUDDLED UP – IN THE SQUARE AND ON THE BRIDGE – KAYTEK'S LOOKALIKE

Mom is in tears and Dad is mad.

"Where have you been all this time?"

"It's such nice weather," says Kaytek.

"Nice weather, so after being sick you run off for half a day? We thought something had gotten into you again. You promised you'd come straight back from the cemetery. I went there to look for you. Aren't you ashamed?"

Kaytek has let his head droop; he doesn't even try to explain. He feels ashamed: he broke his word.

His father says some more, but Kaytek isn't even listening.

It's always like that when the grown-ups get really mad, and the child is so terrified he can no longer understand what and why they're shouting at him. It's just a noise in his ears and his head. He's just waiting for it to be over, and wondering if they're going to hit him or not.

"Today you're staying home, and tomorrow you're going to school. That's enough of this delinquency. You're well, so you can go study. Understood?"

Without saying goodbye, his father goes out. Kaytek is left alone with his mom.

Mom tries to console him.

She's so kind.

"Oh well, never mind, it happened. You won't ever do that again. It's not even your fault. I shouldn't have let you go to the cemetery on your own. You're all we've got, so we're afraid of something bad happening to you. Don't worry – we won't send you to a detention center. Your dad just said that."

Kaytek calms down.

"Apparently there was some fuss going on in town? Is that where you went?" asks Mom.

Kaytek reads the special supplement aloud.

"Yes, yes – there must be another war on the way. They just won't leave people in peace. Your great-grandfather, and your grandfather, and your father . . ."

At once Kaytek asks his mom to tell him how the insurgents hid in the woodshed, and how there were secret books and papers hidden under the wood.

What sort of books were they? Why weren't they allowed? Why were people sent to a freezing cold country as a punishment for having books like that?* Maybe there was at least one of those books left?

It had occurred to Kaytek a long time ago that maybe there were instructions in the secret books saying how to conquer your enemies.

So Mom tells him about the wars that happened in the past, and Kaytek thinks about the one that's going to happen. He even wants a war to break out. Because then he could help – his strong will could be useful.

After that his dad comes home; he talks about the events described in the papers and what he has heard from other people.

"It looks as if there's trouble brewing."

For a long time Kaytek can't get to sleep. Because if he does, at once he'll hear the thunder of cannons, the roar of airplanes, bombs, and grenades.

At once Kaytek's spells are helping to win the battle.

All right, so Poland has Kaytek. But the enemy might have some wizards too – maybe older ones who are more careful? What if Kaytek makes a mistake, or his magic power lets him down at a critical moment, and the enemy wins the war?

Kaytek considers what sort of unknown weapons to conjure

---

* This is a reference to the Polish insurgents who were exiled to Siberia for trying to revolt against the Russian Empire in the period when, together with the Prussian and Austro-Hungarian Empires, Russia had occupied and enslaved Poland.

up, what sort of fortresses to build, what sort of orders to give, what sort of armor, helmets, and masks to dress the army in.

"Maybe a regiment of giants, or maybe some iron cavalry on horses made of steel?"

Dad is moving in bed.

"Dad!"

"What?"

"What's stronger: iron or steel?"

"Go to sleep!"

His father mutters something else too. He's annoyed. So Kaytek went to sleep. He woke up and thought: "Tomorrow I'm going to school. They're going to ask why I ran away from home, and what I was doing in the hospital; they'll start bugging me to tell. Maybe I'd better leave late so I can go straight into class just before the bell?"

Or maybe he should postpone his power for another month?

No, he can no longer do without it; admittedly it hasn't brought any benefit, but that depends on him. He doesn't have to do silly things with it. He must work out a plan of action.

"A strategic plan."

He doesn't entirely understand what that means, but he senses that's exactly what it should be – there should be order, the spells should have a plan, and he shouldn't worry his parents.

Until finally he finds a way to leave the house whenever he wants and for as long as he likes, so that his mom and dad won't be in the least bit worried.

It'll be good if it works.

"I'll conjure up an alter ego. I'll summon up an illusion that looks just like me. There'll be two Kayteks; one will be the apparition, the lookalike, the illusion, and the other one will be the real me. That'll be good. Gradually I'll try things out and learn: meanwhile I'll send the lookalike to school or let him stay home. I'll even be able to go to foreign countries – for a long time. I'll travel; I'll sail on a ship, and I'll go hunt wild animals."

Kaytek thinks and sees what he has read and seen at the movies. His thoughts and mental images all mix together and go racing around his head. Some of the images are distinct, others are foggy, some are near, others far away.

And now he wants to sleep.

But his pillow is making him hot. He tries arranging the quilt first one way, then another. He puts his hand under his head, now this way, now that. He lies on his back, then on his side.

He tries to go to sleep.

"Get up. Time for school."

"Hmmm."

"Hurry up or you'll be late."

He gets up. He sorts out his textbooks and exercise books.

Then he says goodbye and leaves. His father is annoyed.

Behind the wooden fence he summons up his lookalike. It makes him feel sorry, strange somehow. The lookalike is just the same as he is – it's as if he were looking in a mirror.

So they walk along side by side, but they don't talk. They stop outside a store. A lady comes along with a man. She stops too, and stares at them.

"Look how similar they are. Are you boys twins?"

"What's it to you?" mutters Kaytek.

"How rude you are," says the man.

"So what? Why do you have to interfere? Why accost us?"

Grown-ups think they have the right to accost you, make loud remarks, and ask any old questions just because you're a child.

They say: "What fine eyes that little boy has. How old are you? It's not nice to whistle in the street."

Kaytek has always pretended not to hear, or he sticks out his tongue and runs away.

But this time it's lucky it happened, because it has made him realize he shouldn't walk along with his lookalike. What would he say if he ran into someone he knew?

Disappear, double.

The apparition dissolves like the mist. Kaytek sighs with relief because he hasn't a clue what to talk to his twin about.

Then he bumps into a friend who collects stamps. He already has stamps from thirty-two different countries, and he knows a store where you can swap double stamps for others – it's better to swap them at a store than with other boys, because they might cheat you, and there's a bigger selection at the store.

There are stamps that cost a hundred zlotys or more.

Kaytek gets carried away talking, and forgets he's meant to be in school.

But at school no one takes any notice – they're all talking about the incident in town.

In the corridor the lady teacher smiles at him, but she doesn't say anything either. Only in the first lesson does the other teacher start to make jokes.

"Ah, here he is at last, Robinson Crusoe! When will you run away from home again? Did your father tan your hide?"

Kaytek stands at his desk; he isn't even free to respond when his friends laugh at the teacher's words.

Grown-ups often tease children as if on purpose. It's unpleasant when someone you don't like much anyway starts joking and mocking you.

"Come on, Robinson, up to the blackboard. Let's see what you learned on your desert island."

Kaytek reluctantly steps forward. He decides not to say anything, even though he could. Let the teacher lose her temper, seeing she's in such a jovial mood.

And why has Kaytek come to school at all? He could have sent his lookalike, and played truant himself.

"Come along, write it out," orders the teacher.

Kaytek grudgingly picks up the chalk.

The teacher dictates the problem, and it's actually quite easy, but Kaytek refuses to do it.

"Read it out."

He reads it out badly. Just from spite.

"That's wrong. So you know how to travel, but you can't read out a stupid problem?"

Well, exactly. Because it's stupid and doesn't interest him in the slightest bit.

Kaytek is a wizard, and he's not going to let himself suffer. He's not going to stay at school.

He puts down the chalk, licks his finger, and stares sneeringly at the blackboard; then he thinks in his secret way: *By my might and willpower, I command it to be twelve o'clock already.*

Even though it was only a quarter past eight.

None of Kaytek's spells had ever caused so much confusion throughout Warsaw.

Every person who glanced at the clock couldn't believe his eyes. In every home, people started complaining that someone had moved the hands on the clock forward, then ran to the neighbor's to check. They were calling each other left and right, trying to find out what on earth had happened and what time it really was.

The clerks rush to their offices with no breakfast, and the salespeople rush to the stores.

The trams are packed full. The conductors can't cope. Anyone who hasn't squeezed on board takes a shared cab. Everyone's late – they thought it was early, but it's already noon.

The students come pouring out of school.

"Those kids are a real curse, they get in the way when a person's in a hurry."

"What a surprise," the children rejoice. "Who thought of such a good idea?"

"The foreign visitors," says Kaytek, cheering up. "Let's go and thank them."

He goes to the gate, summons up his lookalike, and sends him home. The real Kaytek joins the procession of schoolboys, and off they go to town.

Until they have to stop the trams because such a huge crowd has gathered from all the schools.

Afterward the papers wrote that the young students held a tempestuous demonstration outside the visitors' hotel. Other papers said it was impetuous and spontaneous.

Admittedly there was some shouting.

"Long live the visitors! Thank you!"

The foreign visitors came out on the balcony and bowed and said thank you too.

And then each went his own way, back home or for a walk.

Kaytek goes to Teatralny Square.* He's accosted by a blind man wearing blue glasses.

"Escort me across the road, young man, because I can hardly see."

Kaytek takes him by the arm and carefully leads him across. Then the man says, "Here, have some chocolate."

It's the same kind of chocolate as in the little bags under his pillow. And it tastes just the same.

So he eats it. Then he looks around. The town hall clock is striking one, but the shops are only just opening. He remembers Professor Pootle's lecture. Suddenly he thinks: *I'll change all the names on the store signs.*

This store can be called Dangler's. This one can be Gewgaws and Co., that one's Butterfingers and Sons, that's Mongrel and Hogsnout, that's Kelly Smelly, that's Nopants, and that's Cockadoodledooson.

At once, instead of the familiar, respected names, funny ones appear on all the store signs. But that's not enough for Kaytek. He changes the stores too. There's going to be even more chaos.

On the corner of the square he changes the bank into a fruit store. Instead of money, now there are pears, apples, and plums in the window display. There are nuts, bananas, and grapes on the bank clerks' desks.

Not far from the bank there's a well-known pharmacy.

Let there be birds, monkeys, and goldfish inside it now.

At once you can hear canaries singing on the counters and in the pharmacy jars. Where there used to be cough medicine, now there are tortoises lumbering about, and where the ointment for cuts and bruises used to be, there are humming birds.

And there's a monkey sitting in a locked cabinet for poisons, making faces.

Opposite the pharmacy there's an old store – it's an ironmonger's. There used to be knives, forks, and tools for carpentry and gardening in the windows, as well as ice boxes, scythes, scales, typewriters and razors. Kaytek changes this place into a candy store. And he puts signs in the windows saying: "Special offer! A free cake for every school student!"

---

* Teatralny Square – or Theater Square – is in downtown Warsaw.

Instantly the rascals start flocking into the store.

"A sponge cake please."

"I want one with cream!"

"I want one with jam!"

The store assistants don't know what to do. They're wondering what's going on, and the owner says: "You'd better sell them the cakes."

"But in the windows it says they're free."

"Too bad, we'll just have to give them away, if that's what it says. There must be some explanation for all this."

Kaytek pulls his hat down over his eyes and turns up his collar for shame, then goes to see what's happening at the other stores.

Outside the bank there's a crowd of people.

"Give us our money! We refuse to be cheated! Stop messing with us!"

The bank manager implores them and tries to explain:

"Please calm down, ladies and gentlemen. We're going to open the fireproof safe and the strong room. The cashier isn't here yet. As you know, the clocks have gone wrong."

"So send for the cashier. How long will we have to stand here?"

"So you don't get bored, in the meantime we're handing out fruit – whatever we have, you're welcome to it. It'll be served on trays in just a moment. I'm sending the messenger to the store across the way for some trays."

"There aren't any trays in there – it's Dangler's candy store now."

"Well, you can see for yourselves, ladies and gentlemen. Would you like some plums?"

"We want oranges!"

"Excellent. Get a move on, bank clerks, the customers are waiting."

The clerks are up in arms.

"We're not young ladies whose job is to trade in fruit."

Then the cashier arrives. He opens the safe. But there's nothing in it except figs.

People start screaming and making threats – there's quite a fuss.

It's no better at the jeweler's.

"Excuse me, is the owner here?"

"Yes, I am. Right here."

"Mr. Nopants?"

"What's that? I'll teach you to be funny!"

"I'm not being funny. I'm the agent for a horticultural firm. Please take a look at your own store sign."

The jeweler, a well-educated man, goes outside the store, reads the sign and curses so hideously that I cannot write what he said in a book for young people, or I'll set a bad example.

The sign announced:

NOPANTS AND CO.
TULIP AND MARZIPAN STORE.
ROSES BIG AND SMALL.
TEENSY TARTAN PANSIES.
DING-DONG. HEY-HO.

And just then, in comes the lady baroness.

"What's going on in here? I left my valuable pearls with you. Hand them over at once."

"Your Grace, I have nothing but flowers."

The baroness falls in a faint.

The poor jeweler runs to the pharmacy.

"Mr. Pharmacist, please give me some drops to calm the nerves."

"There aren't any."

"But the baroness has fallen sick."

"I couldn't care less."

"If you're going to refuse to save people, I'm going to fetch the police."

And they start squabbling. Because whenever people are upset, instead of helping each other, they start hurling insults.

So they keep squabbling, while a parrot swings in an empty castor oil jar and shouts: "Stupid, stupid!"

And from a small jar of hair restorer, a little green frog hops onto the pharmacist's sweaty head.

It looks as if Kaytek has caused enough chaos. But he hasn't. Just then he sees a dog chasing a cat.

Let's have a fight between all the cats and dogs in the city, right here in the square, he thinks.

And that's the final straw.

The cats come racing in from Wierzbowa Street, and the dogs from Senatorska Street. They start biting and scratching. There's a big rough-and-tumble, with lots of barking, squealing, meowing, and yelping.

Some people run for it, others simply stand and stare.

"Fifi, Fido, King, Pluto, heel!"

And Kaytek thinks: *Make the dogs blue and the cats red.*

And so it is.

The city council officials are standing in the windows watching.

"Get the firefighters to disperse them with water."

The firefighters fit rubber hoses to the hydrants.

By my will and my power I demand that some green monkeys come and restore order, thinks Kaytek.

At once the monkeys appear, as if they've jumped into the very middle of the fight, and break it up.

The cats run off down Bielanska Street and the dogs up Senatorska.

The foreign visitors have arrived in cars to watch through binoculars.

"What a jolly city this is," says a rich man known as the Ship and Railroad King.

And he turns to his secretary and says: "We must have all this described in our newspapers. Rich people who are feeling bored are sure to come here to see all these curious things."

Kaytek puts the stores and the clocks in order and sets off toward the bridge. He heads across Castle Square and down the slope toward the river.

He used to love watching the ships sailing by here, and the sand dredgers on their flat canoes, digging up gravel using buckets attached to long poles.

Today the ships seem small and dirty, and the River Vistula sailors don't look interesting.

I demand, I command: let there be proper sea here and huge liners.

This time Kaytek gets what he deserves.

An invisible hand seizes him by the scruff of the neck, and an invisible foot gives him an almighty kick.

If Kaytek hadn't been blinded by his own power, he'd have had to admit he deserved that punishment.

He wanted there to be sea. He never stopped to think that the sea would flood the city and the countryside, and there would be a bigger disaster than the biggest flood and earthquake ever. He could have plunged half of Poland into the ocean.

But instead of being grateful that his command hasn't been fulfilled and accepting his sentence humbly, Kaytek is offended, and fixes the evil eye on Poniatowski Bridge.*

Make the bridge stand upright! he thinks.

As if not Kaytek, but the bridge were to blame.

The spell works. The bridge starts to rise, but luckily very slowly, or everyone on it would drown or be killed. Not a single horse and not a single person would be left alive, because at once they've all fallen over and gone spinning, and the cars have rolled downward. No one has been killed, but lots of people have been injured and are bleeding.

Enough! thinks Kaytek.

Well, yes, but it's too late.

The ambulances are on their way. And Kaytek is just standing there, in a state of shock.

Enough! I must go home as fast as possible, to avoid causing any new stupidities.

He runs.

He opens the apartment door and steps back in horror: if he goes into the living room, he'll come face to face with his lookalike. Luckily, just now Mom is sitting with her back to the wall, so she hasn't seen him come in.

He slams the door shut.

"Who's that?" wonders Mom.

"I'll just be a moment, Mom," he hears his own voice from the living room.

The lookalike comes into the hall and meekly waits for him.

---

* Poniatowski Bridge is one of the oldest bridges across the River Vistula in central Warsaw.

Vanish, illusion.

It disappears. Kaytek goes into the living room, and Mom asks:

"What did you go outside for?"

"Nothing. There was a boy calling me."

"Why are you so red?"

"It's nothing. I have a headache."

"Go and lie down. Have a cup of tea with lemon."

He lies down. That's for the best.

He does feel tired. Dissatisfied. Sad. And terribly lonely.

And like the most useless creature on earth.

Chapter Nine

ANTICIPATING FURTHER EVENTS – THE POLICE TRY TO FIND THE CULPRIT – AN INVESTIGATION AT SCHOOL – KAYTEK IS SUSPECTED OF TAKING PART IN THE DISTURBANCES

It's late at night.

Kaytek is asleep, and so are the citizens of Warsaw. But in one large building the lights are still on in all the rooms. No one is asleep; there are meetings in progress and the telephones keep ringing.

What sort of building is it? It's Police Headquarters.

There have been too many disturbing incidents, and now the telegraph has sent news about them all around the world. The police are on alert, waiting to see what will happen next.

"Every police station must have one car, five motorbikes, and ten bicycles at the ready."

"Distribute helmets and gas masks."

"Guard the bridges and clocks. Arrest all suspects; put them in handcuffs and bring them straight to headquarters."

"Both plainclothes agents and uniformed officers must be on guard at the hotel where the foreign visitors are staying."

"Maybe we should close the public gardens to stop children from coming out onto the streets?"

"No. It should all be done in secret. We mustn't frighten anyone. We must post notices calling for public calm and consideration. Tomorrow the papers will report that we are on the right track and the chief culprit has already been caught."

"But who is it? Where's he hiding?"

"Even if he's hiding underground we must catch him. It doesn't matter who he is – not even if he's the devil himself. The whole world is waiting to see what the Warsaw police are going to do. The foreign press is full of descriptions of what happened."

Into the conference room comes the duty officer.

"You're wanted on the telephone, sir," he tells the Chief of Police.

"All right, I'm coming. Mr. Secretary, please write this down too: the firefighters must be on special alert because there could be a fire. The pharmacies must remain open. First thing in the morning, the sanitation department is to catch all the stray cats and dogs. And no one's allowed to sell vodka until further notice."

"Chief, the Colonel is getting impatient on the phone."

"I'm coming. Please take over for me."

The Chief leaves the meeting and goes back to his office.

"Hello, Chief here," he says into the phone.

"I'm calling to inform you that the garrison is fully assembled," says the Colonel. "The sappers have been posted near the bridge. There are armored cars and tanks in the main districts surrounding the downtown area. There are two airplanes circling the city. And the tear gas bombs have been dispatched."

"Thank you, yes. I've already received them."

"If there are any wounded, you can send them to the army hospital."

"Yes, sir."

"And now I'm going to bed. Tomorrow we have to be on the alert and sober. I advise you to do the same."

"Unfortunately, Colonel, I can't."

"Well, do as you wish. Good night."

"Goodbye."

The phone rings again.

"Who's that?" says the Chief.

"This is the Criminal Investigation Department. The judge is asking you to send along the two ladies who were walking down the street backward. They must know something – it all began with them."

"All right. I'll interrogate them and send them along with the file."

"We've also received information about a boy who was found in a field."

"I know: the wizard. I have his address. It's just gossip, pure nonsense, but I'll look into it tomorrow. Instead of running after wizards, I'd be better off trying to catch the criminal."

He said the word "criminal" in a tough, threatening way.

Just then Kaytek squirmed in his bed anxiously and shouted something in his sleep.

"Antek, what's up?"

Kaytek didn't answer: he was still asleep.

The police chief tosses away his cigarette butt, drinks a cup of black coffee in a single gulp, and glances at his watch: it's two in the morning.

The phone rings again.

"It's the Inspector of Prisons here. Please send a car with an escort to the Main Station. Three passengers have been arrested who were planning to cross the border. They're very suspicious."

"OK."

He claps his hands and then gives the order for the car and escort.

"Now bring in those two witches who walk about the streets backward."

The poor women come in, terrified, pale, and in tears.

"Please take a seat, ladies."

They sit down.

"Sir, we are innocent. We are quiet, defenseless women. What are we being locked up for? What on earth do you want from us?"

"My dear ladies, please calm yourselves. There are matters that need to be explained. This is a rather important business."

The phone rings again.

"I'm calling from National Security. Please send a car to the Eastern Station, and send the arrestees to us. What's happening at your end?"

"Not much for the time being. It's calm. Should we send the car at once?"

"In an hour's time. Goodbye."

"Sir, we're innocent," say the ladies. "We could lose our jobs. Fancy being under arrest, at night! What will the neighbors think, or the watchman? We haven't been home all night! We haven't even had our tea."

The Chief claps his hands together to summon his secretary.

"Please bring the ladies some tea," he says. "Do you smoke? Have a cigarette."

"Mr. Chief, Mr. Director, Mr. Minister! Please release us at once!"

"I am not a minister. You are not under arrest, just regular precautionary custody. Would you please tell me what you were talking about in the street?"

"About the fact that I'm having a tooth filled at the expense of the Health Insurance Fund. I even have a wad of cotton wool in my tooth to fill the hole. I can show you."

"There's no need. I believe you. What else?"

"Nothing in particular."

"I'm sorry. If you were just walking along, talking about a tooth, there would have been no reason to arrest you. But do serious office clerks have to walk backward while they're chatting about their teeth?"

"We didn't do it on purpose. It wasn't what we wanted to do at all," says one lady.

"We're willing to pay a fine of a zloty each. Please take pity on us. We are innocent," says the other.

The phone rings again.

"This is the janitor at the Post Office. Two cages full of pigeons have arrived here."

"Well, what of it?"

"They're marked 'Very Urgent'. I don't know what I'm supposed to do with them."

"Make yourself some broth and eat it."

The Chief unbuttons his uniform.

"Oooh, it's hot in here. Please drink your tea or it'll get cold. Now would you please tell me about the car that suddenly flew into the air."

"We don't know anything about it. We didn't see it."

"That's bad. Everyone has testified unanimously that the car was speeding straight toward you. A car is not exactly the size of a pin – you could hardly have failed to notice it, could you?"

"We were embarrassed and scared."

"What were you so embarrassed about, and why were you scared?"

"About the fact that we were walking in such a bizarre way."

"So who told you to walk in a bizarre way?"

"It all happened so suddenly. One moment we were chatting, then suddenly someone seemed to be pushing us and calling us rude names."

"Who was it?"

"We don't know. We did our best to get away."

"From whom?"

"We don't know."

"How can you not know who you're running away from? Was it a man or a woman? Was it someone young or old? Would you recognize them?"

The Chief presses a secret bell, and the secretary comes in again.

"Send a car to the Eastern Station. And call the Post Office – they've been sent two cages full of pigeons. We don't know if the telephones will be working tomorrow, so the pigeons could be useful. And tell my wife I won't be home tonight – ask them to bring me a pillow and a blanket. And summon that baker's boy."

The baker's boy comes in.

"Do you know these ladies?"

"No, sir, I don't mix with that kind of person."

"But do you recognize them?"

"And how! Those are the freaks! I almost dropped a tray of cakes in the mud when I saw them. Occasionally somebody bumps into me because they're staring at something and plodding along like they're blind. But they clearly did it on purpose . . ."

"And did you see the flying car?"

"Everyone saw it. How could I fail to? I've got eyes. I wasn't looking up because I had the tray balanced on my head, but when it took off into the air . . ."

"So, ladies, what do you say to that?"

"Nothing."

"That's bad. I'll note that you refuse to make a statement and are obstinately keeping silent."

"Your Worship, we are not in the least bit obstinate. We were just talking about the dentist, and about the summer holiday trip we'll be taking together."

"Would you please give me the dentist's address."

"I don't know what he's called, but he's very handsome – he has such dreamy eyes."

The secretary comes in.

"OK, the boy can go home," says the Chief. "Take these two dames to the examining magistrate. Then remove this telephone. And no one's to come in here until five o'clock. You understand: absolutely no one. Unless there's a real emergency. Now I must get some rest. Good night, ladies."

"Mr. Chief, please take a look at the cotton wool wad in my tooth," says one of them.

"Show the magistrate. There, it's all signed."

And out they go.

The Chief undoes the last of his uniform buttons, flops onto the couch, and covers himself with the blanket. At once he's snoring.

Three times Kaytek has tried to make everyone forget it all. It had worked that time with the bikes at school, so why shouldn't it work now?

But unfortunately they hadn't forgotten. They could still remember everything.

"I thought up a lot of dreadful things. I've terrified the whole city and injured people, horses, cats and dogs. I've done some stupid things in the past too. I teased the watchman and the storekeepers. I got into fights and I accosted those girls. In those days I was just a regular, annoying little boy, but a wizard can't act like a clown or a hooligan. I have to find a solution. I can't go on like this. I have to find a solution or it could end badly."

It could end very badly.

There are notices posted at the street corners saying:

The Police call on the public to remain calm. Citizens are requested not to gather in crowds, as to do so will obstruct the arrest of the evildoer. There is a reward of 500 zlotys for his capture.

"I've gotten myself into a fine pickle," thinks Kaytek. "Now I'm an evildoer."

The newspaper headlines are printed in enormous letters, saying:

WILL THE GOVERNMENT SUPPRESS THE MADMAN?

GANG OF SPIES ARRESTED

CHANGING THE CLOCKS ALMOST CAUSES TRAIN CRASH

BRAVE CROSSING GUARD AND COURAGEOUS ENGINEER AVERT DISASTER!

And further on:

LIST OF CASUALTIES IN ATTEMPT TO BLOW UP BRIDGE

And finally:

MYSTERY PATIENT IN CHILDREN'S HOSPITAL

"That mystery patient must be me," guesses Kaytek, because it also says that at one of the schools in Warsaw there was recently a mass poisoning caused by an unidentified gas. The school had been closed and disinfected. The school janitor had made a statement to the police. One school student fell sick afterward with a strange kind of flu. He was found in a ditch outside the city and was treated at one of the hospitals.

All this was described rather vaguely, but the newspaper warned its readers that it couldn't write more or it would obstruct the investigation, saying: "In view of the ongoing inquiries, that is all we can print."

Kaytek even finds an echo of yesterday's incidents in the small ads:

Lost: female dog, white with black patches. Reward offered for her return.

Lost: Trusty the poodle. 50 zlotys reward.

Tiger the cat has abandoned his mistress. 20 zlotys reward for news of him.

"I've brought it on myself," mutters Kaytek bitterly. "They're hunting me for a reward, like a dog or a cat. Maybe I shouldn't go to school? Better send the lookalike? But I want to know what happens. What can they do to me, anyway? I'm a wizard."

Just outside school, he thinks of a good solution. "Whatever spell I cast, only make it work if I repeat the command twice," he thinks. "Then it won't just be the first thing that enters my head. I have an impetuous nature, but this way I'll be able to stop and think."

Feeling completely calm now, Kaytek goes into the classroom.

At school no one's talking about postage stamps, or photos, or the new show at the circus, or the latest soccer match, but only about yesterday's events.

One kid saw the bridge go up, another saw a rabid dog, and another was in the Royal Park. Some of them are telling the truth, others are lying and showing off.

There are fewer students than usual because their parents were afraid and wouldn't let them leave the house.

Kaytek's mom wanted to keep him at home, but his dad said: "Our job is to send him to school. The teachers will say what to do next. The worst thing happens when everyone starts exercising his own mind. I know that from military service: there should be discipline and order everywhere."

The lady teacher comes in. The boys are wondering how many classes there will be, and whether they'll be allowed to go home early.

"Classes will be the same as usual," says the teacher. "If anything has to change, the inspector will issue instructions in writing. He knows best what to do."

She has only just said it when a car drives up outside the school, and two gentlemen get out of it. Soon after, the janitor comes into the classroom and whispers something into the teacher's ear.

"Antek, go to the headmaster's office please."

"But what have I done wrong?"

"Nothing, it's some personal matter."

Kaytek boldly marches off to the headmaster's office. The

janitor opens the door as if for someone important. Kaytek bows, and a strange man offers his hand.

Then the man questions him about the bikes, the ink that changed into water, the bell that rang by itself, and the flies.

"What do you know about bicycles?" he says.

"There are new ones and used ones: you can rent them or lease them."

What about the ink? Of course he remembers, but the boys didn't do that.

And the flies in the classroom? That was five weeks ago, says Kaytek, no, a little longer.

And the bell? He says the janitor must have gotten the time wrong.

He says he knows this, but he didn't notice that. That's what he thinks happened.

Then another car drives up, and the doctor and nurse from the hospital come into the office.

"Do you know these people?" the strange man asks Kaytek.

Yes, he does – he was in the hospital, after all. He greets them and smiles awkwardly.

"Well then, what did you talk about when you were in there?"

"When I had a fever, apparently I talked about magic spells. Probably because I know lots of fairy tales."

"You promised to build me a palace on a glass mountain," says the nurse.

"And you threatened to turn me into a jackass," says the doctor.

"I'm very sorry, Doctor."

"And can you show us the place in the forest where you fell sick?"

"It wasn't in the forest, it was beyond a little bridge."

"Do you like to ride in cars?"

"Yes, sure I do. But not for too long, or my mom will be worried."

"Ah, I can see you're a good son – you don't want to worry your parents. Don't be afraid – the school will inform them."

The two gentlemen say goodbye to the doctor, the headmaster, and the nurse. They get in the back of the car and sit on either side, with Kaytek in the middle.

He'd prefer to sit next to the driver, but this is good too. It's a really good car, not just a cab.

"So where are we supposed to be going?"

"To Grochów, and then to Wawer," replies Kaytek.

They're on their way. They pass a tram.

"Oh, I traveled on that line. This is where the conductor chased me off. I walked along here on foot. I had a rest here, and a plane flew by here – very low."

"Do you think a plane can change into a cab?" the man asks.

"I don't know. But there are hydroplanes."

Kaytek guesses they're testing him.

"Stop. It's here. This is the birch forest."

They leave the car by the highway and walk into the forest.

"Show us the way."

"It's straight on. Now to the right. Here," he says – he remembers it well. "But beyond here I'm not sure – I lost my way."

"And do you recognize this man?"

"Who?" says Kaytek, looking around in amazement and staring at a man from the countryside. "I think I've seen him before," he says.

"And where's the little bridge?"

"I don't know. It could be a long way off. I was lost for ages."

"Can we get there by car?"

"Not through the forest, but by road you can."

"So let's go."

"Oh, here are the cut-down trees. And the little bridge. It was right here, under this pillar."

"Yes," confirms the man. "He was lying here, groaning. This is where I found him."

"Good. Here's five zlotys for your trouble," says one of the gentlemen. Then he tells the driver: "Let's go back now."

"How did you know that man found me?" asks Kaytek. "Why do you need to know?"

"Well, my boy, we're looking for some harmful, dangerous people, so it's our duty to know. And it's the duty of every citizen to help us with this difficult task."

They're back in Warsaw again. Now where are they taking him?

They go straight to the restaurant. Kaytek pretends it's the first time he's ever seen it; he looks around and asks: "Why is the window broken? How much did the mirror cost? Who plays the piano?"

"What will you have to eat?" says the gentleman.

"May I have some black pudding? Gee, but this place is expensive!"

"Don't worry. I'll pay."

"Then I'll have some sausage and cabbage, please."

The waiters are looking at Kaytek.

Don't let them recognize me. Don't let them recognize me! he repeats the thought twice.

They don't seem to have recognized him, which may be at Kaytek's command, or maybe out of fear.

They eat their food and talk. Now they've finished, and they're leaving.

"They're sure to take me to the Royal Park," thinks Kaytek.

But instead they go to police headquarters, and into the Chief's office.

"Bring in those two office clerk ladies. Sit down, Antek. Do you know these ladies?"

"No."

"Ladies, have you ever seen this boy?"

They both shrug their shoulders.

"Thank you. Next."

Various people come in. Now he genuinely doesn't recognize them.

"I don't know them. Maybe I've seen them. There are so many people in the streets."

He's feeling bored now, and he starts to fidget on his chair.

Then at last he's free to go. His father comes in.

"You can take him home," says the Chief. "Though we might send for him again."

"Well, too bad, if he's to blame."

"No, nobody's saying that. But it is our duty to check up on every rumor."

"Well, yes, of course. Come on, Antek, let's go home," says his dad.

"So what do you think, sir?" asks the Chief once they've gone.

"I think we have wasted three vital hours for nothing," says the gentleman.

"At least all's calm in the city."

"Maybe he's lying in wait and is planning to catch us off guard."

"Well, he won't succeed."

The Chief lights a cigarette and reaches for the telephone to report to his superiors.

Chapter Ten

KAYTEK CONJURES UP AN ISLAND WITH A CASTLE ON THE RIVER VISTULA – THE GOOD PRINCE – MUSIC, DANCING, MOVIES – EVERYTHING DESTROYED

Kaytek is sitting on the sand by the river.

He's gazing at the water flowing by. He gazes at the clouds, high above. He watches the people working on the ships and boats.

For a long, long time he doesn't think about anything.

Then he sees a sandbank in the middle of the river. There's nothing there but white sand. There's nothing of interest, yet he gazes at it as if he were expecting a new and important idea to occur to him, or as if he were waiting in solemn silence for a decision to come to mind.

He feels strangely calm; partly happy, and partly sad. He keeps gazing and waiting, without doing anything. Then suddenly . . .

"I've got it. I'm going to build a fortress on an island in the middle of the River Vistula. Just a small island, with a small castle on it, with a little tower and a small garden."

In fact, he's been feeling fed up at home. The windows there face the dark courtyard, and the walls are gray and peeling. There are no trees or flowers either. But now things are going to be different.

In the old days, Kaytek used to have all sorts of ideas – some serious, others less so. Every hour, every moment, he had a different idea in a different way. Now he knows just what he wants.

"How many square feet should it be? How big should the island be and how high should the wizard's castle be? How many rooms will it have? Will my parents want to come and live in it? Should there be a drawbridge from the shore to the island? Should there be an embankment around it? Or a wall made of granite, or marble, or stone? What furniture should there be in the rooms? What sort of servants should there be? What sort of plates and glasses? Should I put a clock on the tower? What will I have growing in the garden? How many dogs will there be?"

At home Mom asks: "What are you doing all that measuring and counting for?"

"I'm going to build a house," replies Kaytek.

"Do you have the money for that?" says Mom, smiling.

"You can build one without money too," he says, and he's not even lying.

He's not even going to keep it secret, because what harm can it do anyone? Better than that, there'll be a lamp burning on the tower – there are such things as lighthouses, after all.

But what if they guess he's a wizard? What then? In the past, they used to burn wizards at the stake, though they don't do that anymore. Nowadays there are fortune tellers and folk healers – some of them cure people, others do magic tricks, summon up ghosts, or sell various herbs. No one ever stops them.

They get people to pay them, but Kaytek does his magic for free. He'll be like a knight-errant, like a good prince. That's it: the good prince. That's what they'll call him.

But there's no need to hurry. He won't reveal his secret until later on, one day in the future. It'll be a surprise for his parents and for all Warsaw.

He'll appear to them wearing a huntsman's jacket or a royal coat, maybe dressed as a scout or a rifleman – perhaps on a white horse, or perhaps the first time in a car or in a plane.

He doesn't know yet, but there's no rush.

"The Good Prince."

Maybe he'll find a way to bring Grandma back to life. The fact that it didn't work the first time is no proof that it can't be done. He was only just over his illness then; maybe he went about it the wrong way. So many difficult spells have worked for him by now.

"From now on I must start a completely new life."

One time his father had said: "The boy has character."

That means he has a strong will.

A strong will is very important: if you've decided to do something, then go ahead and do it, and if you've started, you must finish. Kaytek has decided not to waste his spells on nonsense. He'll build his castle on the river as soon as he has worked out all the details.

One time, purely as a test to assure himself he could do it, he tried to conjure up some treasure.

He's all alone in the apartment.

Make a box full of gold and a sack of ducats appear here in the corner of the room, he thinks, and repeats the command again.

There's a roaring noise in his head and he feels an acute pain. Sweat breaks out on his forehead and a shudder runs through him.

Kaytek isn't a coward, but he feels scared when, between the table and the window in the dark room, he sees a large black wooden chest; next to it there's a sack tied with string and a red seal.

They're so heavy the floor has begun to creak under their weight.

I want the key to the chest. I want the key to the chest, he thinks.

He has no trouble opening it. He raises the lid and finds gold. It lights up the room like a flash of lightning.

Then he feels the sack: it's full of hard, round ducats.

He hears familiar footsteps on the stairs.

Make it disappear. Make it disappear, he thinks.

Then Mom comes in.

"Why is it so dark in here? Why haven't you lit the lamp? Why are you so pale? Do you have another headache?"

Nowadays Kaytek looks at things completely differently when he's out and about.

In the old days, the houses didn't really interest him, but now he takes a good look at them.

"Hmm, I'd like to have a small deck like that," he thinks. "And a little round window like that one, a small roof above the entrance to the castle, and a gate like that one set in the wall. I'd like flowerboxes in front of the windows, just like this house has."

Formerly, he never considered whether the houses were pretty or ugly. He never used to look at store window displays with furniture, carpets, lamps, stoves, and mirrors. Now he spends ages standing outside them, looking at it all, and choosing things.

"I'm going to hang curtains like those in my windows. I'll put a bearskin on the floor like that one. I'll put that kind of inkwell on my desk."

He sees a comfortable armchair and a table, but they're too high for him. He wants smaller ones to suit his height, because in most houses and apartments everything's made for grown-ups – it's too big and too heavy.

"That small wardrobe will be good. And that bookshelf."

By now Kaytek knows what the windows will be like, and which stove he'll have for the winter. He chooses a white wash-basin with two faucets: one for cold water and one for hot.

"It'll be good to have hot water when I get my hands dirty digging in the garden."

He once went on a school trip to see an exhibition of paintings. He's been to the gallery before, but he can't remember much, because there were so many different paintings in there. That time he actually got bored looking at them all.

But now when he goes there he looks at things in a different way; he compares, selects, and makes a mental note. He chooses four fine paintings, none of them very big.

"Why are you noting down the picture numbers?"

"Because I like those the best."

So, little by little, making progress in his thoughts, Kaytek builds and furnishes his future residence.

Until finally the time has come.

The hour has struck . . .

He takes a deep breath and repeats twice: *Make an island appear in the middle of the River Vistula.*

The water becomes turbulent and a wave rises. The River

Vistula starts shuddering and is covered in froth. And there in the middle of it, instead of a sandbank he sees an island.

And there are seven stone steps leading from the island to the riverbank because that's just how Kaytek wanted it. That's because in spring the amount of water in the river increases, so the island has to be high to save it from flooding.

"There, I've made a start," he thinks. "And now I'll wait for three days to see what people will say."

But people are just people, they don't really know much about anything. Maybe the river engineers have built a dam, maybe they're going to construct a pier for a new bridge, or maybe it's to regulate the river – perhaps they want to divert the current or something?

People are just people – if something doesn't bother them, they don't spend much time wondering about it.

Kaytek can see the situation is calm, so he waits for three days and then gives the command.

And a castle appears on the island. Exactly the way he wanted it to be – not too big or too splendid.

It's surrounded by just the right sort of stone wall, with just the right sort of iron gate, a terrace, and a small tower.

I want to see what it's like inside.

But he doesn't repeat the command, because people have started to gather on the riverbank and point.

"Now there's going to be an uproar," thinks Kaytek.

But there wasn't – in fact it was strange.

The newspapers reported that one of the foreign visitors had decided to stay in Warsaw forever. He likes it here, and the climate is healthy. And the foreign millionaire suffers from asthma, so he needs fresh air, because he has trouble breathing. That's why he has built a castle on the river, and the eccentric fellow intends to live there on his own.

The papers published photographs showing what the little castle looked like inside. One of them published a made-up interview with the rich man. Others expressed surprise at the fact that someone had gathered items from various shops during the night, and that all these things had ended up in the castle. Four fine paintings had also disappeared from an art gallery.

We are in no doubt, wrote the newspapers, *that Warsaw's new friend will pay for everything. The Americans say that "time is money," so clearly the millionaire didn't want to waste his time on unnecessary conversations and shopping. He sees, he chooses, he pays. Some people talk a lot, others just do it. In a single day, a new building has gone up in Warsaw which will be an ornament for the city. Here is a fine example for our ineffectual city council that it is possible to build something that looks good, and it can be done quickly.*

Kaytek put some money in a large envelope and sent it to the bank with a request to pay everyone twice as much as they were owed.

And when his school organized an expedition to the River Vistula, Kaytek went along with all the other boys to admire his own creation. And it really was a very fine sight.

And suddenly he thinks:

Maybe I should fly onto the island, bow to the whole school, and wave my handkerchief?

But he doesn't repeat the wish. He'll wait three days again to give people time to get used to the wonder: they'll come and see it, and feel calm about it.

To raise funds, the Society for Summer Camps* arranged tours of the castle, for a zloty per ticket. A hundred thousand people visited Kaytek's island by boat and by ship. Then the Society published their thanks for giving poor children the chance to go on holiday to the countryside.

But afterward, Kaytek found his island all covered in litter. The shameful truth is that there were bits of paper, fruit pits, cigarette butts, and broken bottles scattered about the place. Even the papers wrote that the public had shown a lack of good manners. But Kaytek wasn't bothered; his foreign servant had it all cleaned up in an instant.

Finally, on a Sunday evening, for the first time, the lights are turned on in the tower, in front of the gate, and in all the windows. It looks lovely.

"That sort of guy is lucky," people say when they bring

---

* Janusz Korczak was actively involved in this real organization that provided vacations for deprived children.

their families to the riverbank to admire the castle on the River Vistula.

Kaytek tells his lookalike to go home, and spends his first night in his new house.

He's feeling happy, and now he's thinking about other things: how he'll invite his friends, the headmaster (he's kind), the nurse (she's kind), and the lady teacher (she's very kind). He'll invite everyone, and even forgive the boys who teased him.

The servant brings dinner: there's chicken salad, stewed fruit, cake, and tea. Kaytek eats it up, because thanks to the fresh air, he has an excellent appetite. As he eats heartily, he starts making new plans.

Once they see he's a wizard and a good prince, he'll bring a whole mountain from the Tatra range* so the children can ride on sleds and go skiing. He'll make a skating rink for everyone to use. There'll be fun and games and treats.

All Poland will be rich. One day even the Chinese and the Eskimos will be too.

There are some things he'll do himself, by magic, and others he'll pay for, so people will have jobs and an income.

For dessert, Kaytek eats a sweet juicy pear, and then he goes up the spiral staircase to the very top of the tower and looks out at the city.

To the right he can see the Royal Castle, defending the houses that climb up the hill; he can see the lights in their windows coming on and going off like small stars. The glow of the street lamps along the boulevards is reflected in the river like golden sparks.

He feels as if he's looking through a telescope. He can see people like small, dark dots on the riverbank.

He remembers how once, during a school trip, there was music playing on a boat.

Why not give it a try? He could start today. He can entertain Warsaw with some music.

So he gives the double command.

And at once Warsaw hears the concert to end all concerts.

---

* The Tatra mountains are in southern Poland, on the border with Slovakia.

The cars have stopped to silence their engines. People are standing still in the streets and squares, or opening their windows to hear better. Afterward the experts said they had never heard such beautiful music in their lives before.

And Kaytek the Wizard goes down the steep staircase to his bathroom, takes off his shirt, and washes himself with scented soap.

"Sau adan ra?" asks the servant.

"I don't understand."

"May I help you, my Prince?"

"There's no need. You can go to bed."

Kaytek laughs out loud because he has just remembered how when he was little, he once said to his mom: "If I was a wizard I'd do a spell so I'd never have to wash my ears or neck, or brush my teeth."

Kaytek spent four days and four nights in his castle on the island. He only went to the city once.

He clapped his hands, and a motorboat appeared. He boarded it, and put on his Cap of Invisibility. But he didn't play in the city for long. He went home. He prefers to be in his garden. He has added a summer house, and told the birds to sing. He has a dog, rabbits, and a hedgehog (quite like Robinson Crusoe). He has lowered the wall so it doesn't block the view. Why have fortifications if no one's bothering you? He changes details in the rooms too, corrects and moves things. He wonders what kind of new surprise to prepare for the evening, and what he'll arrange for Sunday.

Kaytek reads because he has some fine books; but now and then he keeps putting his book down because all sorts of thoughts are preventing him from reading.

When and where will he make his first public appearance? On the island or up on the castle tower? Or in the balcony at the theater? In the square or at the town hall? Or in a parade through the city streets?

What will he say, what kind of speech will he make?

It'll be a short speech. He'll apologize for everything he did when he was just a frivolous boy: he'll ask each person to say what losses they suffered and what compensation they want.

He'll threaten Poland's enemies, just in case they try to attack or cause harm out of jealousy.

Let them be patient. Kaytek will do his best to make it all good.

He's surprised the newspapers aren't writing about him. It's as if they'd forgotten or didn't know about him.

"When I did stupid things, they printed special supplements, but there hasn't been a single word about the concert."

It's just like at school. There they only shout and make threats when something gets lost or the boys have a fight or break a window or spill some ink. No one says a word about a nice, quiet day. There's only ever a commotion about something bad. But not everything results from idleness and carelessness – there is also effort and good will.

What Kaytek doesn't know is that the newspapers have been forbidden to write about him. He'll find out soon enough, poor guy.

On the second evening, as well as the music, Kaytek provides a display of dancing on the walls and the terrace. There's a beautiful ballet lit up by Bengal lights, and there are tableaux vivants.*

On the third evening he projects a movie on an enormous screen so it can be seen from far away.

The citizens of Warsaw stand on the riverbank for hours. Even the children are allowed to stay up late.

"Let them have some fun," thinks Kaytek, pleased his plan is working so well.

But throughout the fourth day he felt sad, as if he could sense something bad was going to happen – as if he could sense what was going to happen in the night.

That night Kaytek has a headache. He's feeling sleepy and downhearted. The servant gives him a sad look. The dog licks his hand and rests its head on his knee. Even the River Vistula

* Bengal lights are a kind of fireworks. Tableaux vivants are silent, motionless representations of historical scenes, performed by a group of people.

seems to be flowing more slowly. Kaytek doesn't eat the delicious dishes served to him on porcelain and silver plates.

The people have gathered on the riverbank, waiting for a show. But finally they disperse and go home. The millionaire's not in a good mood today, they think. Or maybe he's had enough?

"You can't rely on rich men's favors," they say. "He should have given warning so we wouldn't have come and waited in vain. I'm not coming tomorrow – what do I need music for anyway? The police should ban it; the children should be kept home – they're not getting on with their studying and they'll catch cold out here."

"I'll go to school tomorrow," thinks Kaytek. "A wizard's life is hard. I'm tired. I need to rest. Or maybe I'm sick? Do wizards live forever? In the books it says they're old, but it doesn't say if they die."

He went to bed early, but it took him a while to fall asleep.

When suddenly . . . amid the silence of night there was cannon fire.

Then came more cannon fire, like thunder and lightning. The windowpanes were shaking.

Kaytek jumps awake. He sits up and tries to put on the light, but it's broken. He runs to the door, but it's locked.

There's a second and a third salvo. Now the whole island is shaking.

He runs to the window.

Now there's single fire. He sees a bullet fly straight at the window. Suddenly it stops in mid-air. There's not a moment to lose. Wanting to jump out the window, he breaks the glass with his hand. He's injured and he's bleeding.

Then the door crashes open.

"Run for it!"

He runs.

Boom! Bricks go flying in all directions. By now, Kaytek is on the stairs. Now he's outside the house. It's cold and he isn't properly dressed.

Someone touches him with the end of a stick, and suddenly he's fully clothed.

"This way. Faster! Over here!"

Someone pushes him, and he thinks he's falling into the water. But he isn't – instead he's sitting in the motor boat. It lurches and then drives away.

Boom, crash! Now it's as if all the shells have hit the island.

And then it's dark; all he can hear is the water.

Now he's finally fully awake from sleep and from his terrible experience.

Who on earth was shooting at him? Who broke the light? Who locked the door, and who opened it? Two forces had been fighting over him; one had been trying to destroy him, and the other had rescued him.

Kaytek reaches the riverbank, and sinks the boat as soon as he notices the silhouette of two soldiers on horseback.

I want, I demand my Cap of Invisibility.

I demand, I order my Cap of Invisibility.

At once he's invisible, and just in time, because suddenly an electric light illuminates the spot where he's standing.

"Did you hear that?" says one of the soldiers. "Someone came on shore."

"Yes, I heard, but there's no one here," says the other.

"No, there isn't – no boat and no person."

Now the huge military floodlight is lighting up the river, searching the shore.

"Look at that! They've wiped out the island and the castle. What a pity, it was a fine building."

"It was. But I thought they'd missed."

"How could they miss? It's flat as a table top. An island isn't a battleship or an airplane. They aimed straight at the lighthouse. Our artillery's good."

"They've wiped out the wizard."

"Do you believe it was a wizard?"

"That's what the experts are saying. Either a Star Man from another planet, or a wizard. The sergeant said so."

"But why did they have to get rid of him? He was just sitting there quietly, playing music and singing – people had a jollier time of it."

"It's not my responsibility. The authorities know what they're doing. What about the time he made the bridge stand upright and turned the trees upside down? Who knows what might happen next with someone like that around?"

"You could try talking to him. Poland could do with a wizard."

"Give it a rest. Be slaves to someone like that?"

"Apparently our guys refused to shoot again, the sergeant said. It was the Germans who insisted."

"Well, they've drowned him and that's the end of it."

"Who knows? If he is a wizard, maybe he's managed to save himself? Now he'll really start taking revenge."

"It's not my responsibility. The authorities know what they're doing."

They ride off.

"So it was our side shooting at me! No, I'm not going to take revenge. It's time I went out into the world," thought Kaytek.

With his head drooping and with heavy steps, he walked away.

Chapter Eleven

A MEETING IN GENEVA – THE EXPERTS CONFER – SPELLS OR NOT SPELLS? – MR. X

Kaytek couldn't understand what experts the soldiers were talking about because he didn't know what had been happening in the outside world since the time of his memorable adventures. Nor had there had been anything in the newspapers about it because it was a secret. The authorities had decided to dull Kaytek's vigilance so he would think he could cast his spells with impunity.

Each foreign country has its own consul in Poland. It is the consul's duty to report to his own government about everything that happens in Poland. And in the same way, Poland has its own consuls in all the foreign countries.

It was these gentlemen – the French consul, the German consul, and the British consul – who immediately sent out reports by telegraph.

The German consul telegraphed to his government:

The Poles have invented a way of making bridges stand upward. There is also a secret factory in Poland that makes cars which can fly. Please inform the Minister of War.

The French ambassador sent a telegram saying:

France is Poland's friend; meanwhile it turns out Poland is hiding some secrets from us. Today I went to see the Polish minister and I told him it is a very ugly situation.

The British consul demanded briefly:

Please send a talented detective. There are some important military secrets here. The diplomatic courier left today with a letter in which I have described it all in detail.

In Switzerland there is a city called Geneva. In Geneva, each nation has a delegate. These delegates sit there and confer on what to do in order to make sure there won't be any wars in the world. This group of delegates is known as the League of Nations.*

The reason why the League of Nations is in Switzerland is because it is a small country that doesn't fight.

So the delegates gathered in Geneva and conferred on the matter of Kaytek.

First to speak is the German. "We are Poland's neighbors," he says. "The Poles are in deep trouble. The things that have been happening in Warsaw present a danger to our bridges, our clocks, and our railroads. The Poles like causing trouble."

"The Germans cause more trouble than we do," says the Polish delegate.

Then the Chairman interrupts the meeting, saying:

"Gentleman, we haven't gathered to argue or insult each other. If a delegate has advice to offer, let him give it, but if not, I will not allow him to speak further."

Then the German goes on:

"The Poles are inventing military devices and doing dangerous experiments. They have gained a powerful ally."

"He's not an ally, but an enemy, maybe even a spy," says the Polish delegate. "I have just received news from my government that they have arrested some spies. We only want peace. We were just about to receive a loan from some millionaires, but they took fright and left the country."

"I agree with my Polish colleague. Perhaps Mr. X, the unidentified person, is their enemy. In that case, we want to help them."

"There's no need."

"What sort of help can you provide?" asks the Chairman.

"We'll send our policemen and soldiers, and help them to investigate the case on the spot. The Poles clearly can't manage on their own."

---

* The League of Nations was founded after the First World War to preserve international peace. After the Second World War it was replaced by the United Nations.

"Please don't concern yourself, sir."

"I know . . . I've got it!" cries the Frenchman suddenly. "Gentlemen, we must hurry, because Mr. X really is dangerous."

"So what do you know about him?" asks the British delegate.

"Gentlemen, let us hand the matter over to the experts. A committee of experts must leave for Warsaw this very day. By tomorrow it could be too late."

The British delegate lights his pipe and takes out a notepad and pencil.

"How many experts are to go?"

"Let's say ten."

"All right. Ten experts will go. But who?"

"One learned physicist, one learned chemist, one engineer, one doctor . . ."

"Gentlemen!" cries the German. "We cannot do it like this. We must give this some careful thought. Why should there be ten experts, rather than eight, or twelve?"

"Of course you should give it some thought – who's stopping you?"

"Go ahead and think about it, if you have the time," shouts the Italian, "because we don't! Mr. X is like a volcano that could explode at any moment. I'm saying this because I have had a detailed report from Warsaw."

"Now, now, let's have some patience, please," says the British delegate, calming the assembly down.

The Frenchman takes a crumpled piece of paper from his pocket, borrows the British delegate's pencil, and starts writing.

Everyone waits for him to finish, except the German who mutters: "It should all be done slowly and methodically."

Then the French delegate reads from his sheet of paper:

"So, the following experts will come from London: a physicist, a zoologist, and a spiritualist. From Paris there will be: a chemist, a doctor, and a psychologist. From Rome: a geologist and a lawyer. From Berlin: a philosopher and a historian."

The German leaps to his feet and bangs his fist on the table.

"Out of the question! You are each sending four, and we Germans only one expert? It's outrageous!"

The British delegate takes the crumpled paper from the

Frenchman's hands, and frowns because it's stained with wine and tomato sauce. The Frenchman is embarrassed.

"Sorry, I wrote it on a restaurant check."

"Never mind. Please give me back my pencil."

The British delegate copies it all into his notepad.

"Everyone who agrees, please raise your hand."

"I don't agree," says the German.

They all vote that it's a good plan. Only in Geneva they have a different way of saying it, which is that "the French delegate achieved success."

That's how they say it there.

The League of Nations sends out five telegrams.

At once the experts set off by airplane from London and Paris, and by car from Berlin. The Italian experts arrive in Warsaw by express train from Rome in time for the second session.

The sessions took place in great secrecy at night, at the university in downtown Warsaw.

The meetings are opened by a Polish astronomer.

"Gentlemen," he says, "all the unusual incidents have been gathered and described in writing. There have been three hundred and sixty five of them. The official translator has translated everything into French. Please read it, and you will see how much nonsense and idiocy it contains. Someone only has to have a dream and then they rush off to the police to report it. Drunks come along and talk great streams of garbage. Cheats trying to swindle us out of a reward come and tell plain old lies. A madman has been insistently claiming he is a wizard, and that he did it all. If two old women quarrel, at once one of them says the other is a witch, and that she flies out of the chimney at night on a broomstick. Everyone swears he saw it all with his own eyes. It's impossible to get rid of all these pests, which is making our work much harder."

"I know what it's like," puts in the historian. "It has always been like that. People love to tell fibs."

"I know what it's like," says the lawyer. "Unfortunately, people love telling lies."

The astronomer continues:

"I have rejected the rumors and just left what appears to be the truth. There you have the facts written out on a separate piece of paper, gentlemen. Besides this, we have gathered some material evidence, which is in this cabinet."

He points to a glass cabinet where various things that have been collected and numbered are lying in jars and boxes. There are photographs, stones, knives, paint scraped off store signs, the poster announcing the lecture, a piece of chalk, some mauled cats and dogs in pickling fluid, some flies, some air in balloons, and something one of the elephants did in the Royal Park.

"I will examine the cats and dogs," says the zoologist.

"So will I," says the chemist, "to see if they were poisoned."

"I'll inspect the bridge," says the physicist.

"So will I," says the geologist.

Then the astronomer goes on explaining:

"On this sheet of paper there is a report made by the school's educational board for the inspector. The teachers think someone poisoned the air in the school, maybe with some sort of gas, or morphine. Dentists used to give their patients laughing gas to sniff, then pull their teeth, and the patient didn't feel any pain at all, he just laughed and joked. That is why we saved some air in balloons from the restaurant, from the Royal Park, and Teatralny Square. Our chemists have done tests to see if it contains any additives, but nothing suspicious has been found."

"Let's test it again."

"Excellent. Our employees at the Polytechnic and the Institute of Hygiene are at your disposal. You'll find everything you need for your research there."

Tired by the journey, the experts close the session. They take away the papers to read them carefully, and they examine the material evidence.

"Is that hair?"

"That is the hair of a waiter whom Mr. X stuck to the ceiling."

"And what's this?"

"That is the sleeve from a linen dress in which Mr. X dressed up a policeman. The policeman tore it off and kept it as a souvenir."

The experts say goodbye to each other.
"See you tomorrow!"

At the second meeting they talk about the results of their research, and fully confirm what the Polish experts have already said before them.

Then the spiritualist asks to speak.

"Gentlemen, I know you don't like it when there's talk of ghosts, and so, knowing your mistrust of my kind of research, I won't take up much of your time."

"The only reason we don't trust it is that we've already convinced ourselves time and time again that your stunts are plain fakery."

"I won't deny it. That makes us do our research all the more carefully. We too are often wrong."

"Why do your ghosts do everything in the dark? Why don't they talk clearly like us, when we want to say or demonstrate something?"

"Why? We don't know, but perhaps one day we'll find out. Maybe they choose not to speak clearly, or perhaps they can't. We cannot communicate with ghosts, but maybe one day we'll know how to."

"So are you trying to persuade us that all this was done by ghosts?" asks the historian impatiently.

"No, I'm not saying that. But I have found a medium here in Warsaw, and we held a séance. We put out the light, sat down at a table, and held hands. We put some paper and a pencil on the table."

"We already know how it's done. So then what happened?"

"The table rose off the floor seven times. Some small lights appeared in the air. We heard the sound of someone's footsteps. Then we heard the pencil writing. And here is the sheet of paper it wrote on."

On the page is written:

"Copernicus."

And underneath it says:

"K-t-k."

The experts examine it.

What could the letters mean?

The astronomer stared at the page for a long time.

"That's strange. If instead of the dashes you put letters, it could mean: 'Kaytek'."

There is a long pause.

"Gentlemen," says the philosopher, breaking the silence, "let us be cautious. We may well agree with the words of the school janitor and the guard at the Town Hall: instead of doing all this scientific research, we should be looking for a wizard. We know it only takes one or two people to see something, and at once all the rest are convinced they can see it too. That's just how it was in the past: one person would shout that he'd seen the devil, and at once everyone would start seeing him."

"And nowadays there are fakers who do similar tricks. Huge crowds of people stand and watch, and they all see something that isn't really there."

"We lawyers are well aware of this. Often a witness tells the court what he has seen, when what actually happened was completely different. It's not that the witness is lying, it's just that he's confused."

"So, gentlemen, would you like me to record in the minutes that none of this happened at all? In that case, how do we explain the material evidence? How do we explain incidents number nine, number twelve, and even number four? If we write that the world can relax, and then tomorrow or in a week's time something like this happens again, or something worse, then what? I agree that we mustn't frighten people, but if we tell them they can calm down now, we are taking on a great responsibility."

The experts argue until late at night, and then finally they write:

The committee of experts has confirmed that Mr. X operates principally within Warsaw.

They didn't write "the ghost," or "the wizard," but Mr. X.

All those present sign the minutes.

At the third session the psychologist reads out a character profile of Mr. X, in other words, what he is like.

"I can answer any questions you wish to put to me, gentlemen.

"First question: Is Mr. X just one person, or two, or several? My answer is that there is only one of him – the incidents began at the cemetery, then after half an hour they moved to Nowy Świat Street, and an hour later to the Royal Park. On the second day they began outside the hotel, then occurred half an hour later at Teatralny Square, and then the bridge. It would have taken several thousand people to move all the clocks forward, even in private apartments, and to change all the posters. It's impossible for no one to have noticed it happen, so it must have been done in a way that we cannot identify.

"Second question: Is Mr. X old or young? My answer is that he is young and inexperienced. His acts are jokes, frivolous pranks. Our colleague the astronomer was too cautious when he discounted some of the magic spells (we cannot call them anything else). I believe the market trader's statement – I believe Mr. X did indeed spill her apples, and then helped to pick them up. (Incident number one hundred and forty.)

"Third question. Should we be afraid of Mr. X? My answer is yes, we should be afraid of Mr. X. He is not evil, but he loses his temper very easily. When he does something bad, he's sorry, but he refuses to take the blame. He never stops wanting something different, because everything quickly bores him. He's happy when people are paying attention to him, but he also likes to give serious thought to things. He's impatient, he lacks discipline, and he's a prankster – those are his shortcomings. He has a good heart – that is his virtue. I don't know if he has a strong will. He doesn't make use of any machines or any other known method requiring work and effort – instead of that, he puts his ideas into action through magic spells. And that is dangerous.

"And so here is my conclusion: although I do it reluctantly, I have no choice but to say that he is a young wizard."

The historian is furious.

"Colleagues, are you out of your minds?" he says. "I thought it was my privilege to have confirmed for the last time in history that there are no wizards. I thought we were going to be the last committee in history to finish once and for all with these childish fairy tales about mysterious magical forces. This is shameful. What will people think when they read our minutes? Magic spells, charms, and mysterious powers? How shameful! What a disgrace! For shame, gentlemen, for shame!"

Then the oldest expert of all, a chemist with snow white hair, stands up to speak.

"My dear gentlemen, there always have been, still are, and forever will be magic spells. Is it not magic that out of two gases we can make a liquid – water, and that we can change water into hard ice? Isn't it magic that we can put a patient to sleep and cut him up, while he just goes on sleeping and doesn't feel a thing? Is it not magic that lightning transports people in trams and meekly burns in our electric lights, and that our voices and thoughts can be carried thousands of miles by wire and by wireless? We can even photograph the bones of a living man. And what about the microscope, the telescope, the submarine, and the airplane? Or the radio?"

"That is science, not magic."

"I agree. So now Mr. X has appeared who is capable of doing things we cannot, but he does it in secret, he keeps himself hidden, because instead of benefit he is bringing harm. Our task is to evaluate his strength and decide how dangerous he is; our task is to expose him and communicate with him, render him harmless, and even, if necessary, destroy him."

At the fourth session there is a specialist from America who has invented a new alarm system for emergencies.

"It's a very simple device. It has a bell, a light, a number, and some tinted glass. In case of danger the light comes on, the bell rings, the street number appears, and you can see on the glass if it's a fire, a mugging, or a crowd. One person can keep watch on an entire city. I'm not too eager to distribute my device for use yet – first I'd like to introduce some more improvements. It will only be completely ready in a year, but it may come in handy now."

"Thank you very much."

"So you see, gentlemen, in this difficult situation science has conjured up some help for us."

The experts gather round to examine the device.

"What improvements do you want to make?"

"Firstly, the device only works at a range of six miles; I want to strengthen its power. Secondly, it only captures one incident at a time, but if there's a fire and a robbery simultaneously, or two muggings on different streets, the numbers and images get mixed up and it's hard to know what is happening where. Thirdly, the images on the glass aren't very clear, but I want to see not just the person doing something somewhere, but their face, eyes, nose and mouth – so they can be photographed and identified. I have the plans all ready and there's just one more year's work to do. The hardest bit was the beginning – I've already slaved away at it for six years. Look at this, gentlemen."

The inventor shows them his hand.

"As you can see, I only have three fingers on my left hand because a machine took off the other two. I was in the hospital for five months; I thought the whole project was already sunk because I went completely blind."

The experts bow their heads solemnly.

After that they held several more sessions, but then had nothing more to do, and started to get bored. They all wanted to go home, back to their books and laboratories.

"Things are calm here. We really aren't needed."

"No, you must stay," replied the governments of their countries through their consuls.

"Ah well, that's too bad," replied the experts.

Each of them sits in his room, reading, writing, and studying. They meet up less and less often, every second or third day.

"Nothing new," they say.

They talk about this and that. They have made friends with each other because that's what scientists usually do – they become like one big family.

"You know, colleagues," says the astronomer one day, "if Mr. X doesn't show any more signs of life, I have an idea that might explain the mystery. Well, it's rather fantastical . . ."

"Go ahead, tell us."

"What if someone from another planet has been to visit our

Earth? If it's true that there's life on Mars and the creatures who live there are more knowledgeable than we are . . ."

"So the fairy tale about Star Men would turn out to be true?"

"What's so strange about it? We actually know so little. When man started to learn and discover, he thought he was very clever. Every schoolboy thinks he knows everything there is to know. What's so strange about this idea? Rocks – meteors can fall to our Earth, so why shouldn't a Star Man fall to Earth too? He wandered around, saw there was nothing interesting for him here, and left."

"Except he's a bit too dumb for an inhabitant of Mars."

Everyone bursts into jovial laughter.

And just at that very moment the bell on the emergency device starts ringing. No number shows up, but a foggy image appears on the glass.

"It looks like water flowing. It looks like an island on water."

Then there's another ringing noise – it's the telephone.

Something important has happened because there's a strict rule that no one is to disturb the experts.

"Hello," says the expert who has answered.

There's news: an island has suddenly appeared.

Three days later, there was a castle on the island.

Then they heard that the wizard was living there.

We already know what happened next and how it all ended.

Now let's go back to Kaytek.

Chapter Twelve

TO PARIS – MEETING ZOFIA – A CONVERSATION ABOUT FAIRY GODMOTHERS – THE CHEST OF GOLD AGAIN – KAYTEK'S ONWARD JOURNEY – THE EXPERTS GO HOME

Kaytek's head is drooping as he drags his feet across the city.

The streets are almost empty. It's all so alien and gloomy. The stores are closed and the windows in the houses are dark.

"I'll go see the world!" he decides.

So he goes to the railroad station. He enters a large waiting room and stands at the ticket desk.

"A ticket to Paris, please."

"For whom?" asks the clerk.

"For me," says Kaytek.

"Just the one ticket?"

"Just the one."

"Are you going alone?"

"Yes."

"Do you have a passport?"

"No."

"How much money do you have?"

Kaytek sees there are people looking at him. He starts to feel uneasy. Maybe he's about to have another adventure? Once again he hasn't been careful enough – he's forgotten no one is allowed to travel abroad without the right permit.

"Show me your money," says the clerk impatiently.

Kaytek shows him a zloty.

Everyone starts to laugh.

"Go back where you came from."

"He must want to go to France to find work," someone says.

"Maybe to see his father?" says another person.

"Scram, little guy. Don't take up our time," says a third.

The people are in a hurry. They're all afraid of being late, and they want to sit in the best seat on the train, by the window.

There was a time when Kaytek would have been angry because he doesn't like people making fun of him, but now he doesn't care.

"Watch no one steals your zloty."

"Don't worry, sir."

He walks away and mingles with the crowd. Then he thinks:

I want a ticket and a passport. I want a ticket.

There was absolutely no need to go up to the ticket desk. He just didn't stop to think – as usual.

Keeping his distance from a policeman, he shows his ticket to the inspector. And now he's on the platform.

He sees a train standing there. The locomotive is puffing heavily.

"Are you a passenger?" asks the conductor.

"Yes," says Kaytek.

"Then get on board quickly, we're off."

Kaytek boards the train and it sets off.

He goes inside a compartment.

There are only two people sitting there: a lady in mourning and a little girl who is also dressed in black.

Kaytek squeezes into a corner seat, closes his eyes and thinks: "I've wanted to travel so many times before. Now I'm actually going to faraway countries – it's my dream come true. So why do I feel so sad?"

He sighs.

"Pity about my nice, peaceful house on the river. What did they have to go and fire at me for? What harm was I doing to them? Was it a bad thing to play music and show everyone a free movie?"

He's been unfairly treated by his own home town.

"Don't lean out of the window," the lady says to the little girl. "A spark might hit you in the eye."

At once the girl does as she's been told and sits down.

"Momma, do you remember how last time we came home from Warsaw, Daddy was waiting for us at the station?"

"Of course I do, Zofia."

"Who's going to come and meet us now?"

"No one. Andrew will come in the pony trap."

The girl's voice seems familiar to Kaytek, and he half opens his eyes.

The girl, Zofia, thought he was asleep. She's embarrassed when she sees him looking at her, and quickly turns her head.

"They're in mourning," thinks Kaytek, and is reminded of his grandma.

The lady glances at Kaytek a few times as if wanting to ask him something, but she doesn't say anything. And Kaytek's grateful because he doesn't feel like answering any questions. He knows just what sort of questions they would be, things like: "Where are you going? To see whom? Why alone? How old are you? What grade are you in?"

Grown-ups never talk about themselves, and it's rude to ask them questions, but they always want to know everything about you.

"Lie down, Zofia. Someone else might come in here later, but for now there's plenty of room."

"What about you, Momma?"

"I'll sit for a bit, but you're still weak from your illness."

Kaytek says: "Excuse me, there's room on my seat if you want to lie down. I can go sit somewhere else if I'm in the way."

"Not at all. Not a bit," smiles Zofia's mom.

And Zofia smiles too – such a lovely smile, so friendly. Kaytek notices they look very much alike.

The lady takes a pillow out of her case, puts it down for Zofia, and covers her.

The fatherless girl looks pale in her black clothes.

Kaytek closes his eyes.

"Why exactly is it that I don't like girls? Why have I always teased them? They're quieter than boys and more careful. They have neat exercise books."

Kaytek wonders and thinks back.

"Whenever we play in the yard at school, I make fun of them

and bother them. Whenever they make a garden out of sand and sticks, I smash it up. Whenever they start singing, I yowl and interrupt them. I push them, hit them, and pull their hair. It's just a joke, but they always cry."

Kaytek wonders and gives it some thought.

"Maybe it is quite funny when someone gets mad. But not all girls get mad – sometimes they just go away looking sad. It's bad, nasty, and inhuman to laugh at someone else's tears. What a lot of dumb things a guy does for lack of interest."

Kaytek stands at the window and watches as the sparks fly by like little golden snakes, or fiery fish, a whole shower of stars against a black wall of forest.

The steam train blows its whistle, and Zofia starts moving. Then her mom says in a kind, gentle whisper: "It's all right, little one. Go to sleep."

That makes Kaytek think of home and his parents. And the lookalike.

"They don't know. They can't guess."

And he's getting farther and farther away. Will he be gone for long? Maybe forever? Maybe they'll track him down, or maybe his magic power will suddenly leave him at a vital moment? Kaytek gazes at the black fields.

"How long it is since I talked to anyone! Surely it's because I'm a wizard that I have to be alone."

Suddenly he turns away from the window and asks: "Are you going to Paris, ma'am?"

It happens so unexpectedly that he feels confused and blushes.

It has come out stupidly, like nonsense – he sounded so over-familiar. It's because when you're in the same train compartment as somebody else, you immediately feel as if they're an old friend. He already knows what the girl is called, he knows her father's dead, and he knows Andrew will come to meet them in the pony trap.

But he doesn't really know them, and the lady might be offended, or she might laugh at him. But she doesn't – instead she answers calmly.

"What would we do in Paris? I'm glad to be returning home from Warsaw to my refuge. I wanted to leave Zofia there, to go to school. But we were in the square when that strange fight occurred between the cats and dogs. Zofia was extremely frightened and felt so sorry for the animals – she's so very fond of dogs. Maybe that wasn't what made her fall ill, I don't really know, but I think I'd rather have her at home with me. Warsaw is a large and dangerous city – there are so many different illnesses and unfortunate accidents."

She stops talking, as if she's trying to think what would be better for Zofia.

And Kaytek is grateful she hasn't accused him – she didn't say anything about "the culprit" or "the evildoer."

And then the lady goes on talking – quietly, as if in confidence, as if seeking Kaytek's advice: "At school she'd have friends and more fun. It'll be sad for her at home now. If only she had a sister or a brother . . ."

Suddenly Kaytek decides: "I'll go to their house instead of going to Paris."

He isn't really listening any more, he's just thinking how to arrange it. What will he do in Paris on his own anyway?

He feels tired and starts yawning.

"What does 'refuge' mean?" he thinks. "Is that the name of a village? What does Andrew look like? Do raspberries grow there, is there a summer house, and beehives, and a woodshed?"

Kaytek dozes and thinks by turns, as the train wheels rap against the tracks.

Meanwhile the day is beginning to dawn.

Zofia has woken up. She rubs her eyes and tidies her hair, then goes straight to the window. The sun is just peeping out.

She and Kaytek meet by the window and look each other in the eyes.

"Look, Momma, what lovely sunshine. Come and see the beautiful heather! I must pick some!"

She leans forward and stretches out her arms.

"Be careful, Zofia. Sit down. Let's have breakfast. Here, take this glass."

She hands a second glass to Kaytek. She pours some milk, and gives each of them a buttered roll.

"Go ahead, eat up."

It's all so simple, with such a kind smile.

They've just finished their food and drink when Zofia claps her hands.

"Look, Momma, heather! A whole bouquet of heather. How on earth did it get here?"

"Maybe someone left it behind?"

"We should hand it in to the conductor."

"No, they're just ordinary flowers. Take it, if you like them."

"Ordinary, you say? No, it's a magic bouquet."

"All right. So pick up your magic bouquet because we're just about to get off the train. Goodbye, bon voyage to our dear traveling companion."

She nods to Kaytek and reaches for her suitcase.

Kaytek hesitates, and then says: "I'm getting off here too."

"All the better. And how strange – I thought we'd be the only people getting off at our little station . . . Zofia, go and see if Andrew's there. Here, take the basket. The train only stops for two minutes."

"I'll carry your suitcase," says Kaytek.

"No, it's heavy."

"It's nothing."

He takes the suitcase in his right hand and the basket in his left. He carries them as if they were feathers.

"You're strong."

They alight from the train.

"Oh, there's Andrew. Over here, please. And where are you going, young sir?"

Kaytek is confused.

"Because if you're going our way, there's room in the trap – we can drop you off."

And so without any magic spells everything happens just the way he wanted. Well, except for the bouquet of heather he conjured up for Zofia and the fact that he's so strong – but those things don't really count as magic.

The trap is on its way. They drive up to a small manor house. This is what it must have been like at Grandpa's house. There's a flower bed, asters, and a porch with a vine growing up it.

They invite Kaytek to take a rest, and say he can spend the night in the study on the couch.

He agrees.

"Fine. Thank you."

Only now do they ask: "What's your name?"

"Antek."

"Antek! So what are you children going to do now?"

"Oh, there's a lot to do," says Zofia. "I'll show him the dogs, the hens, the doves, the raspberries, the beehives, and my garden plot – the whole house and garden."

"But mind you don't wear yourselves out – you've been ill, Zofia, and your guest hasn't slept all night."

Zofia is a good guide – she shows him everything and explains it all so understandably. She stops in each spot for just as long as necessary to see and remember. Every time he asks a question she either gives an instant reply, telling what she has seen and knows for sure, or else says at once: "I don't know. Maybe Mom will know. Maybe Andrew can tell us. We'll ask the people from the village."

It's totally different from at school, totally different from a nature trip.

She never once says Kaytek's question is unimportant or stupid; she isn't surprised if he doesn't know something, and she never says he ought to know that by now.

So Kaytek spends the whole day as if he's in nature class, right up to dinner time and also after dinner. He's even forgotten about his own garden on the island.

That evening, her mom hands Zofia some keys.

"I'm going into town tomorrow. I have some business to attend to. I'll be home late. You will have to take care of things for me and Andrew."

Mom explains what she has to see to in town, and what Zofia has to do at home. She even asks Zofia's advice, as if talking to a grown-up, because there are adults who respect and trust children – those are Kaytek's favorite people.

So the conversation he has with Zofia's mom the next day is painful, difficult, and sad.

"Come in the study, my boy," she says. "Sit down."

On the desk there is some Polish and foreign money, and a train ticket to Paris.

"As you know, we met on the train. We alighted together. You're here with us, and you're welcome to stay. You can stay here as long as you like. But on one condition."

Antek looks at her sadly and waits.

"While Andrew was cleaning your clothes, these things fell out of your pocket. Can you tell me what this means? You're going all that way alone with no suitcase and no overcoat. And you have a large sum of money, more than grown-ups usually entrust to children, and if they do have that much cash, they usually hide it very carefully. I don't suspect you of anything, Antek, but I need to know. I'm not going to withdraw my invitation, but I'm sure you understand . . ."

There's a silence.

"I'll tell you what my Grandma used to say about me: I am a troubled, very troubled, but honest boy. I like you, because you have a kind face, so I broke off my long journey. Today, at once, or tomorrow with your permission, I'll continue on my way. A great wrong has been done to me. If it weren't for you, I'd have left Poland with a grudge against the whole country. But you have reconciled me with my homeland. I'm grateful to you for that. And that's all I can say."

He stops talking.

Just then the pony trap drives up to the porch.

"All right, then. Stay until tomorrow. But before you leave, please let's have another chat about your secret. Remember that whatever you choose to tell me or keep to yourself, I will still be your friend. And remember that in case of need, you'll always be able to come and visit us. We aren't rich, but you'll always find good advice and a friendly welcome here."

They're sitting on a bench in the garden. Zofia is weaving a garland and singing. They start to chat.

"It was a fairy godmother who gave me the bouquet of heather. Where else could those flowers on the train seat have come from?"

"Maybe it wasn't a fairy godmother, but a wizard?"

"No, no. Wizards take things away, they don't give them. They cause people harm, but fairy godmothers help them."

"Do you help people?" asks Kaytek.

"Yes, I do, if I can."

"So you're a fairy godmother. And I've often played nasty tricks on people, so I must be a wizard."

"No, Antek, you're not bad, but you need a fairy godmother to take care of you."

"So please take care of me."

"I don't know if I'll manage. Fairy godmothers don't have that sort of power. A fairy godmother only appears for a short while, helps someone, and disappears again. And she only comes when someone has been badly wronged or is in great danger. Do you know the fairy tale about Cinderella?"

"Yes."

"Wizards want to destroy all the fairy godmothers. Dwarves help fairy godmothers, but they don't have much power . . . The fight will continue for a long time, until the moment comes when a good wizard rebels and becomes leader of all the fairy godmothers. He'll capture the fortress where the wizard chief is hiding and free all the imprisoned fairy godmothers."

"So who's this wizard chief? And what does he look like? Where's his fortress?"

"Beyond seven mountains, beyond seven rivers and seas, there is a gloomy castle surrounded by a high wall. In a dark room, on a golden tray, lies a head that gives orders – the wizard chief has no arms or legs or heart or eyes, because long, long ago a rebel wizard cut his head off his body, but the head is still alive."

"How do you know all this?"

"My nursemaid told me some of it, I dreamed some of it, and I made the rest up myself."

"Everything you're saying is so strange."

"Yes, every human thought is strange and mysterious. The world is strange and mysterious. Life is strange and mysterious; it's often sad, but it's sometimes so beautiful and so full of joy."

That night, Kaytek quietly opens the window.

He jumps down into the garden.

The dog begins to bark. Kaytek orders him to be quiet.

He goes into the depths of the garden and stops under a tree.

He concentrates and gives a deep sigh. His head begins to spin.

I want, I command a chest full of gold to appear, he says, and repeats it.

The familiar box appears.

I want a spade. I want a spade.

Night. Silence. Darkness.

Kaytek starts digging, but the ground is hard. Soon his hands are aching. It's hot. He throws off his jacket. He digs, overturns earth, and measures the hole to see if it's deep enough.

By now he has forgotten where he is and what he's doing. He just keeps digging doggedly, just to make it deeper, just to dig harder, just to throw more earth out of the hole. He doesn't rest for a moment.

Finally he has finished.

A cat runs across the path.

Kaytek pushes the heavy box – one, two, three! It shudders and wobbles. He tries again, and it starts to slide.

Something glitters on the ground. He picks it up and looks at it: it's the two twenty-groshy coins he earned at the market that time and kept as a souvenir.

He breathes on them. "For luck!"

He throws them onto the lid of the box and covers it with earth.

Then he gives a careful command: *Let no one know someone was digging here. Let the grass grow over this spot.*

And it happens, just as he has ordered.

He goes back to the house.

He reckons this buried treasure will be his entire reserve when he comes back from his travels, and that Zofia's house is like a quiet haven where he'll be able to rest after the labors of his long journey.

"So you're leaving? Haven't you changed your mind?" says Zofia's mom the next morning.

"No, I haven't."

"Go, then, and keep your secret. Thank you for not telling me lies. I don't like fibs and excuses at all."

They give him a basket of food.

"Here you have some eggs from our hens, and here's some cheese, some jam, and some honey from our hive."

That's probably just what it was like at Grandpa's house.

"Well, off you go, Andrew, or you'll be late for the train."

Zofia waves her handkerchief.

"It's a pity you're leaving, young master," says Andrew. "Our Zofia would have some company if you stayed, because she's all on her own. She's a good child, our little miss. We were sorry when Madam took her off to the city. They say there's a war on there – lots of people have been killed. God forbid any misfortune should happen to our Zofia. Yes, yes, Madam is a good woman, and the late master was a good man too. They're a noble family."

"It's rare for anyone at home in the city to talk so well of people," thinks Kaytek.

As he says goodbye, he gives Andrew a gold coin.

"What's this for? You can't give me this, young master."

But Kaytek swiftly jumps out of the pony trap because the train is pulling in.

The train lets out a whistle. And it moves away.

The compartment is crowded, full of unpleasant people talking about uninteresting things. At the fifth station Kaytek starts hearing foreign speech.

He gives a command to change his clothes, then conjures up a leather suitcase and a first-class ticket. Then he demands: *I want to understand foreign languages*.

Just then the experts were traveling home from Warsaw on the very same train.

"I'm afraid we did the wrong thing," says the Frenchman "We shouldn't have opened fire."

"That's definitely incorrect, my dear colleague," says the Italian. "Mr. X, as we called him, drowned the island himself. I examined the spot with extreme precision. If the cannonballs had destroyed the castle there would have been more rubble left."

"But maybe the water carried it away?"

"No. It happened in some other way."

He takes a piece of rock out of his case.

"Look through the magnifying glass, my friend. There are crystals here that do not exist on our planet."

And they begin a scientific discussion which Kaytek can't understand and doesn't find very interesting.

"Ultimately we can agree we are dealing with a creature from another planet, where the inhabitants know more and can do more than we can. What we think of as magic, for them is as simple and easy as lighting a match."

"What? Students at school don't like new tasks and exercises either. Nor do we scientists like new things that are difficult and incomprehensible. How can we admit that we believe the ghost of Copernicus reincarnated itself as the Star Man and overturned the trees in the park?"

"And yet seeking out what's new, unknown, and ever better is actually the path for us scientists to follow."

Kaytek feels like having a bite to eat.

He opens the basket full of provisions, and right at the top, he finds a sprig of heather and a note saying:

A keepsake for Kaytek the Wizard from Zofia the Fairy Godmother.

Chapter Thirteen

PAUL AND PETE – KAYTEK FIGHTS THE AFRICAN – IN THE PRINCE'S HOTEL – THE NEWSPAPER REPORTER

They say Paris is the capital of the world.

People go there from all over the entire planet to study, to work, and to play.

So Kaytek arrives in the capital of the world.

He stands helplessly outside the station, not knowing what to do or which way to turn.

Thanks to his magic powers he can understand what the people around him are saying, but he feels strange surrounded by a foreign language, as if he's in tight, borrowed clothing.

Crowds rush by, vehicles speed past. No one takes any notice of him.

So he's amazed and pleased when he suddenly hears his own name.

"Look at that – it's Kaytek. I'm sure I recognize him."

"You dope. How could he have gotten here on his own? And so smartly dressed, with a fancy suitcase?"

"All right then. Let's ask him – we'll see."

"You ask if you want to. I'm not going to make myself into a laughing stock."

That's what two boys are saying – one the same age as Kaytek, the other older.

They're staring at him, and Kaytek is staring back.

"Don't I know them? I'm sure I've seen them somewhere before," he thinks, but he can't remember where.

"Excuse me, but have you just come from Warsaw?" asks one of the boys in French.

"Yes, sir," replies Kaytek, also in French.

"Excuse me, but have you always lived in Warsaw?"

"Yes, since birth."

The older boy comes up and says to his brother in Polish: "You see, you dope! Kaytek can't speak French, can he?"

"Maybe he learned it. We haven't seen him for three years."

"And he's already learned French. He was a great one for learning, all right. He was even more of a lazybones than us."

Kaytek feels awful.

"Wait, let's ask. Maybe he understands? Excuse me, sir, but do you speak Polish?"

"Of course I do," admits Kaytek, weary of the long preamble and curious to know who they are.

"So you're Kaytek?" they both cry.

"One and the same. And who are you?"

"Don't you remember us? The time we went to the River Vistula together and some boys stole your clothes?"

"And the time we snitched apples from a stall and a policeman chased you?"

"It wasn't like that – it was you the policeman caught."

"Maybe. It's so long ago. I got a thrashing from my dad that time. Do you remember how we used to smoke cigarettes in the garage, near the gas?"

"And how we put out the lights in the hallway?"

So they laugh and chat. Passers-by politely walk around the jolly trio.

"You know what, come to our place. Leave your suitcase at the station. Why should you drag it around with you? Give me a franc and I'll go fetch you a receipt. You can pick it up tomorrow. Wait here for me, you two."

"There's nothing like old friends! Fancy that, Paul, Pete, and Kaytek together again. Let's go to the circus today."

Paul and Pete pick up the suitcase and the basket. They swap glances, wink, and fail to hand the receipt to Kaytek.

They didn't actually like each other much in Warsaw. Kaytek was a rascal in those days, it's true, but those two were sneaky little thieves. If he weren't a wizard, he'd have to take better care of himself. But it's all right, because they'll show him the way – real people whom he knows, not a conjured-up guide.

They go down some stone steps, deep under the ground, and there, below the street, beneath the houses, is a train station, all lit up.

It's the metro! An underground electric tram system.

They hear a thudding sound, then a bang, a crash, and the train thunders in.

The carriage doors open automatically. They only just have time to jump on board.

They speed down narrow tunnels underground, station after station, stop after stop. A crowd of people gets off, another one gets on. It all proceeds quickly and efficiently.

"Watch out – we're changing trains here."

"Why is everyone in such a hurry?"

"Because this is Paris, brother."

They change trains. They go up one flight of stairs and down another; even though there's a crowd of people, they all carefully pass each other without pushing.

"Get in quickly or the doors will slam shut on you. In Paris you don't have time to stop and stare."

Now Kaytek remembers everything.

"So you left for France, didn't you?"

"Yes. First our father came here, then we left with our mom and we were all together again. Then our father ran away from us and we were left alone. After that our mom found a new husband, a Frenchman. Then our mom died, and we were left with our stepdad, the Frenchman."

"Does he look after you?"

"What does he care about us? He's out all night, and we're out all day. He's a boozer but he's a jolly guy."

"You're jolly too."

"Why not? Should we be weeping for Mom? Waste of time. Gotta earn a living. We feed the Frenchman more than he feeds us. He'd rather see a franc than see us. So do you have plenty of cash?"

"Yes."

"Because you see, we could go see the boxing at the circus. Today the African is fighting the Turk. The African's real strong – he sure hit the Turk on the nose yesterday, he must have lost a bucket of blood. Hats off to you, brother! What great boxers. Today's the big fight. Now we'll show you Paris – you'll see our apartment at the hotel."

"You live in a hotel?"

"*Mais oui!* Like every deadbeat in this town. When our dad wrote that he was living in a hotel, our mom thought he was rich. But the bedbugs sure can bite! In America, every hobo has his own car. Every country has its own customs. I ain't gonna be a chauffeur – it's no better than being a coachman. I'm gonna be a pilot. This is where we get off."

They emerge from the metro into the street and start walking along.

They come to a dirty house on a narrow street.

"Here we are! Come and have dinner with us."

There's a small, dark, shabby room with a narrow bed, a little table, and two chairs.

They fetch a bottle and some glasses. They cut three slices of bread.

"Have a drink. Eat."

"What is it, wine?"

"You'll see. In Poland, the beetroot soup is better than this wine; it's cheap and sour, but it makes your head spin. If you give us a few francs, we can go buy some cold meat."

Kaytek puts fifty francs on the table.

"I'll go buy some," says Paul.

"Wait, I'm coming with you," says Pete.

"No need for that. I'll be back in a moment."

"He won't be back," says Pete, as soon as Paul has shot out of the room like an arrow.

"Why not?"

"It's very simple – because he has fifty francs. I know him well; he is my brother, after all."

He's right. They wait in vain.

"Let's go to a restaurant. Don't be afraid. On your first day in Paris you're sure to spend more money, but once you get to know the place, you won't spend as much."

So they eat dinner at a restaurant.

Kaytek sees the Eiffel Tower, the boulevards, squares, and big stores. He has always liked looking at the stores in Warsaw too, and walking along the streets where colored lights keep flashing on and off. All Paris is full of lights and colors.

"Well, that's enough for today. Shall we go to the circus?"

"If it's a long way, we'd better take the metro."

"Oh, so your feet are hurting. That's Paris for you, brother. You'll soon get used to it."

So they arrive at the circus.

"Give me some cash," says Pete. "Wait here while I go to the box office for the tickets."

Kaytek gives him a hundred francs.

"Ho ho, that's a really fine banknote!" says Pete, and goes.

Kaytek waits in vain. He smiles – he can guess what has happened.

"They've relieved me of some cash. Well, good luck to them."

He goes and stands in the ticket queue by himself.

"Where is everyone going to fit?" he wonders.

But they all fit inside the huge building like sardines – it looks as if there are no seats left at all, yet more and more people keep pouring in, spreading onto all the floors in the auditorium, into the boxes, the stalls, and the gallery.

Until there's just one empty seat left – next to Kaytek.

The band starts to play and the show begins.

First on are the performing horses. Second are the acrobats. But the audience is waiting impatiently for the boxing match to start. Kaytek is curious too. He wonders why no one ever claps – maybe they have a different custom here in Paris.

After the interval, the boxers enter the arena. The African is the tallest – he takes mighty strides. There's a real show to watch.

During the fight between the third pair, a Hungarian and a Greek, Kaytek is so excited that he forgets where he is, and shouts out in Polish: "Whack him! Again! Hit him! Harder!"

Just at that point a beautiful lady comes and sits in the empty seat next to Kaytek.

Kaytek goes on shouting, and she watches, with a smile on her face. Then she takes a golden cup and a flask out of her purse and asks politely: "Would you like a glass of wine?"

Kaytek's throat is dry from all the shouting. So he takes the cup, drinks the wine, and thanks her. Then he hands it back to her.

At last – out comes the African. The whites of his eyes are shining. He smiles, flashing his white teeth. He bows. There's thunderous applause. Someone throws flowers, someone else throws tomatoes. The African eats them, licks his lips, rubs his stomach, and says: "Yum, that's tasty!"

But where's the Turk? Send in the Turk. What's keeping him?

"Hurry up! Get started!" people shout.

Then the circus manager enters the arena in a black tail coat.

"The Turk has fallen ill," he explains.

"It's all lies! It's a swindle! Show him to us," shout the people in the gallery, louder and louder. A doctor and a nurse bring in the Turk; it's plain to see he can't possibly fight.

"He has a fever. His nose is bandaged."

"Why didn't you warn us? We want our money back. You won't get away with this!"

Suddenly Kaytek leaps up from his seat, but no one takes any notice. He covers his face with a red mask, but no one has spotted him yet. He pushes his way through to the aisle, runs down the steps and shouts in a mighty voice: "I will stand in for the Turk. I'm going to fight in his place!"

Ushers in red livery try to stop him, but they fail. He's already in the arena.

"The Red Mask! The Red Mask! Who is this boy?"

The circus manager turns and stares at Kaytek. He can't understand what's going on.

Meanwhile the people in the gallery are shouting: "Quit clowning around! You grafters! Quit playing dumb!"

But the people in the stalls and the boxes – the rich members of the audience – are laughing. They're curious to know what sort of a surprise the manager has prepared for them because he's famous for his quirky ideas. And it really is a comical sight – in the entire history of boxing, no one had ever seen a pair of fighters quite like this one.

The African also thinks the white guys are having a joke. He goes up to Kaytek smiling, then tries to take him by the hand to lift him up, so they can have a better look at him . . .

But Kaytek breaks free and leaps in the air. Somehow he hits the African so nimbly with his entire body that he falls over, and Kaytek jumps on top of him. The African clumsily gets to his feet, but Kaytek is already in boxing gloves and has hit him twice. Now Kaytek is standing, and the African is lying down.

Everyone is laughing.

"The little guy's putting on a good turn. Let him show his strength. Let him show what he can do."

Kaytek nods to the circus manager, and whispers something in his ear.

At once the ushers bring in an iron bar with two heavy balls at either end. Kaytek spits on his palms and stands with his legs apart, but pretends he can't shift the bar.

"Too heavy!" cries the gallery. "Bring something else."

The ushers try to take it away, but Kaytek gives them such a hard push that they stagger back. He throws off his jacket, blows a kiss to the gallery, gives a shout, runs up and grabs the weight with one hand. He lifts it, throws it up, and catches it. He spins it in the air twice, and then hurls it onto the sand. Landing with a dull thud, the iron balls stick into the ground.

"Well then? Am I good enough?" cries the Red Mask to the audience.

"We'll take him! We're on!"

"All right. Let him fight."

The confused African looks at Kaytek. He alone may have realized Kaytek's secret, because some Africans believe in magic.

"Look! The African's afraid. Long live the Red Mask!"

The band starts to play, and the manager sends for sportswear at high speed.

Kaytek attacks in a casual kind of way. The African just drives him off, as if he were a persistent fly.

It's clear he's just pretending to be on the defensive. The white guy knows what he's doing, the white guy is smart: he pulled some kind of joke with the barbell.

But the people in the gallery are on the alert – they won't let themselves be taken for a ride.

"Enough! This ain't what we want!" they shout, dissatisfied.

Just at that moment the African takes three mighty punches, short and fast as lightning.

At once the audience falls silent.

The African is spitting blood. Now he's defending himself more carefully. Kaytek makes a sharp attack. His nimble leaps arouse even greater admiration than his strength.

"It looks as if they really are fighting," says the president of the boxing club, who is sitting in a box.

"Indeed. But the African's not attacking at all."

"Maybe you'd like to see him slaughter the kid?"

"No, I wouldn't, but I'm worried. You see, the African is sore now. If the gallery gets him steamed up with their shouting, the fun might end badly."

And the gallery is shouting: "Don't give up, African! Well done, Red Mask! Down with the monkey! Chimp! Gorilla!*"

The African isn't laughing any more. He isn't letting Kaytek out of his sight. He has a plan: he'll push Kaytek to make him dislocate his arm – he might even break it, but he has to punish him. The boy will scream with pain, and his arm will hang helplessly.

But Kaytek's feeling encouraged as well as mad because the African isn't attacking – he keeps skipping around him, battering him from all sides at once. But the mask is getting in his way, he's out of breath, and his heart is aching more and more.

The umpire blows his whistle.

Kaytek slumps onto his chair. The attendants rub down his numb arms and legs. The circus manager fans him with a towel.

"That's enough!" some people are calling.

"Don't stop the fight! We want to see more!" shout others.

The African gets up and waits. He's seething with rage.

---

* See Translator's Afterword.

And so the second round begins.

Wham, wham! The punches rain down thick and fast like hailstones. The African leans forward and takes a punch. He sways and staggers backward.

He clenches his teeth. Now he's coming back at Kaytek.

Total silence – the entire audience has frozen in anticipation.

Sheer terror – he'll kill him. The more nervous people have closed their eyes. Two duchesses and a marquise have fainted. Afterward the circus manager will say he has only seen a scene like this one at the circus once before, five years ago in London, when a lion got ready to jump on his tamer.

It's a terrible sight.

Rocking and leaning forward with bloodshot eyes, the African is coming toward Kaytek.

Quietly Kaytek says: "Stop. I command you: stop!"

The African stops. He raises his arm.

Make my face change. Make it change, thinks Kaytek, and tears the mask from his face. *Now!*

"Snap, snap, snap!" the photographers click away. The movie cameras whir and the flash lamps hiss.

The African aims an enormous black paw at Kaytek's head. He holds the other one low, ready to parry a blow. His teeth are clenched, his face is contorted.

Kaytek is done for!

The police chief takes out a revolver. Too late.

A dull thud resounds as the African's swing sends him tumbling to the floor because Kaytek has dodged in time. Kaytek's small hand showers punches on the African, whose muscles are twitching under the skin. Sluggishly the African gets up; he has lost faith in his lucky star. His fame has been eclipsed, and he's not even pretending now. He tries to defend himself awkwardly. Yes, this really is a fight.

The whistle goes.

Everything has gone dark before Kaytek's eyes. He can't hear the shouting or the applause. He sits torpidly on his chair.

The African comes up and places Kaytek's foot on the back of his own neck. Kaytek opens his eyes, and stretches out his arms with an effort. The African rests his head on Kaytek's

knees; Kaytek kisses him on the head, and strokes his curly hair.
People are crying. There's a hurricane of applause.
The giant gently picks Kaytek up and carries him out of the arena.

Once again Kaytek is in a hotel, but it's a different, expensive one. He's lying in a wonderful bed, in the royal suite. And crowds of people have gathered in the street outside.

"I'm taking him to America for ten thousand dollars," shouts a man.

"I'll give him a hundred thousand," cries another stout gentleman.

"I'm here to offer congratulations on behalf of the boxing club."

"A basket of flowers from the Marquise."

A man with binoculars pushes through the crowd.

"Please let me into the little boxer's room. I'm from the press agency. I must write for the papers where he came from, and who exactly he is."

The doorman bows low, lower, right down to the ground.

"I am sorry, but no one is allowed to see him. I am sorry, but it is not permitted. I am sorry, but not today."

"But my papers have to know. My readers cannot wait."

The circus manager comes out in front of the hotel.

"It's not possible, gentlemen. The doctor has categorically forbidden it. The boy is very tired."

"But I must see him. Where did you find him? I'm a journalist."

"Jump in my car, sir. Let's go dine together."

They get into the car and start talking.

"So you really don't know much about him? That's too bad. In two hours they'll start printing the morning papers. We must write about him. Is he French? Is he Parisian? Does he have parents? Is he an orphan? What has he been doing until now?"

"The doctor has forbidden him to speak. You understand, sir – it's his heart. He's made such a big effort."

"That's too bad. But we must have some information. I've

promised it to four newspapers. And to cap it all, I'm as hungry as a wolf."

The car stops outside a restaurant.

"You order something to eat, I'm going to make a call," says the journalist.

He calls the first newspaper and says: "The Red Mask who beat the African is the son of a drunk. His father sold him to the Gypsies and he's been performing with a traveling circus. This is his first time in Paris . . ."

Then he calls the second newspaper and says: "The mystery boy is the son of a lord. When he was six years old, he was already strong – he killed his own brother in a fight. Their dad threw him out and he hid in a fisherman's hut. Then he took part in some whale hunting expeditions . . ."

Next he calls the third paper: "The little boxer comes from a family of miners. He was born during a fire. He used to haul coal and earned a living for his entire family – his mother, two sisters, and brother."

Finally he calls the fourth one: "When he was a year old, he got lost in the woods. He was brought up in the mountains by a female brown bear. That's why he's so strong. He only heard human speech for the first time recently. His grandpa is Oaktoppler the Giant and his grandma is Mountaintoppler the Giantess. Anyway, write whatever you like. I'm hungry and that's enough."

He slams down the receiver and goes into the dining room.

The circus manager is sitting at a table with some literary types and some bankers.

At every single table, they're all talking about Kaytek.

"Well, what a ball we had with that kid! In all my life I've never seen anything like it, even though I've reported from three wars. I've been on expeditions to the North Pole and the Gobi Desert. I've seen ten royal coronations. I've been to the top of all the pyramids and the Tower of Babel. I've fought twenty-six duels. I've been hunting for eagles high in the mountains. I've been torn to pieces twice – once by a tiger and once by a cannonball. I've drowned, been poisoned, and strung up on an

Indian gallows – in Africa I was boiled by cannibals in a stock made of hawksbill turtles. But all that's nothing compared with today's fight."

The circus manager knocks gently on the door of Kaytek's room, and out comes a doctor in a white coat.

"What's the news?"

"He's asleep. He's breathing calmly now. He even has a good pulse. Tomorrow I'll let you talk to him, but only you, and only for five minutes."

"That's good. Well, I'm off to sleep, I'm tired too."

Outside the hotel, the manager bumps into the African.

"What are you doing here?"

"I come to see boy. I want him to live. I want him not be sick. I love little boxer kid! Him fight real great! Attaboy, he's a gem!"

Chapter Fourteen

THREE PERFORMANCES AT THE CIRCUS — A SWIMMING DISPLAY — ON THE SHIP — KAYTEK THE MOVIE STAR

They say the circus manager is a drunk who's always playing cards, and they say he's greedy and he's mean.

Well yes, it's true. He does like a drink, and he does play cards, and he haggles with the performers because he wants more money. They say he has luck, he "has a nose," which means he can sniff out a good deal when it comes his way.

But they don't say why that is so: it's because the manager loves the circus, he loves the horses, and he loves people with talent.

He spent two months bargaining with Baron Berg before buying an Arabian stallion from him for the circus; the stallion was the grandson of Almanzor and Bela, the son of Reshal and Flora. He entrusted the training of the wonderful Arabian horse to Paulo Dorini, who was still young and unknown at the time.

And didn't he buy the most expensive Bengal tigers for Leopardi, the famous animal tamer?

Wasn't it he who set up the aquatic pantomime show for Mironov, the dancing lady?

And who do the twin clowns Flip and Flap have to thank for their fame?

And who looked after Valetti the acrobat when he broke his leg at a foreign circus in Boston? Who arranged a big birthday party for old Potin, when everyone else had forgotten him?

In order to make money, you have to be smart, and in order to spend the money you've made, you have to be clever.

The circus manager recognizes and appreciates Kaytek's value. Kaytek couldn't have found a better guardian.

"Listen, my dear pal," says the circus manager, "they want to give you a hundred thousand dollars for a boxing tour in America. They want to give me three hundred thousand francs for you; but I'm not a middleman. I've consulted the doctors. They say you'll be fully recovered in a week. But if you overexert yourself and cause this cardiac dilation to happen a couple more times, you'll be crippled forever. You'll have a chronic cough, you'll be short of breath, and you'll have swollen legs – you'll be like a sick old man for the rest of your life. I advise you not to do it."

"What do you advise me to do?" asks Kaytek.

"My plan is this. You give three performances at my circus because the whole of Paris wants to see you. Each performance will only be ten minutes long. They'll be easy displays of agility, not strength. Then at my own cost I'm sending you to Hollywood in America. You'll be accompanied by a doctor, a gymnastics coach, a music teacher, and a secretary. You'll have a house and garden there, your own car, and a horse. I'll buy all that, I'll pay for it. You're going to be a movie star, not a circus performer. When you grow up, you can go back to the circus if that's what you want."

"It's a deal," says Kaytek.

"I'm very pleased you have confidence in me."

They seal the contract with a warm handshake.

"Three appearances by the Red Mask," announce bills posted on pillars and walls and advertisements in the papers, all showing Kaytek's picture.

He's a strong man. A boxer. He's famous!

"In three days . . . The day after tomorrow . . . Tomorrow."

Each performance will last seven minutes and forty seconds – that's what the doctors have ordered.

Kaytek enters the floodlit arena riding the Arabian horse and wearing a leotard with a sash glittering with gold and green sequins. The band is playing. The horse is proudly shaking his mane. Kaytek is waving to the audience.

The African brings in a table. On it there are various rings, bars, banners, and balls. It's a display of agility.

"We refuse!" someone shouts, and then everyone else joins in, shouting: "We refuse! We won't let him! No tricks! Don't tire the boy! Give him a coat or he'll catch cold! Let him grow and be healthy . . ."

Kaytek gestures to show he's not tired at all. The circus manager comes out and tries to calm the audience.

"Just five minutes."

"No! No tricks. Not for a moment. We came to show him to our children and to see him for ourselves."

There are lots of children at the circus. They clap and throw flowers.

Kaytek feels regret, but the circus manager says the spectators have the right to make demands – they have the right to say no.

And night after night the same thing happens three times over.

Each time, every seat in the circus has been sold to the very last one. But Kaytek isn't in a leotard any more – instead he's wearing a leather jacket trimmed with white fur. The African leads the horse as people shout and take photos.

"Bravo, long live the Red Mask!"

The lights keep changing as Kaytek releases balloons of various colors, and fires arrows made of chocolate from a bow, which fall into the hands of the youngest children.

And so the noble city of Paris celebrated its triumphant favorite.

"How good the Parisians are, how kind," says Kaytek to the circus manager. "But I can't take their money for nothing. I want to thank them, I want to do something for Paris – I want to give them a surprise. Please think of something – I can do anything."

The circus manager lights a cigar.

"Wait a moment – I've got it. Let's give a free show for the school kids. But what sort of show should it be?"

The manager gets up and paces the carpet. He stops and pours himself a glass of wine. He drinks it. He mutters under his breath, then stops in front of Kaytek.

"Can you swim?" he asks.

Of course he can. They wrote about it in the papers, didn't they? About the time he went whale hunting.

"Excellent. We have a big swimming pool in Paris, surrounded by a stone amphitheater with fifty thousand seats. We'll invite the schools to a swimming display."

It's a deal.

The swimming display is attended by the Minister of Education, the sports clubs, and the students from four hundred and ninety schools.

They've filled the seats on the stone steps. The weather is excellent and the sun is shining. A kayak appears on the pool, with Kaytek in it. He's doing the paddling. He paddles around the pool, then the boat flips over, and Kaytek changes from a paddler into a swimmer.

The African gives explanations through a megaphone.

"Here's how the Cossacks swim, here's how the Ashanti swim, and here's how the Singhalese swim.* Here's how a dog swims, and here's a frog, here's a seal, here's a fish when it's escaping, when it's catching prey, and when it's caught on a rod. Here's a shark, here's a crocodile, and here's a hippopotamus."

Kaytek swims on his side, on his back, and underwater. He pretends to drown and call for rescue, and he shows how to rescue someone who's drowning. He spins in the water, head down, feet up. He bounces off the water and turns a somersault in the air. Finally he does something incredible – he walks on all fours across the water.

He dives from the first, the second, and the fourth levels.

There's a hurricane of applause.

The minister signals to say he won't allow any more.

"He's the king of the water!"

"The wizard of rivers and seas!"

The schools are given two days' holiday because there is no way to keep the students at their desks.

For two days, crowds of them gather outside the hotel, and the cars are forced to use other streets.

---

* The Cossacks are a people who live in southern Russia and are famous for their horsemanship, the Ashanti are tribesmen who live in Ghana, and the Singhalese are the main ethnic group who live in Sri Lanka.

One night, Kaytek leaves Paris in secret, in the saloon car of the train. The manager sees him off at the port.

It's the first time Kaytek has ever seen the sea and a really big ship. The ship's captain shows him around and explains everything.

"This is your cabin," he says. "This is the dining room for first-class passengers; this is the reading room and the movie hall; and this is the swimming pool. Would you like to see the engine room?"

Kaytek looks at everything and can't believe his eyes. Can it be possible that people made all this, and not wizards?

"What is this machine for?" he asks. "What does that one do? How does it move?"

"That's enough for now," says the doctor. "It's hot in here, and the air's not good for you."

"Just a moment."

He peeps into the furnace.

"It's like a volcano in there," he says.

He insists on staying in the engine room until the ship starts moving because he wants to see those big wheels and pistons going into motion.

"Can they break? What happens to the ship then? Why is this machine working although the ship isn't moving yet?"

"That's the dynamo – it lights and ventilates the ship. Well, let's go now."

No, he wants to wait. He insists that he absolutely must see the engines start up – he loves powerful things. Will there be a big bang? Will the ship move at dizzying speed?

There's no helping it – something incredible happens and the ship leaves port an hour ahead of schedule. A smaller boat bringing the passengers and sailors who arrived late only catches up with it on the open ocean. Kaytek's whim costs the circus manager a fine of five hundred dollars.

"Never mind. It's a good advertisement. Kaytek has done well – celebrities are supposed to have whims."

The oldest sailor on the ship squeezes Kaytek's hand.

"Forty years I've been carrying people across the ocean. I'm proud to have a passenger like you."

That evening there is a banquet in Kaytek's honor in the ballroom. The gentlemen are in tail coats and the ladies are in white dresses, observing Kaytek through their opera glasses.

The ship boys stare at him in admiration and envy. They've read about him in the papers.

"So it's all true, and not a magic spell or a dream? So as long as they pay the money, ordinary people can have ships and trains like this, all these entertainments and comforts? If you're rich you can have anything. So why did Grandma and Dad say money doesn't bring you happiness?"

Late that night he went back to his cabin with the doctor.

"From tomorrow, my pal, you belong to me. In the morning you'll take a bath after some light exercises. Then breakfast: milk, rolls, and fruit."

"What sort of fruit?"

"I don't know yet. I'll consult with the head chef and look in my medical books; it seems the healthiest thing to eat on a ship is grapes."

"And what happens after breakfast?"

"A walk about the deck, then a music lesson. Three games of checkers or a movie. Then ten minutes of gymnastics or swimming. Dinner. Then a rest. All timed by my watch."

"So I'm a sort of prisoner?"

"Yes. We are all the prisoners of our duties. And the more someone is worth, the more he is supervised. You, my dear pal, have great talents. People need you. You don't belong to yourself. It's extremely necessary to keep an eye on you."

He says this in a weird way. Kaytek looks the doctor in the eye and sighs, as if he's guessed what's coming.

"You're not allowed that, it's bad for your health."

"You're not allowed that, it's dangerous."

"You're not allowed that, it's too early, it's too late, it's raining, and you're not allowed that because it's hot."

Every day it's the same.

"Can't you get it into your head that I'm bored?!"

"Too bad. Yesterday you lost three and a half ounces."

"I want to go up to the crow's nest."

"It's windy up there, so you can't go."

"I want to go to the engine room."

"No. Remember last time you had a cold afterward. The thermometer showed two degrees above normal."

"I want to play soccer with the ship boys."

"You know the gymnastics coach has forbidden it."

"What about tag?"

"No. You might catch something off them. They're ordinary boys – one of them has tonsillitis, and they all sleep in a single cabin."

Three times Kaytek tries to get revenge by playing a trick on the doctor.

He'll jump off the deck into the sea. He'll bathe in the great big ocean like a dolphin, not in the narrow little pool. Imagine bathing in the ocean!

I want, I demand, I command. I want to jump, I want to dive deep, to the very bottom of the sea, to the depths of the ocean.

He repeats the command, but nothing happens. His strength and magic power have gone – but why?

Kaytek has grown during the journey: he's an inch taller and weighs three ounces more. The doctor is pleased, but Kaytek is furious.

"You see, you're not coughing, your back doesn't hurt and your head doesn't ache. You have red cheeks. The thermometer says . . ."

"I couldn't care less about the thermometer! And I don't give a hoot about the red cheeks. Even school was better than this because there I had recess and the yard. I could do what I want. I don't like Hollywood at all."

He's just about to say he'd rather be in Warsaw, but he stops himself in time.

So what if there's a beautiful house with a garden here? "The most comfortable, most expensive house of all" – that's what the circus manager ordered by telegraph, and that's what he has rented for Kaytek.

"You're not allowed this, you can't do that, there's no need for that."

On the ship, it was the doctor who annoyed him, and now the

secretary and the movie director are being even more annoying.

Rehearsals, rehearsals, rehearsals.

"Once again. Scene one hundred and ten."

"What for, when I already know how to do it?"

"You know how, but the others are acting badly."

"What do I care?"

Sometimes he acts badly out of spite; if only they'd stop tormenting him, dressing him up like a doll.

He's acting the part of an orphan. The picture's going to be called: "Child of the Garrison" or "Little Jack's Secret." He's a spy, and he creeps through barbed wire fences.

If only they'd get on with the filming!

But they don't – one time the hat's no good, another time the pants are torn the wrong way, or his bag's too big and it's shielding his left leg.

Once again the tailor measures him, and once again the barber rearranges his ruffled hair yet another way. They argue whether the wound should be on his cheek, or on his brow. And Kaytek just stands there like an idiot, waiting for them to finish.

"That's enough," he says.

"Just a moment more."

In scene thirty, where the orphan is supposed to cry, Kaytek suddenly sticks out his tongue and laughs into the camera.

"So you see, dear boy. This time you have only yourself to blame," says the director. "You deliberately spoiled the tape. You'll have to do the scene again."

He prefers acting alone or with other children – worst of all is with the grown-up movie stars.

"The scene's okay already," sulks Kaytek.

But the grown-up movie star isn't satisfied, because she raised her hand too high or held her head too low. So they have to go back to the beginning again.

Once again Kaytek runs up, throws himself into her arms and shouts: "Momma!"

And under his breath he says: "For Pete's sake, hold your head the right way, lady!"

The movie star is offended, and Kaytek has to apologize to her.

At last they take a break. Oh no! The editor of a British newspaper has come along and wants to talk to Kaytek. The head of the film studio is here too. A sports representative has come to thank him for the swimming show. And there's a millionaire's wife who wants to kiss him.

"Tell her to go kiss a dog on the nose."

They're all staring at him like a monkey at the zoo. But Kaytek refuses to play ball.

"You signed a contract," says the secretary.

Oh yes, so he did – he committed himself to all this.

"Just do the scene one last time. You're an artiste, aren't you? Don't you want the picture to look good?" says the director.

"I'm not an artiste and I couldn't care less about the picture."

"This is an important scene, my dear friend."

"I am not your friend. I don't like you, in fact I can't stand you!"

"But why not?"

"Because you're so nice and sweet to me, but not to anyone else. Why did you push that old lady? Why did you tug those boys by the ears and throw them out without paying them a penny?"

"Just be patient and I'll explain it to you. I took on the little girl out of charity, because her mother asked me to. I gave her a mirror and told her to learn it in a week."

"Learn what?"

"First she had to smile, then look a bit surprised, then a bit scared, and then she had to be pleased. The lazy creature failed to learn it. I lost two days because of her. Those boys were meant to be fighting in the street and a car was supposed to run them over."

"I know. They fought badly because they were afraid the car really would run them over."

"That's it. So I chose some brave ones instead of them. They spoiled thirty yards of tape for me. I had to pay a fine for that."

"You have an explanation for everything."

"You just don't get it, pal."

"I refuse to be your pal. I'm going to tell the studio head I want a different director."

"He'll agree, he's sure to agree. He'll give you a different director, and he'll throw me out. And I'll lose my job, though I have a wife and child to keep. He's been wanting to get rid of me; he'd rather take on a younger, cheaper director who's even stricter with the actors. Because he says I'm not energetic enough, I'm too lenient. You just don't get it, boy. You live in a grand mansion and you have no idea what life is really like here."

"I don't," thinks Kaytek, "but I'm going to find out. I want to know."

The doctor shuts the door of Kaytek's room.

"Goodnight."

For a while, Kaytek lies in bed quietly. Then he silently gets up, gets dressed, puts on his Cap of Invisibility and leaves through the garden.

He wants to know what's really going on and what life is like for the unemployed people in this rich city full of movie stars.

Here's what he saw . . . and what he heard . . . .

He sees a poor room and its inhabitants.

"There's no work," says the father of the family. "In a month they're going to make a new picture where they need crowds. Maybe I'll manage to earn something."

He looks inside another small room and sees a widow and her children.

"I have no luck getting work in the movies," she complains to the woman next door. "Either I'm too fat, or too thin, or my nose is too long, or too short. I heard they needed children. So they went along. But right now they're looking for an ugly child – mine are too pretty. So we're empty-handed again."

In another apartment a young worker is boasting: "I have a job. I've as good as earned three dollars. I just stand in the window, I look at a big crowd outside, and then I throw a brick at them. I must practice in front of the mirror because I have to have an animal look on my face. They're also looking for a one-armed hunchback – they haven't got one yet, but they'll pay him ten dollars when they find him."

Until finally Kaytek hears something about himself too.

"It's all right for that little puppy. They treat him like a soft-boiled egg. The papers say he's gonna earn a fortune. The director is giving us all that grief because he doesn't want to come to rehearsals. The tender little punk says he's bored. But isn't it a mercy to spend five hours a day just pretending to choke in front of a mirror?"

"He won't last long. In a year the public will tire of him. They'll find themselves someone else. I can't wait for 'Child of the Garrison' to be over. The worst thing is to act with a star who's playing up."

Later, still wearing his Cap of Invisibility, Kaytek overhears a conversation in his own mansion.

"He's a strange boy," says the music teacher. "Sometimes it's a pleasure to have a lesson with him and sometimes it's hard to put up with him. Sometimes he plays exquisitely, and sometimes he has fingers made of wood."

"You never know what crazy idea he'll have next," complains the secretary. "If it weren't for me, he'd have broken his contract by now. He won't let anyone make the slightest comment. He instantly takes offense and says: 'I won't do it,' or 'What do I care?' He's obstinate, ambitious, and capricious. He'll probably go to waste, which would be a pity."

"He's spoiled and impudent," says the gymnastics coach. "There's no place in this world for insubordinate types."

"He's weak willed," complains the doctor. "He's impatient, he wants everything at once, straightaway. When he had a toothache, I took him to four different dentists. They all tried so carefully. But at once he shrieks: Ayeeee! He jumps up, gets mad, and runs away. He wants his tooth cured with his mouth shut. Sometimes he really does take too many liberties."

"I've sent a telegram to the circus manager asking him to come and take care of him. The kid insists on driving the car himself, and then speeds like crazy; he could get killed. He's also insisting the picture is finished in a week."

Yes, Kaytek is bored and he's rebelling. He's refusing to obey orders. He didn't become a wizard just to do as he's told. He has signed a contract, so let them get on and finish the movie at last – then the circus manager will have his money; after all, he spent a lot on Kaytek's journey. So he'll be patient for one more week, and then it's goodbye.

He never wants to see the director, or the secretary, or the doctor, or the teachers, or the tailors and photographers, or the editors and movie stars ever again.

He wants to be alone and free.

He's bored. He's not happy in this foreign city among all these strangers.

Just one more week: he's started, so he'll finish.

Chapter Fifteen

TO GREY'S CONCERT IN SEVEN-LEAGUE BOOTS – KIDNAP – THE MIND – AT THE MILLIONAIRE'S MANSION

At last the movie "Child of the Garrison" is finished. This evening there's going to be a ball for the movie stars and newspaper editors. The scene where the little spy is brought out to be executed and the soldiers start to cry has worked brilliantly. The studio head thanks Kaytek.

"All right then. I'm hungry. Let's go home now," says Kaytek.

A car drives up, and the director helps Kaytek get in. Quite unnecessarily – he can do it by himself. The secretary sits next to Kaytek, and the chauffeur drives off.

"Have they paid us?" asks Kaytek.

"Yes, they have. Yesterday I sent off the last twenty thousand dollars you owed the circus director. Tomorrow you'll be signing a contract for a new film, 'Gulliver Among the Giants'."

Kaytek yawns. He gazes idly at the houses and gardens, and responds reluctantly to the people who keep bowing to him – they all recognize him here. It's so boring – he keeps on having to take off his hat and smile, again and again.

He doesn't want to eat his dinner.

"You said you were hungry."

"So what if I did? I just felt like saying it."

He doesn't like the turtle soup, the venison is too soft, the stewed fruit is too sweet, and there's too much vanilla in the cream. Finally he eats two portions of ice cream.

"You must lie down after dinner," says the doctor. "You're tired, and the ball will end late."

"I'm not going to lie down," replies Kaytek. "Please get the smaller car ready for me."

"You want to drive yourself again?"

"I do know how."

"But you don't take enough care. Last time you almost drove into a tree."

"I'll be careful."

"I'm coming with you."

"There's no need. I want to go out on my own."

He puts the latest newspaper in his pocket.

"But maybe you'll let one of us accompany you?"

"Stop bugging me, doctor."

The secretary winks at the doctor to tell him to leave Kaytek alone.

"But you promise you won't go swimming in the sea?"

"I promise. I won't go swimming."

"And you'll be back by evening?"

Kaytek doesn't answer.

He got in the car, drove off, and wasn't back by evening, or by night – he never came back at all.

They have no trouble finding the car on the beach, at the place where Kaytek usually relaxes after tiring rehearsals. The paper he took with him is lying under a tree. The only other thing they find is a cane with a silver handle. In one spot the grass is flattened: he has clearly been sitting there, reading the paper. There are footprints leading toward the road, but not toward the sea.

Police dogs are fetched, but they just stand on the spot, howling pitifully.

If Kaytek has drowned while bathing, why aren't his clothes here? If he has been kidnapped for a ransom, why aren't there any signs of a struggle? Why is there no evidence that anyone else was here, or that another car drove up?

It's a mystery – is Kaytek alive or not?

Yes, Kaytek is alive all right. He has run off to New York in his seven-league boots to attend a concert by a brilliant violinist called Grey. That's what he felt like doing because his music teacher has often talked about Grey, and is proud of being his student.

"Anyone who ever hears Grey play is different for the rest of his life – a better person," the teacher said. "If only everyone loved music, if only everyone could hear him, there would be no bad or unhappy people in the world. Grey is not a musician, he's a wizard. Even greater than a wizard."

How could Kaytek fail to go and hear him? Especially now, when he wants to start a new and better life?

Before Kaytek became a wizard, when he was just an ordinary boy, troubled and spiteful, he had wanted to change and improve himself so many times.

"I'm never going to be like that anymore," he used to think. "From now on things will be different. From tomorrow. From Monday. After the holidays. In six months from now. Right now!"

Once he became a wizard, he still felt as if there must be something else, something better than magic spells. After all, hadn't they continued to complain about him? "He's capricious – a vagabond – stubborn – unruly."

He doesn't want to be a boxer or a movie star. He wants to be like Grey: greater than a wizard.

"What if Zofia really is a fairy godmother?" he wonders.

And then fate took a very strange turn.

As he is sitting by the sea, full of troubled thoughts, he casts an eye across the front page of the newspaper and sees two pieces of news.

The first one says: "The long awaited movie 'Child of the Garrison' has been completed."

The second says in big letters: "TONIGHT GREY WILL PLAY A CONCERT IN NEW YORK FOR THE BENEFIT OF THE UNEMPLOYED."

Kaytek glances at his watch. It only takes him a moment to decide. He could get there in time, but not by car or plane. Will he make it or not?

I demand and I command . . . he begins.

What's so extraordinary about it anyway? He just wants to listen to some music, some beautiful violin playing. That's all.

I want, I demand and I command, he continues. *I want a pair of seven-league boots to carry me to New York*.

He waits. He takes a deep breath. He stares hard at his feet. And he repeats the spell.

He pulls his Cap of Invisibility down over his forehead and is carried away by a whirlwind that isn't a whirlwind, a hurricane that isn't a hurricane, over fields, forests and mountains.

It's a wonderful crazy journey through the sky!

The first and second hours of the journey go by, and at home they're starting to grow impatient wondering why Kaytek isn't back yet. The third hour passes, and the doctor and the secretary refuse to wait any longer. Kaytek's sure to be at the seaside as usual, isn't he? The fourth hour passes – now the police and whole city know he's missing and they're all out looking for him.

Evening falls. There are bonfires burning on the seashore, and the fishermen have gone out with their nets; maybe Kaytek has sailed off in a boat and gotten lost, or a wave has flooded his vessel. Cars rush back and forth, telephones keep ringing.

Meanwhile Kaytek has reached New York safely – he's free and he's happy.

He pulls off his cap and his magic boots. In an instant, an invisible tailor has dressed him in a new suit of clothes.

He gets in the first cab he can find and tells the driver: "Take me to Grey's concert!"

He pays for a box directly opposite the stage. And there he sits, in the great big concert hall.

Tired by the journey, he leans back in his armchair. Weary from traveling, he lets his eyelids close, and falls asleep.

Is he dreaming? Can he see? Can he hear? Is this earth or sky? He's floating, surrounded by waves of music that are gently rocking him.

He wakes, looks up, and far below he sees . . . who is it? It's Grey – just one man standing there. He's holding . . . what? A small wooden box – for what else is a violin? He's drawing a stick across four strings – for what else is a bow?

And at once thousands of hearts are filled with all sorts of gentle whispers – memories and nostalgia, incomprehensible words giving unfamiliar orders. There's a strange clarity and warmth, silence, beauty, and sweetness all together.

"Yes, this is greater than magic," thinks Kaytek as he listens.

Suddenly he realizes the music is coming to an end, and that soon Grey will stop playing. What a pity.

Someone disturbs his concentration. There's a man sitting in the box next to Kaytek's; he's still young, but his hair is white. He's all on his own, dressed in black. He's rich. He has a tie pin with a big diamond in it.

He's looking at Kaytek with sad eyes.

Someone used to look at him like that in the past. Who was it?

Grandma! Kaytek shifts nervously in his chair. He stands up.

I want a violin. I want a violin, he thinks.

Kaytek's fingers are trembling and his heart is thumping. He can feel a strange warmth in his hands and his chest. His heart is beating fast. The violin is burning. His fingers are trembling.

He starts to play – softly – softly. Now they're both playing: Grey down there on the stage, and Kaytek up here in his box.

"May I please?" Kaytek's violin asks timidly.

"Yes, please do – be my guest," replies Grey's violin.

The engrossed audience hasn't noticed that they are playing together. No one has noticed the young boy in the box – except for the man with the diamond, the sad eyes, and white hair.

Kaytek plays louder and louder, more and more boldly. He's smiling. Grandma has appeared to him – dear, unforgettable Grandma! She gazes gently at Kaytek and whispers: "Be good, be good. The greatest treasure a man can have is a clean conscience."

Kaytek plays louder. Grey plays more quietly, barely moving his bow across the strings.

Kaytek sees a wide river, and beyond the river, a city on a hill. What city is it? Oh, it's Warsaw. What river is it? The gray River Vistula. Here is a poor street, and a familiar house, and in the house, a very modest room, up on the first floor, down a dark corridor. He sees the table where he sat to do his homework, and his bed, a flowerpot on the windowsill, and a coffee mug – and his dad, and his mom.

As he plucks the strings of his violin, he catches sight of his lookalike.

Kaytek plays music describing his school and the boisterous school yard. He plays music describing the noisy recess. He can see the bench he sits on in class, and as he plays, his violin sings about that fair, decent man, the headmaster. It all seems so far away . . .

He plays music that tells the fairy tales he heard when he was little, before he went to school. He plays Little Red Riding Hood, Cinderella, and Puss in Boots. His music is about dwarves and fairy godmothers, about the fatherless Zofia and her widowed mother.

Kaytek sees the cemetery and his grandma's grave. His playing tells about Grandma, and how weak she was, how stooping, and how good – he tells it all with his violin.

Two tears have appeared in the corners of his eyes; he flutters his eyelashes to stop the tears from falling.

Kaytek's violin sings of his grandpa who was impetuous, of the mysterious clock and the wild vine, of the guard dogs, and the hen that stopped laying. It was all long ago . . . long, long ago . . .

"Who are you?" asks Grey's violin.

"Guess," replies Kaytek's violin. "Listen to me, and guess."

And again it sings of the Vistula, and the fishermen's wooden cottages on the river banks. More houses appear, then villas and mansions arise. The forest is still sighing, but there are fewer trees now, fewer tall trees by the gray river. It was all long ago, a very long time ago.

Kaytek plays a fanfare, like a military band. He can hear the horses neighing and the flags fluttering.

"Who is that?"

"The king."

Kaytek plays music describing battles and fights, victories and defeats, invasions and fires, grim captivity, war, and resurrection.

"Where are you from?" asks Grey, with a soft whisper of his strings.

"From Poland," answers Kaytek.

He wants to stop now because he's very tired, but he can't.

The ancient River Vistula keeps flowing, just as it flowed long ago, and very long ago. The forest keeps sighing as cranes fly over it. The river flows from the mountains to the sea, fast and stormily, then slowly and quietly, in a broad sweep toward the sea.

"My city. My river. Me."

He has finished. There is no applause. Just silence.

Then everything happens in a flash, at dizzying speed, in an instant.

Strong hands seize Kaytek, pick him up and carry him out of the hall.

He wants to scream, but a heavy hand covers his mouth.

He's too tired to give any commands. He doesn't even try.

An experienced wizard by now, Kaytek knows when the mind is agile and capable of performing magic spells, and he knows when it is idle and unfit for action.

The mind! Strong, young, and rich all at once! The mind! Pure, clear, and ardent. The mind! Wise, bold, and daring. The mind! Wild, proud, free, and independent.

The mind! Quiet, good, and sad. The mind! Fearful, alarmed, and entangled. The mind! Weak, drowsy, and heavy.

Kaytek is very, very tired. He's exhausted and his wizard's mind is idle. Idle and helpless.

Someone is carrying him, but he doesn't care. They move along a corridor and down some narrow stairs, but it's all the same to him. There are four of them, strong grown-up men, and Kaytek is just one little boy. They're armed with revolvers, and Kaytek is unarmed. They've even taken his violin and bow from his powerless hands.

"Don't be afraid."

He isn't at all afraid.

"Nothing bad will happen to you."

He isn't afraid or surprised.

There are four of them.

They run out into the street. One of them is carrying Kaytek. There are two others on either side as the fourth one opens a car door.

A policeman has noticed, but it's too late!

Kaytek sits in the back with a man on either side. A third sits in the driver's seat, and the fourth sits next to the driver.

They zoom past brightly lit houses and stores. Kaytek can see, his eyes are open, but his mind is asleep. He doesn't care about a thing.

He's been kidnapped!

The car stops outside a beautiful garden, and at once a gate lights up and opens all by itself. They drive up to a fabulous mansion, and at once the lights come on above a marble terrace and in all the windows.

A footman bows very low, and then escorts Kaytek along a carpet to the millionaire owner's study.

"Please wait here," says the footman

He picks up a phone from the desk and leaves the room.

Kaytek is left on his own. That's fine.

One wall of the room is occupied by a huge bookshelf full of books, large and small. On the table there are some expensively bound volumes. On three walls there are pictures, including portraits above the desk: one is of a young woman, and another is of a boy. On the desk there is an inkwell, a paperweight, an ashtray, and all sorts of expensive souvenirs.

Kaytek sits down at the table in a comfortable armchair and looks through the drawings in a book. Some of them are interesting, others are not. Inattentively, impatiently, he flips through the pages, waits, and stares at the wall.

Who is that boy? Who does he look like? Who does he remind him of? He has seen the boy's eyes somewhere before.

Kaytek stretches. This is boring. He yawns. His mind is asleep.

The mind! One moment it can remember, but the next it wanders and forgets. The mind! One moment it is asking questions out of curiosity, wanting to know, seeking, calling and pursuing, but the next it runs away and hides, it simply can't and won't do anything.

The mind! Either it works obediently, or else it stubbornly refuses to obey.

The door opens gently, and there before Kaytek stand the white-haired stranger from the box with his diamond tie-pin, and the violinist, Grey.

Grey comes up to Kaytek, takes his hand, strokes it, and refuses to let it go.

"It's wonderful that we've finally met. I've waited a long time for you," he says.

"You were expecting me?"

"You're surprised," says Grey, "but you'll understand when I explain it to you. Is it true you weren't playing from a score but from memory? Is it true that if I asked you to play that music again, you wouldn't be able to? Is it true you don't know what to call the music you were playing? Well then, I will tell you its name. That song is called Sorrow. That song is called Nostalgia. Sorrow and nostalgia can make a man's spirit wither or blossom. And the flower of the spirit is inspiration."

"At school, the teacher told us that only poets have inspiration when they write their poetry."

"Oh, no. Anyone can have inspiration, not only to write, but also to play and sing, to dance, to recognize, and to sense things. Through inspiration you can find a friend, discover new truths, and say your own prayers. Through inspiration you can talk to the ghosts of those who have already died and those yet to be born, you can talk and vow loyalty to those whom you have never seen, you can fraternize with man and with dog, with star, stone, and flower. Now do you understand why, without knowing who you are or where you might be, I've been longing for you, looking for you, and waiting for you?"

"No, I don't, maybe only a little," admits Kaytek. "The things you're saying are very difficult and new to me, Mr. Grey."

The footman brings in supper on a silver tray. Only now does Kaytek notice that he's very hungry: all day the only thing he has eaten is ice cream.

"All right then," says Kaytek, "Here I am, having supper with you. It all tastes very good – the wine and the sardines and the cake and the caviar. I'm sitting in a comfortable armchair in a fine study. I like it here, it's a mighty fine place. I've made a long and difficult journey, and all that inspiration has tired me. I'm happy to take a rest, and I'm not in any danger here. You're not mad at me, are you, Mr. Grey?"

"Why should I be?"

"I interrupted you during your concert without permission. I'm very sorry."

"There's no need to be. You don't have to apologize for performing a beautiful act."

"Well, quite. So now please explain to me, gentlemen, what happened, who were those people, and why was I kidnapped? Where am I?"

"You're in a millionaire's mansion."

Now Kaytek's neighbor from the box at the concert speaks up in a quiet voice.

"Yes, I'm a millionaire. Here on the wall you can see two paintings: this is a portrait of my wife, and this is a portrait of my son. They're not alive any more. On the same day, at the same hour, they were both killed in the same car crash. Ever since, I've been living alone among strangers and people who aren't friendly. I am rich, but I'm very unhappy."

"I think I understand. Is that why you had me kidnapped?"

"Yes. I want you to stay with me. I'll buy you whatever you want, I'll give you whatever you desire. I'll obey your every wish. You can give the orders. I'll show you your rooms – my son used to live in them, but I can change anything, just as you demand. If you want to travel, we'll travel; I have my own railroad car and my own yacht. We can live in the mountains or by the sea, in America or in Europe. I just want you to stay with me."

There's a long silence. The only sound is the clock ticking.

"So who were those people, those four . . . er, gentlemen?"

"Those are my detectives, my bodyguards. They make sure no one attacks me and no one shoots at me."

"Do you have enemies?"

The rich man smiles painfully.

"There are plenty of people who wish me ill. Hungry, unemployed people think it's my fault, and rich people are jealous of me, because I have more money than them – they'd like to have even more, but I get in their way."

"So don't get in their way, and give bread and work to those who haven't any."

"If I tried not to get in their way I'd have to close down all my mines, factories, and warehouses. That's because anyone who buys from me isn't buying from them. And if I did that, there'd be even more poor families with no work, thousands more unemployed."

"So do the thousands of people who work in your mines, offices, and factories like you?"

"No, they don't like me either."

"Perhaps you don't pay them enough?"

"If I paid them more, I'd have to sell my coal and iron at a higher price, and the price of my cloth, my coffee, and rubber would go up too. No one would buy them from me. I'd lose everything at once."

"So why . . . ?" Kaytek begins, but he doesn't finish the question, because although his eyes are open, although he can see and hear and feel, his weary mind is asleep.

Grey glances at his watch.

"It's late already . . . You see, my boy, people think, give advice, and try to do things in various ways. Some do it slowly and laboriously, others rapidly, with inspiration. It's late now, but if you stay here, you'll have plenty more conversations with your guardian. He is very eager for you to stay with him. Now it's entirely up to you."

The millionaire shifts nervously in his armchair.

"Yes, it's entirely up to you. I see there's no phone on my desk. The footman must have removed it. No, I don't want to keep you prisoner, and I have no right to do that. You can call anyone you like, you can write letters and put them in the mail box yourself. You can lock yourself in your room or go into the city on foot. Don't give me your answer today. Or even tomorrow. Have a good think about whether you want to be my adopted son. And now just one question: will you be afraid to sleep alone in your room?"

"No, I won't," replies Kaytek.

The millionaire rings for the footman.

Chapter Sixteen

THE RETURN JOURNEY HOME — KAYTEK RECOGNIZES AN ENEMY — A RAILROAD CRASH — THE CONFESSION AND DEATH OF THE DETECTIVE

The mind! – Strong, young, clear, and ardent.

The mind! – Independent, generous, wild, and daring.

The mind of a wizard! – A weak, sleepy, idle mind.

An idle, helpless, defenseless mind . . .

Kaytek can see and hear, and his eyes are open, but his mind is asleep. He doesn't care about a thing. He isn't happy and he isn't sad. It's all the same to him.

Kaytek's playroom is a huge hall with a glass roof. There are several smaller rooms inside it. One of them contains a fortress with soldiers and cannons, some small cars and railroad cars that work on electricity. There are tanks, infantry soldiers, and cavalry. Kaytek has spent two days playing happily in this room.

The second room is a dwarves' cottage, but he doesn't like playing with dolls.

The third room is like Robinson Crusoe's island. There are real talking parrots and funny little monkeys. There are trees which can be moved from one spot to another like Christmas trees. There's everything for building a tent, and various animal hides.

Kaytek has spent two days playing a great game in there.

In the fourth playroom there's a pond with real water. There are small boats, ships, motorboats, sailing and fishing boats. There are live fish in the water, which you can catch with a rod or in a net.

And so? So he switched on the fountain, caught a fish, and threw it back in the water. Then he threw some gingerbread to a swan, but there was nothing much to do here.

He spent a whole week in the workshop, but he broke more things than he made. Everything was all ready, all cut to fit together, and he never hurt himself once.

In the library there are too many books, so you don't know where to start or what to read first. None of it seems interesting enough.

As for the boys and girls invited by the millionaire to play with Kaytek, none of them are interesting either. The boys pretend to be tough, but they'd rather play with dolls than play at war, and they want nothing to do with bandits – they're such a bunch of scaredy-cats.

"What else can I buy you? Who else should I invite?" asks the millionaire.

"I don't want you to invite anyone. There's everything here already – don't buy or bring me anything – I don't want you to, that's enough!"

Kaytek feels like a bird caught in a snare, or like a swallow before it flies away to a distant country – because he has decided to go home to Warsaw.

They must have forgotten about him by now, they can't be looking for him anymore. They flooded his island in the River Vistula, and they're sure they shot him.

"Why don't you play the violin?" asks the millionaire.

"Why should I?" answers Kaytek.

"Why don't you read a book?"

"Reading ruins your eyesight."

"Why don't you play a game?"

"All right, I will. Later on. Tomorrow."

Kaytek plans to go home to Warsaw and get rid of the lookalike who has taken his place and is hanging around there for no good reason.

Even if he has lost his magic powers, he'll go home the regular way. His old, small spells are working, but something has gone wrong. Either he needs to rest, or start over again from the beginning.

I want a bag of chocolates under my pillow, he thinks. One time it's there, another time it's not.

I want a zloty in my pocket. And he's pleased when he finds one there. He kisses the small, silver coin.

He tries outside in the street. *I want that man's briefcase to fall from under his arm . . . I want that lady to sneeze . . . I want that dog to bark at the girl*. Sometimes it works, and sometimes it doesn't – that's how it was at the start.

He'll just have to be patient . . .

Finally his moment has come.

The millionaire has gone away because the workers in a faraway mine are threatening to go on strike.

Kaytek manages to leave the park on his own. He quickly mixes in with the crowd of people and boards a tram. And once he feels sure there's no one watching him, he makes his face look different, changes his clothes, and heads for the port.

The days and times when the ships leave for Europe are posted on a big white board. As Kaytek is reading it, a young man accosts him: "Hey, pal. What do you want?"

"I want a job."

"Give me a dollar and I'll take you to the right place."

Kaytek hands him five dollars, but he doesn't get any change.

"Come along then, you scamps."

Only now does Kaytek notice about ten other boys; the man leads them into an office in a dirty wooden barracks.

"Wait here, you urchins."

They're called inside by turn for an examination.

"What's your name? How old are you? Where do you live? Have you been to school?" asks a man with a pipe between his teeth, but he asks in different languages: "What's your name? Wie alt bist du? Où demeures tu? Andato a scuola?"

So Kaytek replies in English, German, French, and Italian. He tells fibs in four different languages. Never mind: they write it all down in a register.

"Show us your hands. Show us your teeth. Hmm, hmm! Read that."

They hand him a greasy, dirty piece of paper on which there are two phrases: "Don't steal. Do as you're told."

"Got it?"

"Yes."

The young man whispers something to the man with the pipe, who picks up a stick in his left hand, taps Kaytek on the nose with his index finger, and threateningly repeats in his four different languages: "Be obedient! *Gehorsam sein*! *Sois obéissant*! *Sii ubbidiente*! Got that?"

"Yes."

"Sign your first name and surname. Just don't make a mistake. You must write the same name as in your fake ID."

"My ID isn't in the least bit fake."

"Silence! A fine one, you are."

That was how Kaytek ended up on the ship – the same one that brought him to America, but now he wasn't going home as a movie star, accompanied by a secretary, a doctor, or a teacher, or as a first-class passenger, or as a spoiled, sulky little lord, the darling of beautiful ladies and elegant gentlemen.

The other boys, his shipmates, give him a cool reception.

"Well then, what have you got with you?"

"Nothing. I didn't have time to bring anything."

"How much of a bribe did you pay them?"

"I didn't pay them any bribe," says Kaytek.

"Tell that to the dopes, not us. We could get along fine without you. Knows four languages, but his boots are full of holes. Hands like a little lady, but he's sure to have lice in his hair."

The cabin is cramped and dark. Kaytek sits down on a storage chest because there's no spare chair.

"Who gave you permission to sit on my chest? Get up and wait until we find room for you. Where's he going to sleep? It's stuffy in our cabin as it is – you take him in yours."

"But there are already five of us in there too."

"Are you trying to be clever?"

"They took him instead of Mike, so he's going to sleep where Mike slept. You're the smartass."

"Shut your trap! Two months he's been in service, and look how sure of himself he is. Just wait till you've sailed a whole year like I have, then you'll have the right to gab. I make the rules here."

"And the world stands in wonder! He's sailed a whole year. What a pro! My dad's been a sailor for twenty years – he was on the Poseidon under the late captain. He won two medals for saving people from drowning."

They're just about to grab each other by the hair, when in comes the Redhead, the senior butler from the scullery. It's his job to supervise the boys.

And he gives Kaytek a bad reception. Fairly drunk before the voyage, he's mad that someone has wangled a boy onto the ship without involving him.

"Where's the new boy? Stand up straight, you freak. What a wimp! He's sure to get seasick right away. He sure will. He'll mess up the cabin. Have him sleep in the vestibule. Silence! You'll sleep where I tell you. Show me your teeth – are they clean? Show me your hands. OK. Stand by the door. Feet together. Make a bow."

Kaytek bows.

"Do it again. Who taught you to bow like that? Think you're bowing to an equal? Head down, don't raise your mug! Lower, lower than that."

He grabs Kaytek by the arms and squeezes, shakes, and pushes him.

"Serve me a glass of water. Get a move on! Not like that! Not from this side. Smile, you sourpuss. That's no good! Do it again. Take the matches. Put the box in your pocket."

The Redhead sits down, puts a cigarette in his mouth, and shouts: "Give me a light, boy!"

Kaytek doesn't move.

"A light, you dope! Give me a lighted match."

Kaytek's hands are shaking. The boys are laughing. The matches scatter on the ground. Kaytek starts picking them up, with tears trickling from his eyes.

"That's enough, you gimp. Don't come within my sight until they've taught you the ropes."

So they started to train Kaytek. They gave him a green tail coat with gold buttons, and his service began.

They test Kaytek to see if he's obedient, if he's hard working, if he's a big-mouth, and if he's going to snitch on them.

"Hey, sourpuss! Take my place in the kitchen, I have a headache."

"Hey, go to the reading room, I'll be at the club."

"All right," agrees Kaytek.

The club is where the passengers play cards; it's easier to get a tip there, it's more fun, you can find money on the floor, and even very carefully sweep a banknote off the table while you're serving drinks.

He mustn't say he was asked to swap places.

"Why are you in the reading room?"

"I made a mistake. I didn't hear the order properly."

"Penalty shift, all night on restroom duty."

Kaytek's a good pal! But he seems a bit weird or sad – he says yes to everything. He never makes a joke or laughs. The boys don't know how chirpy Kaytek used to be – too chirpy even!

How good they are at smelling out money whenever Kaytek gets a tip. At once they say: "Wanna play cards?"

"All right," he agrees.

He knows they use marked cards. He soon loses a dollar and goes to lie down in the vestibule. He knows he'll be hit by the door three times when the boys on night shift come back to their cabin. But it's all the same to him – not long to go. Just as long as the ship reaches port.

After his shift, Kaytek comes out on deck, stares at the sea, and thinks: "Poor Mike. He's lying in the hospital, he may even have died by now. He was already sick then."

Kaytek has taken Mike's place. He remembers the pale boy who smiled so sadly. Because Kaytek knows them all, these mates of his – they're the boys the doctor wouldn't let him play with on the outward journey. He gave them ten dollars each as they stood and bowed low to him – when Kaytek was "King of the Ocean" and victor over the African – as he left the ship with the movie starlet.

One time Mike was on shift at the swimming pool. He was handing Kaytek a towel when he'd started coughing. He'd gone so red, it was clear he was trying to stop coughing as hard as he could. At once the gymnastics teacher had wrenched the towel away from Mike, and Kaytek had only seen him once after that, as he held out his hand for the tip and whispered: "Thank you."

Kaytek stares at the sea and thinks: "Are these boys bad or good? Are they really bad, or just ruined?"

Today he can hear them quarreling.

"Just wait, you thief. If you don't give me back those twenty cents, I'll tell the Redhead where you got that pencil. You think I didn't see? Don't you worry – I can see well in the dark too. That actor brat was writing something in the movie theater and he put it down on the table. You served him lemonade and you lifted it."

"All right, go ahead and tell, and I'll tell about the bottle of wine you took from the pantry. I gave that pencil to the Redhead, but you swigged the wine yourself."

Only now does Kaytek understand why he hadn't been able to find his pencil in the silver holder that time. And he's amazed that you can smile so nicely at someone and steal from him at the same time, or bow double to someone while calling him a brat behind his back.

There's here and there, there's then and now. Why are there rich people and poor people anyway, and why do they dislike each other so? After all, the sun shines the same way for everyone.

One evening, Kaytek is gazing at the sea and the sky and the setting sun. He can hear a first-class passenger singing in Italian; it's the Italian diplomat to whom the Redhead told him to be extra polite.

"You know how to 'parlo italianno', so do it. You'll earn something, and you'll be giving the ship a good advertisement." But the Italian only examines Kaytek carefully from a distance, and never once addresses him.

Whereas there's another passenger who has often spoken to Kaytek and smiled at him. The boys call him Grandpa because he's always carelessly dressed, or "the blind man" because he wears dark glasses.

And he's in those glasses now.

"Ah, cabin boy, aren't you asleep?" he says.

"No, I'm not, sir," answers Kaytek.

"And you're looking at the sea?"

"Yes, I am, sir."

"And are you having a think?"

"Yes, sir, I am."

"Feeling sad, eh? Are you homesick? Have a drop to drink, dear boy."

Kaytek stretches out a hand, but the wine smells the same as the time he was offered some at the cemetery, and the time at the circus in Paris too.

"Drink it up and you'll sleep well," says the man.

With an abrupt movement Kaytek knocks the glass from his hand and says: *Vanish, you vile illusion!*

The old man grabs the handrail, emits a lengthy groan as if starting to howl, and vanishes as suddenly as he appeared.

Kaytek looks around anxiously, but there's no one else on deck. In the distance the Italian is standing with his back toward him, still singing; he hasn't seen a thing.

Kaytek goes back to the cabin.

"Tonight you can sleep with us," says one of the boys. "We've decided you're a good pal. And it's uncomfortable in the vestibule – you keep being woken up."

"Thanks."

Inside the cabin no one wakes Kaytek up, but he can't sleep anyway.

So now he has recognized his enemy. He was trying to get him drunk again, and maybe drown him, or cause a new rumpus. "No, I won't go crazy," thinks Kaytek. "That's not why I became a wizard. Any old clown can do that, even without drinking wine from a silver cup. He's sure to get revenge. But I don't care. Now I'm sure I'm stronger than him. What will happen tomorrow when they notice the old man has gone? Should I admit I was the last to see him and talk to him?"

But the old man in dark glasses is there at breakfast, just as if nothing ever happened, as if it wasn't him at all.

"Why do you want to destroy me?" Kaytek angrily questions him.

"You must have imagined it, dear boy. I don't know what you mean. I can't remember a thing."

He smiles, but he can't fool Kaytek.

"Just watch your step. Don't get in my way or you'll be sorry," whispers Kaytek.

On the last night on board, the ship radio announces that the latest hit movie, "Child of the Garrison," the masterpiece of a mysterious star, is now on in Europe and will be shown in all the movie theaters.

"If he has been kidnapped, we will find him to take part in a new picture," declares the bulletin. "If the sea has swallowed him, 'Child of the Garrison' will be the one and only memorial to his acting, all the more valuable for that."

"Hey, sourpuss. We'll buy you a movie ticket so you don't think badly of us. We know you ain't got no cash because you've lost it all playing cards."

Kaytek smiles. He says goodbye and goes on his way.

Once again, he changed his face and clothing.

His train was due to depart in four hours. So what was he do in the meantime? He went to see the movie.

He thinks it might be grand to see himself in a picture. But it's not in the least bit grand. He was naïve to dream of being famous. The flowers wilt, the applause dies down, the lights go out, and then you go home feeling tired, sad, and even more lonely than before. There's only one good thing about fame: it entertains people and moves them, it attracts and captivates them, and brings them something positive. But that's a benefit that can be quiet and intimate, that you give your loved ones and the people you meet in person, not one provided by your picture or your name.

In the crowd scenes, Kaytek recognizes the impoverished, pushed-around actors from the cruel city. And he finds himself watching his own memories, not the pictures on the screen.

Until he's had enough.

He glances at his watch and leaves without waiting for the end. He walks down rich streets, and then poor ones.

"It's the same everywhere. It is time I was at the station."

He buys a newspaper and looks for news from Warsaw; tomorrow he'll see it again.

As the train moves off, his heart is beating fast.

Maybe on the way he should drop in at Zofia's mother's retreat? They'd be sure to give him a happy welcome.

He's on his way back – to his folks – to his home!

There's just one other person sitting in the compartment, a man with a long black beard. There's enough room for Kaytek to stretch out on the seat after all those nights spent in the uncomfortable ship's vestibule.

He's longing to sleep.

He takes a blow-up pillow out of his case, inflates it, stops it up so the air won't escape, and lays it under his head.

The rail car is rocking, and the wheels are rattling over the joints. It's a pleasant melody, a railroad lullaby.

Suddenly there's a deafening crash, the car leaps in the air, comes to a halt and leans on its side, then shifts violently once more and turns over.

The lights go out. Screams and groans ring out in the darkness.

Kaytek has been thrown off the seat.

"I'm alive, I'm in one piece, and I'm not hurt."

How is he to get out of there? The part of the car where the door is located has been smashed.

Kaytek climbs toward the window, which is now where the ceiling should be.

The moans and cries for help are getting louder. Until the worst thing happens: a fire breaks out.

Kaytek comes close to being burned alive, but the car breaks free and falls from the railroad embankment. The fall smashes a hole in the side of it.

Kaytek is just about to abandon the unlucky train, when suddenly he hears a voice begging him: "Antek, save me!"

Who could be here who knows him and is calling him by name?

"Save me! I'll tell you everything."

His traveling companion is groaning, crushed between two

wooden boards. The firelight illuminates his deathly pale face. Kaytek stares at him in amazement. His beard has come unstuck, and he can see that the injured man is the Italian from the ship.

"Help me! It's easy for you because you're a wizard."

Indeed, it's true.

Shortly after, the stranger is lying on the grass, far from the burning train.

"Thank you. Listen. I am Detective Philips. You deserve a reward. I know everything. I sent a telegram to Warsaw to tell them to arrest you at the station. I wanted to make a deal with you, but he got in my way – the 'blind man' from the ship. I saw it all in my mirror – I always have it on me. Watch out for him – he's traveling on this very train. I've been following you every step of the way. You drowned the island yourself, it wasn't the cannonballs. The ticket clerk told me you tried to buy a ticket to Paris. You must have stopped somewhere along the way. I didn't see the boxing match, but then came the swimming display and Hollywood. In your Cap of Invisibility you handed out golden coins to the unemployed . . . but they lost them. With one hand you pulled a car out of the mud. Then you vanished from sight. At Grey's concert . . . our detectives were keeping an eye on you, and so was I . . . You escaped from them . . . but I was with you on the ship . . . Your collaborator . . . is sheer evil . . . He's . . . following . . . Enemy . . . Derailed . . . It hurts. It's not me . . . Don't be mad . . . It's a beautiful death . . . Even for a wizard . . . Yes . . . Report . . . You . . . Report . . . . Philips is dead."

Kaytek unstuck the rest of the dangling beard, closed Philips' eyes, and folded his hands across his chest.

Chapter Seventeen

KAYTEK IS ARRESTED TWICE — THREE TIMES HE AVOIDS DEATH — THE CAP OF INVISIBILITY IMPROVED — CAUGHT UP BY A WHIRLWIND

Philips the famous detective had been killed in a train crash.

"That's bad, it's very bad. That's sad, it's very sad," said the Chief of Criminal Police. "We've lost our most talented employee. No one can ever replace him."

"That's good, it's very good. That's amusing, it's very amusing," said the international criminals, con men, and burglars. "No one can ever replace him."

For twenty years Philips had tirelessly pursued and tracked down criminals. He took on the hardest cases. He worked alone. By train and plane, yacht and motorbike, from city to city, from hotel to hotel, he was always on the move. Often, no one knew where he was for whole weeks on end. Only when he had identified an entire gang and its ringleader did he give a sign of life.

When a case was hard, his jealous colleagues would say:

"Philips isn't showing his face because he's ashamed. This time he won't succeed."

Suddenly a telegram would arrive, saying:

Please send five yards of canvas and ten yards of cloth to such and such an address.

That meant they were to send five policemen and ten secret agents.

During the arrest he always stood at a distance, disguised as a woman in a dress. He always kept his revolver ready to fire, but he never did shoot.

He always used to say:

"Your task is quickly and firmly to catch whoever needs catching; my task is to make sure none of the rubberneckers gets a bullet."

The rubberneckers are the curious bystanders who gather in a crowd whenever there's a fuss – they're the biggest obstacle.

"How can you catch a wolf when the trees in the forest are obscuring him?" Philips would say. He was proud that no one had ever been wounded during any of his arrests.

"A healthy police force should catch healthy criminals among healthy bystanders. I arrest people, not mincemeat."

His colleagues didn't like the fact that he held back for too long. Once he'd identified a bandit, he would follow him step by step, but he never let them lock him up in jail immediately.

"Their haste helps us to catch them, and our careful work prevents them from hiding. If we're in a hurry we catch a less guilty person, but if we leave them at liberty for a while, we catch the guiltiest person possible. You have to cut wide across an abscess to let out all the pus."

Once when the police were looking for two bandits in Berlin, Philips caught not two, but nine, and not in Berlin, but in Vienna. And it was always like that – more than they reckoned, and not where they thought.

The "dandy with the suitcase" was a dangerous criminal. He was the ringleader of a gang of conmen, and he always carried a small suitcase with a highly explosive bomb inside.

"There's a high price for my freedom," he threatened.

For two months Philips followed him, on foot and by car. Finally he caught him, with just one single policeman in uniform, at a theater, during a show.

"There he is – put the handcuffs on that guy."

"Handcuffs on me?" said the dandy, showing his suitcase.

"No problem. I swapped cases. I've got your bomb, and my bomb won't do anyone any harm."

"You're lying."

"You can check. I'm not a conman. I even put my business card in there."

The dandy went pale.

"Would you please be quiet? You're spoiling the show!" said Philip's neighbor angrily.

"I'm so sorry, excuse me please," replied Philips modestly.

So they sat there quietly to the end of the show. The dandy went on watching it too, but he couldn't applaud because he was wearing handcuffs.

Philips had sent a telegram to the Warsaw police saying:

Tuesday. Sell the colt. One hundred yards of silk, a hundred of velvet, and a hundred of plush.

That meant: "Arrest the boy. One hundred policemen are to wait for him at the station, one hundred are to escort him to jail, and one hundred are to guard him there."

"Surely it's a mistake. Let's wait for a second telegram," said the police.

They thought they would receive some more precise instructions because Philips always sent several telegrams; if one of them fell into the wrong hands, it wouldn't give much away on its own.

But no more instructions have come, and it's already Tuesday. People are wondering why there are so many policemen at the station. The train is pulling in. The police are on the lookout, scanning the passengers as they emerge from the train.

Philips isn't there, but out of the first-class car steps Kaytek, with a bandage on his head.

"Stop. Who injured you?"

"No one. It's just a scratch – it happened when the train was derailed."

"So where are the mother and father?"

"The train didn't have a mother or a father."

"Don't play dumb. Who were you traveling with?"

"With Mr. Philips. He only just had time to introduce himself."

"Why's that?"

"Because he bit the dust."

"Handcuff the kid."

"My pleasure," jokes Kaytek.

The senior officer is furious.

"What's the meaning of this? It's true he's a wily, brazen little colt, but why does it take a hundred guys to arrest one small kid?"

He sends the policemen back to base and puts Kaytek in the paddy wagon himself.

They set off.

"Sit down! Why are you standing up?" says the senior officer.

"I have to look through the bars to make sure you don't take me too far," says Kaytek.

"So where do you want to go?"

"Not to the cooler, just home. What a lot of questions you ask!"

Kaytek is kind of joking, but he's feeling nervous and irritated.

"My home city is welcoming me the same way it said farewell."

He smiles painfully.

"Well, that's the limit."

He takes a deep breath, glances at his own hands, and at the officer's hands.

He frowns and gives a command.

"What are you gaping at me for?" says the officer.

"You're just about to find out."

He takes another deep breath and repeats his command.

"Bon voyage, Chief," says Kaytek politely, and opens the door of the paddy wagon.

And so the senior officer trots off to jail with handcuffs on his wrists and a gag in his mouth, while Kaytek the colt runs free. Now the know-it-all officer realizes that Philips was right.

Kaytek is looking around the city in curiosity. Nothing here has changed – he sees the same old stores and movie houses, the same ads on the pillars, and the same passers-by. Nothing has changed – it's only Kaytek who is different now.

He walks past his school. He stops at the gate and listens to the buzz of voices. He puts on his Cap of Invisibility and goes into the yard. He recognizes his friends – they've grown. But they're kids – what do they know? They just play games, chase about, push each other, and laugh in a carefree way.

"That's not true! They have their own childhood sorrows and fears, and obligations too."

Kaytek scowls when he sees his lookalike playing in the classroom. What sort of life does he live, that strange phantom whom he called into being? Why does it bother him and make him feel nervous? After all, it was his choice.

"I'm off. I have nothing to do here."

He opens the gate out of the school yard.

"Hey, who goes there?" calls the janitor.

The invisible Kaytek goes through the gate, with the janitor after him.

And just then a boy comes across the street.

"What are you hanging around here for? Why did you open the gate?"

"What? I didn't open the gate. What do you want from me?"

"You know what I want, you rascal!"

"No, I don't."

"Don't answer back or I'll give you a thrashing! Now scram!"

"I'm on my way."

Kaytek can see a flush of anger and sparks of rebellion in the boy's eyes. He remembers how many times he was unfairly judged in the past.

What can you do to make one person trust another? Unjust suspicions prompt vindictiveness, and mistrust kills the truth in a person. If only you could tell everyone everything! It's enough to bring tears to your eyes.

He quickly jumps over the wall and goes back into the school yard. Just then the bell rings. In the confusion, it's easy for him to stop and destroy the lookalike. He goes back to his usual appearance and takes off his Cap of Invisibility.

"I'm me, it's me again. I'm the old Antek again."

He whistles as he runs to his classroom. He strokes the familiar bench like a trusty steed. He stands up when the teacher comes in. He takes a book and notepad from his schoolbag and listens attentively, as if he has entirely forgotten everything that has happened in the past. And so a not very interesting arithmetic lesson goes by quickly.

It's the end of the school day. He runs to the cloakroom and bumps into the lady teacher in the corridor.

"Antek, how did you injure your forehead?"

"It's nothing, miss, just a scratch."

Now he's outside, he's on the steps, and now he can see Mom. He throws his arms around her neck and gives her a big hug.

"Momma!" He can't say another word.

"What's happened to you? What's this? How did you hurt your head?"

"It's nothing, just a scratch," he says.

But his mom demands a proper answer.

"Oh, all right – I cut myself. I hit my head."

"Tell the truth, Antek."

"Well, the train was derailed. Didn't you read about in the papers?"

"What train? What are you saying?"

"It's really not worth talking about. When will Dad be home? We'll all be back together again. Life's so hard when I'm not with you."

"Anyone would think . . . Is someone after you? Is that why you never stay home for long?"

"So what's new?"

"Not much – this morning I made coffee, and now I'm making soup, and that's the biggest change."

Mom doesn't know it was the lookalike who went off to school this morning, but now it's the real Kaytek who has come home.

"So Mom, wouldn't you like to go on a long voyage by ship?"

"Who'd darn your socks if I was away traveling? Look what a big hole you've made."

"It wasn't me who did that."

"I know, it wasn't you, it was your feet. Goodness, boy, when will you ever settle down?!"

"From today . . . from right now!"

"I'd say that would be magic!"

So Mom does her darning, then she puts the soup on the

range and stirs it, while Kaytek sits on a low stool. It feels so strange and so good, better than in a long time.

"Yes, Antek. You're off at school or out with your pals, and your father's at work, so I'm left alone with my thoughts. Since Grandma died I have no one to talk to, or ask for advice, or complain to. I spend my whole time worrying about the two of you."

Kaytek gently kisses his mother's hand.

"So tell me, who gave you that scratch?"

"I'd rather you told me what it was like when you were little. Tell me about Dad and Grandma, and about me and Helenka."

"Helenka was a quieter child than you, maybe because she was a girl, or perhaps because she was little. Though you've always been a scamp – even in your cradle you couldn't be left alone because you'd start kicking and want to get up, and you'd chatter away from daybreak."

Mom talks, and time passes quickly. Finally, Dad comes home.

"Here's your little imp. Look, he's all scratched – he was in a train crash. He reads the stupid papers, then he makes up garbage. Oh dear, what a son you've given me!"

"You gave me the little ne'er-do-well. Show me your face, Antek. You know what? Your old man has just gotten a new commission. Things were getting tough – I just didn't want to tell you. Now I'll have work again for a few months. But you know, Antek, those wounds of yours are strange – they don't look like fresh ones from today, they look older than that."

"That's right. The crash was the day before yesterday."

"Watch out, boy, or I'll have to punish you."

"If you lose your patience?"

"Yes, I sure am losing it."

"His head's full of jokes," says Mom, "but I shudder every time he leaves the house, the little madcap."

They eat supper. They talk about his father's work and the new commission. And Kaytek thinks: "I told the truth. They only have themselves to blame for not believing me. But now things are going to be different. Dad's not going to worry about losing his job, and Mom's not going to be afraid. From now on

I'm going to have a peaceful life and a kind heart. From tomorrow. No, from today."

He helps his mom with the dishes and sits down to do his homework. Poor kid, he doesn't know what's ahead of him.

A famous writer has died. There's going to be a grand funeral with music.

Big cities like fine funerals. If the weather's good, why not go watch, why not meet up with friends, why not have a chat? They'll be making speeches at the graveside – why not go listen?

Everyone is heading for the funeral, so Kaytek has gone there too. But as he's small, he's having a hard time in the crowd.

Thieves love going to crowded funerals too, because it's easier to get into people's pockets and pinch their wallets or watches. The police are aware of this, so they send along plainclothes agents.

But Kaytek doesn't know that. As the crowd presses him from all sides, he puts on his Cap of Invisibility and invisibly pushes his way through, using his knees and elbows.

Soon he's getting close to the funeral cortege, because it's much easier to advance like that. He might tread on someone's foot or stick a fist in someone's side, but he's gone before they have a chance to turn round. At once they start arguing that it's rude and ill-mannered to push, but meanwhile Kaytek is far away, causing more confusion and taking full advantage of it.

The regular rubberneckers don't realize what's happening, but one of the plainclothes agents is on the alert. As soon as he feels someone touching him, he waits for his moment, and then seizes Kaytek by the arm, even though he can't see him.

"Let me go."

"Oh, no I won't. Take off your cap. You're the wizard."

So he's been caught. That's too bad. He takes off his Cap of Invisibility and meekly follows the agent.

The agent leads him away, wondering what to do next. The wizard is no ordinary catch. The greatest detectives have failed to arrest him. He led the senior officer up the garden path, and Philips died because of this little colt.

"If I hand him over to the cops, I'll get a reward. But I'd do better by becoming his accomplice."

Kaytek has changed his face because they might want to take his picture. He's not afraid – he's in good form, as the sportsmen say. He'll soon get out of jail.

The agent seems to have guessed his thoughts because he gently asks, almost begs him: "Please don't run away. I'm not going to do you any harm."

He takes Kaytek to a regular jail.

"Who's this boy?" asks the duty officer. "From the funeral, I guess?"

"Yes, from the funeral."

"Aren't you ashamed? You're a fine rascal. Show me what you've stolen."

"He hasn't stolen anything," says the agent. "He may have wanted to, but he wasn't quick enough. Or maybe I just thought he wasn't."

He waits until they're alone together, then he says to Kaytek: "Listen, boy. You're in my hands now."

"Yes, I am. So what?"

"You know there's a reward on your head?"

"Yes, I've read about it."

"But I feel sorry for you. If we make a deal, it'll be good for both of us. You can see for yourself you've goofed. Haven't you? How smart is it to wear a Cap of Invisibility in a crowd? You're too small. You can't do it alone. So teach me to do magic and we'll help each other out. Well? How do like the idea?"

"Fine. Very well."

"So it's a deal?"

"No, it's not a deal."

"You'd rather die in the cooler or dangle from a rope?"

"What do you mean, a rope?"

"They'll hang you. Mind you, I'm not so interested in your magic spells, but I like you."

"I like you too, but I have to go home now because my mom will be worried."

"You're dumb."

"We'll soon see who's dumb," says Kaytek, and vanishes.

The agent feels and fumbles, running about the room like a madman as he tries to find him – just as if he were playing blind man's buff. But Kaytek has changed into a fly. However, Philips' last words will prove to be true: Kaytek has a more powerful enemy than the police.

He tries to keep still on the wall, but he falls into a spider's web. He buzzes pitifully, but the spider is already hanging over him on its crooked legs, and has just thrown the first thread at his wings.

I want, I demand, I want to be a mouse, he thinks, and changes into a small gray mouse.

He jumps through the window and into the yard. His head is spinning and he hasn't yet recovered when a big black cat leaps at him.

He thinks his last moment has come.

I want, I demand! I demand, I command!

Just in time – and from under the cat's claws a pigeon flies away.

Kaytek perches on a roof, but it's cramped and he can hardly breathe. He flies off, but keeps looking for a place to return safely to the ground, because he knows he can't keep this up for long.

Suddenly there's a third attack on Kaytek's life. He's about to stare death straight in the eye a third time over as a hawk attacks him, falling from the sky like a stone. The hawk's talons are touching his feathers, when in a crazy effort, the pigeon breaks loose and falls heavily among the trees in the Saxon Garden.*

A person. I want, I demand to be a person!

Now Kaytek is sitting on a bench, weighing up an important issue.

"My Cap of Invisibility doesn't guarantee me safety. What's the use of being invisible when, even if they can't see me, they can catch me and shoot me? I'll have to do it a different way. I want to have a watch, and I want there to be four letters on the watch face. And I want it to have a spring. If I press on the

---

* The Saxon Garden is a park in downtown Warsaw.

spring once, the hand will stop at the letter A, and half of me will change into air. If I press the spring twice, the hand will stop at the letter B, where an ordinary watch has six o'clock, and then only my head and hand will remain solid. When I'm threatened by great danger, I'll press the spring three times, and the hand will stop at the letter C, which is where the nine should be. And then the whole of me will change into air; only the watch and the finger will remain, and with this one finger I'll be able to press on the spring to return to my solid, bodily form."

Kaytek thinks through the entire mechanism once again very carefully, then conjures up a watch of this kind.

Maybe because he's tired, or maybe because the spell is difficult, something stabs him in the heart, causing him pain. He shudders, and then everything goes dark before his eyes. He leans against the bench to stop himself from falling over.

But now he has the watch. For once and for all, he has freed himself from his pursuers. Now he'll never have to escape as a fly, a mouse, or a pigeon again. And the enemy wizard is evidently too weak to kill Kaytek as a person.

"Were you at the funeral?" asks Mom.

"Yes, I was."

"Did you see it?"

"Yes."

"You look very tired."

Poor Mom can't sense the truth. She doesn't know a thing, the lovely, kind woman.

Anyway, his secret is exhausting Kaytek too.

"Just once I've met my enemy face to face. But who gives me my strength? Who has me in their power?"

He can tell this is just for now, that eventually everything will be explained, and then he'll understand.

One Sunday he goes to a soccer match. The first half of the game isn't very interesting; only later on do both teams start to liven up.

Kaytek has a sudden, willful idea to obstruct them and get them riled up.

He presses the spring on his watch to position A, and dashes onto the field.

Strange things start to happen. A player kicks the ball straight, but suddenly it stops and changes direction. It's heading for the goal, but suddenly it flies backward all by itself, as if someone had thrown it. As if someone else was playing, someone agile and invisible.

The referee and the teams have noticed something is up, but there's no time to stop and think – they can't work out what's going on and they can't interrupt the game.

But there's a lieutenant in the crowd watching the game who has noticed and realized what's happening, because he can see a shadow moving about the field on its own. The shadow keeps changing – now it's the distinct shadow of a boy, though he isn't on the field at all; now it's just half of him, now just a hand and a head. That's because Kaytek keeps pressing the spring to different settings so the players won't run into him, kick him, or knock him over. And wherever he darts, the most extraordinary things start happening to the ball.

The lieutenant has heard at the officers' mess that they're looking for a boy-criminal in a Cap of Invisibility. So he takes out his revolver and creeps up very quietly.

There's just about to be a penalty kick. The lieutenant sneaks close to where the shadow is cast on the ground; he can hear a watch ticking and the invisible Kaytek's breathing. He takes aim and is just about to fire . . .

But just then a whirlwind rises up, pushes Kaytek high into the air above the field and carries him away in an unknown direction.

Chapter Eighteen

IN THE WIZARD CHIEF'S FORTRESS – THE AUTHOR TELLS THE READERS WHY HE HAS DELETED PARTS OF THIS CHAPTER ... – ZOFIA IMPRISONED

Kaytek tries in vain to come to a stop.

He demands and commands, but it's no use. His commands and wishes have no power, as nothing but a stream of lifeless words pours from his pale lips.

There's a whistling noise in his ears and his mind is full of confusion. All he can see are the rectangles of fields and forests, unfamiliar villages and towns, strange stretches of water and gardens. Until finally his courage and strength of mind give in to the opposition, and he's too weak to fight.

As the whirlwind carries him away, he's like a drop of water in an ocean wave, like a feather tossed by the power of the elements. He swallows gulps of air, but it is sharp and painful to breathe.

Whatever he wants, let it happen.

The last thing he sees is a lofty mountain, a high rampart and a stone wall, and the towers of an unfamiliar fortress.

And then he falls. He closes his eyes. His mind goes numb.

Now he's lying on a stone floor, in darkness and silence.

He's in a stuffy cellar – it smells damp and musty.

"I'm a prisoner."

He stands up and reaches out a hand. He touches a low ceiling. He paces his prison cell to measure it – it's four paces wide and five paces long.

"Is this a punishment or revenge? I want to know."

Two shining eyes are staring at Kaytek without blinking.

A flaming fireball nine times bigger than Kaytek's head goes spinning round it.

Then it's black night again.

"How long will I be here for? What happens next? Is this forever?"

Kaytek walks around the dark cell, wetting his tongue against its damp walls.

Some agonizing minutes or hours go by.

And there on the other side of the stone walls, the sun is shining as before – the good, warm sun.

"I'm a captive in the pitch dark, while out there is brightness and freedom."

He has eyes, but he cannot see, he has ears, but he cannot hear. All that's left is his mind, which he sends back to Warsaw, to his home and his school.

And then he starts to cry.

Suddenly the walls begin to swarm with thousands of tiny, flickering sparks . . .

. . . .
. . . .
. . . .

From the Author

Before I started writing my story about Kaytek, I talked to some boys about magic spells, and to some girls about fairy godmothers.

Then I read them various chapters. I made some corrections, changed some things, and rewrote the story. I wanted the book to be interesting, but I didn't want it to be terrifying or too hard to understand.

When I read out Chapter Eighteen about Kaytek in the wizard chief's fortress, one of the boys said: "That's scary!"

And he moved closer and held onto my hand.

Then I said: "But stories about wizards are scary."

And he said: "Well, yes . . . but this is something else."

That night he had a dream about Kaytek and it frightened him.

As I couldn't change what I'd written, I crossed out all the scary things that had appeared in his dream. Then I read it out to him again.

And he said: "Now it's OK."

. . . .
. . . .
. . . .

Kaytek swallows the refreshing drink to the very last drop. Then he puts his hand against the stone, leans his face on it, and goes to sleep.

These are the first peaceful hours of his captivity.

He wakes up in darkness.

He doesn't immediately remember what happened the day before.

There on an iron table, written in fiery letters, is something that might be a verdict or a sentence.

Some black bats make their presence known by rustling and fluttering their wings.

A large feather pen slowly runs its golden nib across a black metal board, writing line after line:

"You will not be destroyed by bullet or sword."

"You will not be struck by fire or lightning."

"You will not be poisoned by venom."

"You will not be thrown from a cliff."

"You will not be stifled by rope or gas."

"You will not be drowned."

"You will not be buried alive."

Beside each sentence there are some incomprehensible signs and numbers. They must be paragraphs from the wizard's penal code.

So is his trial over?

The sentence has been passed.

There is a small barred window in the stone wall. There is a low door in the stone wall, and the floor is made of wooden planks.

Kaytek rejoices. His heart is trembling with hope.

He counts the knots and nails in the floorboards. Now and then he casts a glance toward the bars.

He tries to climb up to the window: although he's tired and weak, he tries to jump, to catch onto a hook that's sticking out underneath it. If he can reach the window, maybe he'll manage to see the free world one more time beyond the walls and the iron bars.

I wish, I demand, I command!

The only answer is malicious laughter and the boom of distant thunder.

. . . .
. . . .
. . . .

There are laws and there are obligations.

. . . .
. . . .
. . . .

There is the power of free will, and there is the power of discipline.

. . . .
. . . .
. . . .

That day he doesn't receive a meal.

Hunger . . . hunger!

Maybe they're trying to break him by starving him?

Maybe this is the harshest punishment of all?

. . . .
. . . .
. . . .

Seven days and seven nights have gone by.

Kaytek wakes up in bed in a bright room.

There's a table, a bowl, and a jug of water. On the wall there's a clock and a mirror.

Kaytek is afraid to move for fear of scaring away this welcome vision.

Has he been forgiven? Or is this an illusion sent to deceive him?

A small bag of candy would be a sign of forgiveness, he thinks.

He reaches under the pillow – and something scalds his hand painfully.

Never mind. He's enjoying the sunlight and the warmth. There's a fine window with transparent panes of glass, and there's a door with a regular handle.

But is it locked?

Boldly he leaps out of bed. He pours some water into the bowl and washes up. Now he's feeling strong and brave again.

He can cope – he's been toughened by all his adventures.

He sees an envelope lying on the table. Instead of an address, on the envelope is written:

Do not break the seals.

He picks it up and takes a look: there are five red seals – a secret kept locked away by blood-red sealing wax.

It's a new test. A warning.

....

....

....

Here is your right, your strength, and your power.

He opens the door.

He walks boldly down a long, dark corridor.

A resounding echo counts out his steps.

There's no guard. But he is not under any illusion – there's no way out of here.

He wasn't kidnapped by a whirlwind and imprisoned just to be able to walk out of the chief wizard's fortress.

He goes into a high-ceilinged hall.

There are stone columns and marble walls covered in inscriptions in strange letters. Are they the names of famous wizards, or a list of murdered victims? Are they decrees and prohibitions, with their dates?

"I didn't know, I didn't understand, I went astray. It's easy to obey when you know the rules."

. . . .
. . . .
. . . .

He has seen a similar hall before, on a school trip when they were taken to visit an armory.

Lying and standing, leaning against the wall or hanging up, there are swords, sabers, and all sorts of firearms, both new and shiny, and old and chipped. There are breastplates, helmets, steel gauntlets and chainmail, machine guns, cannons and bombs, executioner's axes, and instruments of torture.

There's a guillotine and a gallows.

Just like in an armory.

. . . .
. . . .
. . . .

From the Author

I left out three pages here.

. . . .
. . . .
. . . .

Kaytek remembers an incident from a long time ago involving a spell that hadn't worked. It was in the days when he was just starting to try magic, and it often didn't work.

So that day, he was on his way home when he saw a small boy tugging at the hand of a man who was drunk.

The child is begging: "Please come home. Daddy, Momma's waiting for you."

"Go away, I keep telling you, go away," mutters the drunk.

There he stands in front of his small son, swaying on his feet.

"Daddy, Momma's waiting for you. Come home, Daddy."

"Home? Why home? How do you mean, home? Here you are, go buy yourself some candy."

The small boy doesn't take the coin; it falls and rolls into the mud.

Then he begs his father a third time: "Come on Dad, come back to Momma."

Kaytek feels sorry for the kid. He wants to help. He takes a deep breath and says:

I command: make him go home, make him obey his son.

No sooner has Kaytek said these words than an electric current stabs him in the heart like a needle.

The drunk pushes the child away, shaking him off his sleeve in a brutal way, and then rolls into the nearest bar.

In front of an iron door into the next hall there are two wolves on guard. They start growling and barking, sniffing the air and baring their teeth.

Kaytek shows no fear – he boldly enters the treasury.

There are shelves filled with royal crowns, scepters and maces, rings, brooches and necklaces, diamonds, pearls, rubies, and corals. There are old silver jugs, candlesticks, goblets, and sculpted vases.

There are chests and barrels full of coins, and sacks of gold.

Kaytek looks at it all and thinks:

"Here is the treasure from Ali Baba's cave, like in my childhood dreams."

. . . .
. . . .
. . . .

Suddenly he hears – what is it? Someone crying and calling? He strains his ears to listen and hears a familiar voice calling for help.

It's coming from up there – up at the top of an iron spiral staircase.

Kaytek takes off and runs toward the staircase. He listens.

Can he be dreaming?

A shout rings out from the tower, repeated three times over:

"Antek! Antek! Antek!"

He runs up the stairs. He's in no doubt – it's Zofia's voice.

He tugs the door open.

There's a burst of flame, and acrid smoke fills his eyes and throat. But he's not daunted – he steps into the flames and keeps running despite the burning heat, shielding his eyes with his hand.

"Antek . . . Antek . . ."

He pushes another door open, leaving the fire behind him.

Now he is standing on the edge of a cliff, with a bottomless abyss gaping below him. He leaps, hangs in mid-air, and just manages to grab hold of the opposite side. He throws his entire body forward, and clambers onto the rocks. Now he's sure he can hear Zofia crying for help.

He leaves the second obstacle behind him and enters a third door.

On he goes – he's determined to reach Zofia, even though snakes are winding around his legs, spitting poisonous venom. Swaying, they raise their flat heads in the air and lean toward his face. They're trying to coil around him, tangle him up, and suffocate him.

. . . .
. . . .
. . . .

The last door is locked with five seals. He has understood their convoluted speech.

"Who's there?"

"It is I, the imprisoned fairy godmother."

"It is I, Antek, Kaytek the Wizard."

"I know. I am Zofia, your Fairy Godmother."

He breaks the first seal. There's a flash of lightning. He breaks the second seal. There's a clap of thunder. He breaks the third and fourth seals. A thunderbolt strikes just above his head. There's a brief pause, and then with his final effort he tears off the fifth seal. At once, bright red zigzags of lightning flash and there's another clap of thunder.

Kaytek falls in the doorway.

"You will not be burned."

"You will not be thrown from a cliff."

"You will not be struck by lightning."

Kaytek opens his eyes and sees Zofia's tear-stained face leaning over him.

"Are you alive?"

"Don't cry."

He struggles to his feet. Leaning on his fairy godmother's arm he slowly descends some broad steps of gray granite.

There's a glass door leading into a garden.

They sit down on a bench beneath a tree.

"Have you been a fairy godmother for a long time, Zofia?"

"I don't really know. For ages I longed to be one. As I was picking berries in the forest and weaving garlands of flowers, I often used to think about what I would do if I were a fairy godmother. I longed to know if there really were dwarves, and to be good to all the children, protect the orphans against harm, help the sad and the poor. I didn't know it would be so hard, so very hard."

"But how did you come to be a fairy godmother?"

"I don't know. When I was little, I was happy. Why do I have such good parents, I thought, why do I have such a nice bright room, and a warm coat, and books, and toys, while others go hungry and suffer misfortune? There's so much poverty in the countryside."

"And in the city too."

"I didn't know that. I was too small. I thought the cities were filled with nothing but royal palaces and monuments. A child confuses everything so strangely: fairy tales, dreams and real life."

"It was the same for me. It must be that you have to believe in the truth, but you'd rather believe in fairy tales – in fairy tales and fine dreams. And that's called daydreaming."

"I did my best to be useful. There's not much you can do when you're little – give a slice of bread to the poor, or a sugar cube to a child. My daddy used to laugh and say: 'You'll give the whole house away!' But I wasn't very good at it; I gave my doll to a sick girl called Marysia, then I was sorry I'd done it. Momma let me give away my white dress, but afterward I cried. Once I gave away some bread and honey, then I felt hungry, but I was ashamed to ask for more. My daddy used to laugh and say: 'Don't give everything away!' But what can you do if someone asks you?"

"Well, you may be right, but if you give something to one of them a whole gang of brats will jump on you. Do you know any magic spells?"

"No. But I could hear more and more clearly when someone was calling for help, when someone needed me. Either I ran to help myself, or . . ."

"Or what?"

"Or I sent the dwarves. I'd say: 'Go and help, my little servants.' It didn't always work."

"What do they look like?"

"I don't know – I've only ever seen them in pictures. But I know they're there. They've often told me about you, Kaytek."

"What did they say?"

"Do you remember the time when you were standing outside a bookstore? There was a boy and a girl standing next to you. They were looking at the books too, and then the boy said: 'What a fine book.' And the girl said: 'Go in and ask how much it costs.' And he said: 'I'm too shy.' And she said: 'Go on.' He said: 'I can't buy it anyway – we only have twenty groshys.' Do you remember that? You caught up with them and gave them the book, and you gave a magic rose to your teacher at school . . ."

"How do you know?"

"The dwarves go bustling about everywhere, so they see what happens, and they tell me."

"I see. But my gifts weren't the same as yours. If I give someone a gift I think – 'That'll make the little squirts wonder!'"

The wizard and the fairy godmother haven't finished their conversation when a bell rings.

. . . .
. . . .
. . . .

"Be gone from here!" he says. "In one lunar month you will return for your trial. Do not forget the oath we have sworn, and your promise to come back. Now I'm changing you into dogs! Be gone!"

Chapter Nineteen

CHANGED INTO DOGS BY MAGIC – THE WRETCHED LIFE OF A STRAY DOG – ZOFIA'S RETURN HOME – THE TEACHER'S TEARS AND COMPLAINTS – THE LAW FROM THE YEAR 1233

Kaytek never thought his mysterious magic power could leave him. But it has come and gone, like a dream, like the memory of a very weird dream.

In the past he would have regretted losing his power, for how could he go back to being a regular schoolboy and the son of a carpenter? But sometimes he wanted to be ordinary again because this restless life was wearing him out.

Kaytek thought his unknown enemies could kill him. That made him feel sorry for his parents and for his life.

But he hadn't foreseen this sort of punishment, revenge, and humiliation.

Whenever he changed his face, or suddenly disappeared leaving just a hand, a head, and a torso visible, it felt very strange. "Is this me or not?" The day he changed into a mouse and then a pigeon, there had been no time to think about it. He was in danger, so the first thing he had to do was escape, and later he could become a person again.

It was a terrible moment when, tossed far from the wizard's fortress, he and Zofia landed on the highway – on four feet each.

Antek looks at himself, then at Zofia, and lets out a long howl.

"Don't cry, Antek," he hears Zofia's gentle voice.

There's a long silence, until Zofia says: "Isn't it better to be a good dog than a bad, spiteful person? Isn't it better to be a free dog than a prisoner in a tomb made of stone?"

"No it's not," snaps Kaytek angrily. "Our imprisonment would have ended eventually."

"How can you be sure? If we'd tried to escape or committed some other offense, they could have thrown us in a dark dungeon forever!"

"Sure they could. But can you imagine being a dog for the rest of your life?"

"We mustn't lose hope of being saved, and it might happen sooner than we expect. No one knows what tomorrow will bring. I know our enemies are strong, but justice is stronger."

Kaytek sits on his back paws and pricks up his ears in a doggy way. He's listening.

"I don't know what real dogs feel," Zofia continues, "but like us, dogs have happy moments and outbursts of joy as well as regret and longing. Anyway, aren't you still a person? Remember the saying: it's not the clothes that make the man!"

Kaytek is amazed Zofia is talking so calmly, as if nothing major has happened.

"Well yes, it's easy for you, because you're a fairy godmother, but there's always so much rebellion, impatience, and anger in me."

Kaytek bites at a branch hanging from a bush. If he weren't ashamed, he'd start barking and scratching at the ground with his claws.

"You see, Antek, things happen in life that are stronger than us. Anger and rebellion don't help in the slightest. It's important to be able to cope when it's up to us alone. The main question now is how to get home."

"You want to go back to your mother? But she won't recognize you, will she?"

"But I will recognize her and I'll be close to her. I'll do my best to get her to like me. I'll guard her and try to make her happy."

Kaytek starts growling the moment he remembers his lookalike, who isn't at home, taking his place with his mom and dad anymore. His parents will be getting worried. He hadn't thought of that. Zofia is good, whereas he is bad – whether he's a person, a prisoner, or a dog, he's bad, bad, bad . . .

Side by side they run fast, along the edge of the woods. How easy it is, pleasant even. They keep going, sensing that if they stop, worrying thoughts will fill their tired heads again.

They've decided to go back together. They don't yet know how hard it is for one stray dog to feed himself, let alone two. They're soon going to find out, poor things, what torture it is to be a hungry dog.

But their strong, reliable canine paws carry them more nimbly than human feet. A dog's heart doesn't tire so quickly.

Zofia is the first to stop.

"How lovely it smells here. How many hundreds of wonderful smells and sounds there are – the smell of pine needles, oak leaves, tree bark, grass, and resin. They play on the nose like music, like singing. You only have to raise your head, turn it to the right, turn it to the left – and you sense a different tune each time."

"Shut up!" Kaytek interrupts her impetuously. "There's nothing lovely or wonderful about being a dog. You're lying."

"I'm telling the truth."

"You're lying! It's a bad, rotten, low-down dog's life. I'd rather be the most wretched man on earth than be a dog."

Kaytek refuses to admit that he can sense the same things as Zofia. Now he's getting to know the world and its images through his sense of smell rather than his eyesight. As he runs along, he scents interesting smells, both strange and familiar. He keeps turning his well-tuned nose in different directions, and pricking up his ears in response to distant noises.

Perhaps a dog knows the world in a way that's different, but not any worse, than the human way. Perhaps he doesn't just use his senses, but also understands things? No – no! Kaytek won't betray his human pride – it's shameful to be a dog.

They're hungry, but there's no bread to eat, and no one in sight.

Then they catch a scent of wild game, and Kaytek turns into the forest, sniffing carefully. He finds a burrow under a bush. He has to exert his will power to stop himself from digging at the ground with his paws to open up the burrow and attack the young baby hares. He presses his nose to the hole. He barks once, then again, and dashes back to the road.

As their hunger grows, they stop running. They walk along in silence until late evening. At last they meet a man.

The poor old fellow is dragging himself along, groaning under the weight of a bundle of twigs.

"I must have a rest," he says.

He sits down in a ditch and notices Kaytek and Zofia.

"Hey, doggies."

He clicks his tongue and holds out a hand. They run up to him.

"Where are you going, doggies? Are you hungry? Have you come far? Come along with me, as we've met. There are two of you, but I'm all alone in my old age."

Kaytek feels the sincere warmth of a human hand.

"Good doggies."

Kaytek responds to his petting with a dog's kiss – he licks the old man's wrinkled hand. The old man gets up, groaning, and tosses the bundle of wood on his back. In the distance, the smoking chimneys of a nearby village are coming more clearly into view.

They reach a small cottage at the edge of the village.

"You good dogs, you kissed an old man. You can stay the night here, but tomorrow you'll have to be on your way. I'm too poor to have friends."

He pours a tin pint of water into a bowl, whitens it with a drop of milk, and crumbles some brown bread into it.

"My supper's not a rich one," says the old man regretfully.

He tells them how, one after another, his children have gone out into the world and left him on his own.

"They've gone to the city, little dogs. There's more fun to be had in the city. It's jollier there than with their old father in the country."

Two hot tears roll down his withered face and fall onto Kaytek.

They fall asleep, but with the vigilance of dogs, who go on hearing in their sleep. Now they hear a mouse scratching, now a rooster crowing, now a cart passing down the road. And they can sense the smell of a sad man and his poverty.

But they do get some rest, and Kaytek feels calmer. Zofia was right – it's not worth thinking about what might happen. Life is so full of surprises. They'll just wait and see what comes along. At least they have a goal – to reach home.

"Well, off you go. I can't let a living creature starve, but I've no food to share with you."

And so they say goodbye.

Kaytek and Zofia wander from village to village, from cottage to cottage, in search of some bread and bones.

They're growing weak and thin. They approach people mistrustfully, and keep at a cautious distance whenever they see a dog near the fence, because often people shout: "Scram! Go away!"

And along with the sharp claws of the farm dogs . . . They've also had to run away and hide from whips, sticks, and stones.

"Don't be sad. Don't get mad, Antek," Zofia comforts him.

But Kaytek is mad and rebellious when he has to sit down and scratch with his paws and teeth to fight off the vermin that keep a stray dog company. People don't know what a great gift it is to have hands for work and for self-defense.

On and on they go, in silence, without talking. They have no strength left now and no more thoughts. Nothing but painful delusions – is that the smell of milk, or soup?

"Food!" cry their eyes, legs, and ears.

Until they drag themselves to a forester's cabin. And it's high time.

"Hey there, hound dogs. What are you doing here without your master? How did you get lost? But you're starving, you poor things. And you're fine dogs, not just any old kind. I'm sorry for you. Do you want to stay?"

Oh, how happy they are! Properly bathed, well rested, and full of food.

"Now let's have a little chat," says the forester. "A dog sometimes understands things better than a man. These days the world isn't very kind to men, or dogs, or trees. Everything's done for profit or for entertainment. The timber merchants are chopping down the forest. To them a tree is just a commodity, not a living thing. The sins and the injuries just keep multiplying."

For several days they rest. What should they do next?

"Just you wait," says the forester. "I'm going to the town today. I'll leave the female here for myself, and give the male dog to an actress as a birthday present; I must teach her that dogs are better than cats."

What should they do? There's no choice. Kaytek will have to part from Zofia. In the town it'll be easier for him to find out where to go.

The forester leaves Zofia locked in the hall, and Kaytek runs along after his carriage. He's not ashamed to be a dog anymore; he sniffs, barks, and jumps up at the horse's muzzle – he breathes deeply, his chest full of canine joy. There's so much to run around, so much to sniff at.

"I have brought you some presents, dear lady – some mushrooms and a little dog," says the forester. "It's such a shame you have three cats and not a single dog! What use is a cat? All it does is fawn, while a dog understands you and responds to you with his eyes."

"I don't want it," says the actress. "You're a schemer. You're trying to put me at odds with my friends. It's a waste of time."

Kaytek is left at the actress' place.

Things go badly. He fights with the cats. They might seem refined and well raised, but they pick fights, they're jealous, and they scratch on the sly.

As soon as he can, Kaytek slips away, back to Zofia, back to the forest.

"What's up?" Zofia asks him.

"We need to wait patiently," says Kaytek. "It's a long way to Warsaw. We'll have to go by train, because we'll never manage on foot. Our journey hasn't ended badly so far, but we could have died on a trash heap by now. A dog has to be careful – there are so many dangers threatening him."

The forester isn't pleased to see Kaytek back again.

"So you're here again? You ugly big mutt! You've got yourself all muddy. I found you a good home, so why did you run off? If I were your mistress, I wouldn't let you in the house, you slob."

A couple of times Kaytek slips away to the railroad. They

soon get to know him there. He runs about the station, examining the trains to see how to jump on board and hide under a seat. He comes back from his reconnaissance with muddy paws, and dirties the floor. And keeps having rows with the cats.

"That's enough, doggy," says the actress. "I don't want you here. You see, my dear, I used to live in a big city, I was famous – I had more flowers than I now have potatoes. But it's no good there, it's too noisy – there are more tears than joys, so I hid away here in seclusion, far from the city strife. But thanks to you I'm being disturbed again."

What could he do?

One cold night, as the wind blew and the rain lashed down, Kaytek and Zofia set off on their way, and managed to board a train.

They're lying quietly under a seat. They hear a whistle, and the rumble of the wheels.

Only a boy, who's on his way back to school after the holidays, has noticed them.

"Lie still or the conductor will throw you out." He feeds them the food his mom has given him for the journey: a roll, an egg, a tart, and a pie.

But then their over-eager caregiver betrays them.

"What have you there under the bench, young man? What's that you keep fussing over? Who are you fetching water for?" asks the conductor. "Aha, dogs! Well, well. You'll have to pay a fine."

"They're not mine," says the boy in his defense. "What harm are they doing you?"

"It's not allowed."

They've only gone six stations, but at least they've had a feed and a rest. Whatever you do to help a stray dog, it'll be easier for him to survive another day.

So they run along, counting the telegraph poles. In the evening there's cold rain again.

They dig out a rotten board with their paws and take shelter in a stable. One horse is standing up, the other is lying down.

They cuddle up to the horse that is lying down; he sniffs at them and lets them stay – one animal often helps another.

But in the morning the cart driver chases them out and whips them with a strap. Zofia starts to howl, and Kaytek bares his teeth and growls.

"You're gonna bite me, are you? Proud, are you, you tramp?"

And he throws a stone at Kaytek.

Things are bad for a dog when he's hungry, even worse when he's sick. The injured Kaytek drags along on three paws, while the fourth hangs in the air. The road is even longer now as they try to avoid human settlements, because healthy dogs and spiteful boys love to provoke a lame animal. Perhaps they don't even do it out of spite, but just because they fail to stop and think.

"Does it hurt?" asks Zofia.

"A bit."

So they go on, without food, for two days, then a third.

Zofia is growing more and more restless, turning her head this way and that. Although nearly at the end of her strength, she runs fast, outstripping Kaytek by far. She keeps turning round, wandering about, and sniffing.

"Antek, it's here."

Impatiently she snuffles the air close to the ground – and seeks the scent higher up too.

"It's here, it's here. Our pony trap's wheels went past here. Here are our pony's hoof prints."

She speeds along like an arrow. But Kaytek stops and licks his wounded paw, struck by the cart driver's stone.

"Leave me here," he says.

"No, I won't," insists Zofia.

Sometimes a long journey seems short, and sometimes a short one seems infinitely long. Late that night, they finally reach Zofia's home.

Zofia's mom is sitting on the deck, with a child's bonnet and slipper on her lap.

Zofia rests on her paws, looking her mother in the eyes. She licks her feet, whimpers, and jumps up at her.

"What's this? Where have you come from? What do you want?"

There's anxiety in her voice, as if she can guess.

"She'll recognize her," thinks Kaytek.

But she doesn't, because people only trust what they can see with their eyes.

She doesn't recognize her own daughter.

"Come on, doggy. Perhaps you can find Zofia, since people don't know how. Here, give her cap a sniff. We'll search for her together."

She hugs Zofia, who kisses her mother's face and eyes.

At last the dogs can rest and drink warm milk again. Kaytek's wound is dressed and soon heals.

"Stay longer," begs Zofia.

It's sad to part after so many adventures together, but he must be on his way.

It's easier to find food on his own, though it's harder to bear the miserable life of a dog in solitude.

On his lonely journey, Kaytek finds out what it's like to be sold, to have everyone looking at you and judging you. He finds out what it's like to be kept on a short chain. He finds out how a spoiled little boy behaves when he's given a dog to play with. Fate does not spare Kaytek the worst misery a dog can suffer, when the dog catcher snares him on a rope. What did he do that for? Is it because Kaytek wants to live, just because he's alive?

He tugs at the rope once, and again. Then in a human way he cunningly waits for his moment; as soon as the bars are just about to close on him once and for all, in a dog-like way he stabs his teeth into his tormentor's hand, bites him, and runs away.

He spends only two truly fine days with a poor shepherd. Here he goes hungry, but it doesn't matter, because here he's not treated like a toy, or even an animal, but as an equal, a close friend and brother.

As Kaytek and the shepherd part ways sadly, they gaze after each other for a long time, sure they won't forget each other in a hurry.

Once his strength has run out, Kaytek tries his luck at the

railroad station again. Twice he is unsuccessful – the first time the door is locked, and the second time he is kicked down the steps and thrown from the moving train.

But the third time he is noticed by a kind-hearted girl who is traveling to the city on her own to work as a servant. She throws a slice of black bread under the seat for him.

"Eat it up. You're alone and so am I. But we'll help each other on the way."

So finally Kaytek reaches Warsaw – his hometown, with its own special smell and memories. Taking the side streets, he reaches his parents' apartment without any mishap.

But here there is a painful surprise awaiting him.

He stands at the door and scratches impatiently, breathing in the smell of the room. Longing to go inside, he presses his nose to a crack, and freezes on the spot when he hears his mother's voice.

"Go and see what's making that scratching noise," she says.

He crawls forward, keeping his head lowered.

They don't recognize him.

"It's a dog. No, you've no business here. Off you go . . . If Antek were alive, you'd have a pal."

"Father, Daddy," he whimpers.

"Maybe he's hungry," says Mom.

"All right, I'll feed you."

But Kaytek doesn't want food. He's only hungry for a kind word, for his parents' caress.

"If you don't want food, be off with you, before I lose my patience."

Kaytek jumps up, leans his paws against his father's chest and stares him in the eyes.

"Get lost!"

"What if he's rabid?"

He goes outside, and the watchman chases him out of the yard.

Where should he go now? Why did he ever come back?

"How big the world is. There are so many towns and villages, so many people and animals in it. And they all have a home, a roof over their head and someone who loves them."

He won't go back to Zofia. He's ashamed to, and anyway, he hasn't the strength for all that wandering again.

So Kaytek walks along, not knowing where he's going and what for.

He remembers the old man with the bundle of sticks on his back, he remembers the shepherd and the schoolboy who fed him in the railroad car, and the girl, and the forester. He remembers the people who have helped him, and also the ones who have hurt him.

He sighs.

Suddenly he scents a familiar smell. He looks around and sees he has dragged himself to his school.

He sits in the gateway of the house opposite, lays his head on his paws, and gazes at the window.

He waits. Living the life of a dog has taught him patience.

He waits for the kind lady teacher.

He waits. He dozes. One person pets him, another jostles him. One person says something kind and clicks his tongue, another grumbles that the mutt is taking up space and getting in the way.

He waits for the kind teacher, until finally out she comes.

Kaytek follows her very closely.

She looks around and he stops. Then she goes on walking. When she goes into a store, Kaytek waits outside.

She only really notices him when they reach the door of her apartment.

What will happen now? Kaytek can hardly breathe, his heart is beating fast, and there are stars before his eyes. He feels hot and cold by turns.

"Are you following me? Are you coming to see me? Come in then, since you're here."

She doesn't welcome him like a dog, but like a student.

Kaytek goes inside and looks around the shabby room.

"Why did I always think teachers were rich people?"

As if she has guessed his thoughts she says: "It's a poor life here at my place. You won't get fat on a teacher's pay, poor dog."

They have some food.

"Yes, doggy, I thought things would be different. I fooled

myself that the children would be kind to me, and that I'd find support among them. Well, what can you expect when they don't know any better? I can't just do what I want, or what they want. I'm not allowed to because the headmaster keeps an eye on things, and the inspector checks up on me. They say there's too much noise during my lessons and not enough progress. The teachers they like are the ones who know how to punish the children, but I want to be friendly and kind to them."

Kaytek has noticed the rose he once gave her, such a long time ago. The rose has withered, but she has kept it as a souvenir; it's standing in a small vase on a shelf.

"Yes, doggy. I wanted to be a teacher and spend my time with children, but now it's just that I haven't any choice. Nowadays I'm happy when it's Sunday or a holiday; I don't long to be at school anymore. Why should I make an effort if the children couldn't care less? I'm sad about Kaytek, I liked him very much. I tried so hard to help him improve. But it's not easy to improve a person. Yes, doggy, there was a time when I was happy, but these days I'm sad."

She holds Kaytek under the chin and presses her face against his head. He can tell she's crying.

But there's an ancient wizard law which says:

When a human changed into an animal by magic,
drinks human tears of complaint against humans,
he will be changed back into his human form.

That law dates from the year 1233, so it's seven hundred years old.*

* *Kaytek the Wizard* was originally published in 1933 in Poland.

Chapter Twenty

KAYTEK CHANGES INTO A WILLOW TREE –
AMONG FOREIGN RACES – AT THE BOTTOM OF THE SEA –
AT THE NORTH POLE – BE DISCIPLINED

The ancient law says:

When a human changed into an animal by magic,
drinks human tears of complaint against humans,
he will be changed back into his human form.

Yes! As the teacher presses her face against Kaytek's head and cries, he licks up her warm, salty tears of complaint against the children.

And suddenly he feels as if his bones are breaking and bending inside him, he feels his veins stretching, his heart beating differently, his lungs breathing, and his skin bursting.

He struggles, hunches up, leaps free, and jumps to the door, then pushes it open with his paws and runs into the hall.

He races down the stairs and hides behind a fence.

And his transformation has taken place.

Kaytek is on human legs again. He feels wobbly, but now that he's a person he has regained his magic powers.

With his first command he satisfies his hunger.

With his second command he recovers his Cap of Invisibility.

With his third command he anxiously asks to know the fate of Zofia, his companion.

I wish, I demand, I command!

"Here I am!"

And at once he sees a strange messenger from his fairy godmother, her secret envoy – it's a real life dwarf, peeping out from behind the fence. He clumsily climbs onto a board, shakes his white beard, winks his left eye and says:

"Zofia is waiting to be rescued, O Great Good Wizard."

"Why do you call me a good wizard?"

"Not for yourself do you summon up favors."

"I don't understand."

"You will understand after the trial."

Oh yes. He still has the trial ahead of him.

He has forgotten all about it, but the chief wizard's trial still lies ahead of him, and Zofia too. No! Zofia will not go to trial.

"I will go alone. I alone will be brought to trial."

And he gives his fourth command since regaining his powers.

To Zofia's home, in my seven-league boots and my Cap of Invisibility.

No sooner has he spoken than Warsaw disappears from sight.

In moments he has made the journey that cost him such an effort only a short time ago.

He stands at the window of the familiar house and looks inside.

He sees Zofia's mother sitting in an armchair holding a newspaper in her hand, but she is not reading. He looks more closely and notices that her hair is turning gray.

And there is Zofia, sitting on her mother's lap, excitedly sniffing the air and pricking up her ears.

She has recognized him.

"Come on, doggy, off you run," says her mom.

Zofia jumps off her lap and runs to the door. Her mother opens it.

"I'm here," says Kaytek, full of emotion.

"I know," replies Zofia.

"It's me, Kaytek."

"I recognize you."

They walk along, Kaytek at a human pace, and Zofia taking small dog steps.

They go through the garden, out the garden gate, and down the road across the field into the woods.

They look around; there's no one in sight, so Kaytek takes off his Cap of Invisibility.

"Antek, how did this happen?"

He strains his eyes to stare hard at Zofia, takes three deep breaths to clear his mind and lungs with forest air, and crosses his hands on his chest.

Speaking slowly, clearly and solemnly, he repeats twice:

O Fairy Godmother cursed by an evil spirit, by my secret powers and wizardly command I release you forever and ever from the order to stand trial. I alone will stand trial before the hostile forces. By my supreme indisputable right I guarantee you freedom and a permanent place at your mother's side. No evil enchantment and no vengeful spell will have the power to change my order, my will and command.

A dull thunderclap rings out.

Wearily, Kaytek leans against a tree. Zofia looks at him anxiously and waits.

Kaytek breathes in deeply, once, then again, and a third time. He clears his mind and lungs with forest air.

Then he speaks: *I demand and I command! By my might and power I decree. I call on the sun, the sea, and the mountains, on air, fire, and water to assist me. Return to human form! Become a person again! Return to human form!*

He closes his eyes. His lips have turned white. His arms drop to his sides.

"You are a great wizard," whispers Zofia and smiles, as she tidies her tousled hair.

He has fulfilled his duty. He has freed her from the spell.

Now he's in a hurry.

"Be well and happy," he says.

"Stay here. I'm frightened for you, Antek."

But Kaytek has already gone.

Kaytek has written two letters.

To his parents he wrote:

My dearest darling Mom and Dad,

You are sad. Although I wish I could come home, I don't know if I can. Please be patient. I have suffered a lot. Happiness doesn't come easily. Not everyone reaches his goal by a straight road free of danger. Forgive me, although it's not my fault. I kiss your hands and I miss you.

Antek

And to the teacher he wrote:

Please do not be mad at the dog who ran away so suddenly, and to whom you provided the greatest possible service that one person can provide to another. Please go on being good to the children. They are not to blame. You don't know how much we want to improve and how hard it is for us. A person isn't always master of his own deeds. And not everyone travels a quiet path to his goal. Our minds are full of trouble and we don't always believe things can get any better. Please be patient.

He addresses the envelopes, sticks on stamps, and tosses them in a mail box.

"Either I'll be victorious or I'll die," he thinks.

There are three days left until his trial. He is running out of time.

He'll have to hurry to find out, but he longs to rest.

Kaytek has his quiet corner among the bushes on the River Vistula. He has had it since way back when. That was where he used to go whenever he felt sad. Down there on the riverbank was where he learned to read, and it was where he first practiced his magic spells. He connects his love of the river with his love for Poland, his homeland.

Children don't only like running around. And the more of a scamp a child is, the more he longs for peace and quiet, though he doesn't even know it himself.

So Kaytek has his corner among the bushes by the river where he tried to improve himself and start a new life, and where he used to think about the days when he was very little, because children have past memories and keepsakes too. It's not just grown-ups and old people who remember past times.

"When I was very little, when I wasn't yet born . . ."

So Kaytek goes to his quiet corner. He sits down on the sand and gazes at the water and the trees. It's so quiet, so good to be here. The silence is so refreshing.

He gazes – his eyes are open, but his mind is asleep; he's so very tired. Because it really has been too much and too difficult . . .

And suddenly he hears voices in the distance, and sees some boys approaching. He realizes it's a school outing, and they're coming this way. Any moment now they'll accost him and start asking him questions. But he wants to be alone – he doesn't want to talk to anyone.

He glances at a clump of trees and remembers what the forester said: "To a timber merchant a tree is a commodity, not a living being."

Well, yes, a bush sprouts from a seed, it is nourished and it grows, it thirsts for food and water just like a person – and it also falls sick, grows old, and dies. Maybe it feels joy and suffers too?

I wish, I demand . . .

And Kaytek changes himself into a tree. What an amazing initiation into life on this earth he has achieved! His roots grow deep into the ground. Hard bark protects his outside. His arms lengthen and fork, and he is wrapped in a coat of green leaves. The wind gently rocks and strokes his branches.

He breathes greenery and drinks cool water from the earth. And in a rustling whisper, his sister the willow tells him it's good to be alive and to enjoy the world.

The boys reach this spot. They're running around, calling to each other.

One of them stops next to Kaytek.

"I'll break off a stick for myself," he says. And he seizes Kaytek by the branch, trying to bend and break it off.

"That hurts!"

The branch cracks and hangs helplessly. The boy yanks at the broken piece and rips it off.

"That hurts a lot!"

But the boy can't understand the broken tree's groaning, because it's hard to interpret a plant's complaints.

But his friend says: "Leave that. Let's keep going. You can find yourself a straighter stick than that one."

And they're off. Their voices fade away. All that's left behind is the damage to the injured tree.

It hurts, and Kaytek feels ashamed. Hasn't he done things like that in the past? He never thought about the fact that a tree hasn't any legs to help it run away, or arms to defend itself, or teeth, horns, or claws. Any old coward can attack it. It is defenseless. Totally defenseless!

Kaytek remembers how one time he threw a stone at a dog. And his pal Stefan said: "Don't you think a dog is a person?" Stefan was trying to say that a dog has feelings, just like a person, that dogs and cats and frogs feel pain too.

But what had Kaytek done? He told everyone in the yard and at school. They all laughed at Stefan and teased him, saying: "You're the dog's uncle!"

Stefan had cried.

"Crybaby!" they shouted.

How thoughtless and cruel a person can be if he doesn't stop to think. And if he realizes he's in the wrong but doesn't want to admit it.

Some kids prefer to go everywhere with a pal. Not Kaytek – he'd rather be alone. He's always been like that.

He's walking along the street, looking at something over here, stopping for a moment over there. He keeps seeing something new. One thing he understands, another he finds interesting, and yet another amazes him.

He's walking along slowly and aimlessly when he sees a policeman escorting a man he has arrested. The man's face is pale and gloomy. They're going to lock him up in jail.

Kaytek remembers his own captivity in the wizard's fortress. He knows what torture it is to be locked up for hour after miserable hour.

In the past, Kaytek used to like watching arguments in the street and arrests. He liked to read about fights and robberies in the papers. He liked conversations about thieves and bandits. And adventure movies.

In the past he felt curiosity, but now he feels sympathy.

Sympathy!

I wish and I command! I want to visit a prison.

No sooner has he spoken than he's walking down a gloomy corridor wearing his Cap of Invisibility. He makes a tour of the condemned men's dismal cells.

There are old guys and young guys. What about the poor children of these men who have been locked away for years on end? How are they to blame?

"My dad's doing time!"

Kaytek knew a boy at school who wasn't good or nice. But is that a surprise when, in every quarrel, at once the other kids said: "You're the son of a thief! You'll end up in handcuffs just like your dad!"

There really is a lot of distress and disorder everywhere, among grown-ups and children too.

A lot of distress and a lot of disorder.

Kaytek has understood it and felt it.

He leaves the jail, and breathes the air of freedom once again.

He walks from one street to the next.

Just then a siren starts to wail, and an ambulance comes speeding toward the hospital. Kaytek jumps onto the running board.

The ambulance is taking an injured man to the hospital. It stops outside, and the paramedics carry the man in. A doctor examines him, and says they'll have to do an operation.

They take off the man's blood-stained clothes and lay him on a wheeled stretcher. In his Cap of Invisibility, Kaytek goes into the operating theater and stands very close.

They stick a needle into the injured man to give him an injection of medicine. They put a mask on his face and pour drops on it to make him go to sleep. They tell him to count: "One . . . two . . . three . . . four."

"That's it, he's asleep. Let's get started."

The doctors wash their hands very thoroughly. They cover the injured man's chest with a cloth, and then the surgeon cuts his skin with a scalpel. In a spot where blood appears, he clamps the bleeding with a pair of pincers. One young doctor helps him, while another passes them the instruments. No one says a word, but they can understand each other without talking. Each of them makes the right move at the right time. They cut and sew a live person while he sleeps.

It's not magic, it's science.

Still invisible, Kaytek goes into a hospital ward. There are two rows of beds. One patient is moaning, another starts coughing, and a third one is chattering.

Suddenly Kaytek hears laughter in the corner by the wall.

There's a boy sitting on the bed, laughing and describing his accident.

"... So after the tram ran me over, I started trying to get away, because I saw a policeman. I was so scared it didn't hurt much. I would have high-tailed it out of there, but some people stopped me. They said: 'Look, you idiot.' And there was blood sloshing in my shoe, and my foot felt hot, though it didn't hurt yet. It only hurt later, when they carried me into a store."

"You shouldn't have tried jumping onto a moving tram."

"Yeah, I know. If Dad was alive, I wouldn't have to be out selling newspapers. But what can I do when there are four of us at home, and the little ones are bawling because they're hungry? I gave my mom two zlotys and just had a slice of bread and some soda water for myself because my throat was dry from shouting."

"Cold water's not good for a warmed-up throat."

"I know. They were going to cut my foot off because the doctor said the wound wouldn't heal because my shoe was dirty. But it did heal up. I've only lost two toes. It's nothing."

Kaytek wanders through the hospital wards.

"There's a lot of distress and disorder in the world."

Suddenly he thinks: *I want to see the world. I want to see the whole world. I want to know what there is on the earth, under the water, and in countries where there's eternal ice and winter. I want to see the lives of Africans, cowboys, and the Chinese . . . I want to see it all.*

No sooner has he spoken than a whirlwind carries him away to the wild land of Africa.

He sees tall palm trees, strange animals and birds, and people with black skin. They live in poor tents or mud huts and have miserable bits of junk for utensils and equipment. They have weird decorations in their ears and lips. When you study history, it's incredible to think that white men lived just the same way as them, a long, long time ago.

Next the whirlwind carries Kaytek to the ancient land of the Chinese. He remembers what he learned at school – these amazing people were printing books, producing glass and beautiful silk cloth when Europeans hadn't yet learned to do anything.

"Why did they let themselves be overtaken? Why have they

fallen into slavery? Why are there so many lame people and beggars here?" thinks Kaytek. "Don't they have any doctors? Why don't their compatriots help them? Poland shouldn't and mustn't let itself get overtaken. People have to study and read books, they have to work and help each other, including the Chinese and the Africans."

Kaytek walks along the streets of a Chinese city, thinking hard.

"I was a bad student. I wrote sloppily. My exercise books were a mess. I wasted so much time. I kept falling out with my classmates, I quarreled and had fights. I was a bad citizen."

I want to see what's at the bottom of the sea! says Kaytek.

No sooner has he spoken than he's wearing a diver's helmet and has weights attached to his feet as he plunges deep into the ocean.

Through a green curtain of water he sees a whole new world, hidden from human sight. Startled fish dart away in all directions. On the sea bed lies the black wreck of a ship resting against a large rock. He sees the transparent veils of jellyfish, the tentacles of octopuses, snail shells, starfish, crabs, sponges, and corals.

"How much life there is on Earth that no one knows about!"

But Kaytek is wrong. People do explore the bottom of the ocean and its secrets, and they write countless books about it. As a heroic explorer, man reaches every corner of the globe through his thoughts, words, and deeds. He encompasses the stars, the past, and the future.

I want to see the North Pole, says Kaytek.

No sooner has he spoken than a magic carpet carries him away.

He passes forests and fields – then he sees nothing but stunted bushes and moss. He sees reindeer, strange birds called penguins,* polar bears, whales, and seals.

Finally he can see nothing but snow and icebergs and Eskimo

* Penguins are actually only native to the Southern Hemisphere.

settlements. What strange people! They love their homeland and its lifeless white plains.

Kaytek blinks because the brightness is so dazzling – there is pure white silence, a sharp wind, and a sun that doesn't warm. The wind is cruel, and there are deep crevasses, abysses made of ice.

Silence.

Hush!

Here is someone's sled, a broken sled.

Inured to the climate, Kaytek walks across the snowdrifts. Tiny needles of cold air sting him like mosquitoes.

He looks around him, scanning the white plain.

Silence.

Hush!

He sees a sign left by man: a solitary mound of stones. Between two of the stones there's a faded flag fluttering. This is the grave of a fearless man.

Kaytek stops and bares his head.

Hush!

He hears a voice, quietly saying:

"Be alert! Be disciplined! Be brave."

Kaytek replies in a whisper.

He raises his hand and says:

"I promise."

Translator's Afterword

TRANSLATOR'S AFTERWORD

"Who would you like to be when you grow up?" Janusz Korczak asked a class of boys. "A wizard," one of them replied. The others started laughing, and the boy felt embarrassed, so then he said: "I'm sure I'll be a judge like my father, but you asked who we'd *like* to be." That was in 1929, and four years later *Kaytek the Wizard* was published, the story of a wayward boy who develops extraordinary magical powers.

Janusz Korczak is a household name in Poland, but this remarkable man really deserves to be far better known to the wider world, as a writer and as a pioneer of children's rights.

Who was Janusz Korczak?

Janusz Korczak was the pen name of Dr. Henryk Goldszmit (1878–1942), a pediatrician and child psychologist who famously ran a central Warsaw orphanage for Jewish children, using his own innovative principles. He not only wrote books for children, but also about children, in particular how they should be treated by adults.

As an educator, he was one of the first defenders of children's rights. In the words of Marek Michalak, Poland's official Ombudsman for Children since 2008, Korczak "very clearly stressed that children are not just the object of care and concern on the part of adults, but that they have their own subjective existence because – as he justified it in a simple way – 'there aren't any children, there are just people.'" Describing him as her hero, writer and academic Eva Hoffman says Korczak's "educational beliefs were informed less by theory than by large-minded humanism. He believed in the full dignity of children . . . and their need for love and respect."

On gaining his medical diploma in 1905, Korczak worked at the Berson and Bauman Children's Hospital in Warsaw, an institution that provided free health care for Jewish children. After serving as an army doctor in the Russo-Japanese war of 1905, in 1909 he became head of the city-center orphanage established by the Help the Orphans Society. As Eva Hoffman puts it, "he ran it like a microcosmic democracy." The children not only helped with domestic chores on work shifts for which they were paid, but had their own parliament and court. If anyone broke the internal legal code – including Korczak and the few other staff members too – their case was "tried" and a suitable penalty applied, though forgiveness, fairness, and leniency were the defining features of this justice. The orphanage also had its own newspaper. So the orphans learned not just practical skills for life and how to be responsible citizens, but ethical values, such as love, sympathy, respect, and how to act for the common good.

Korczak managed to exercise these principles in difficult circumstances within the atmosphere of prejudice against Jews that prevailed in inter-war Poland. Society was divided, with Jews at best treated as second-class citizens, and at worst abused, making it doubly hard for the orphans to find their way in life. Raising money for the orphans and for deprived children to go on summer holidays in the countryside required a constant effort to which Korczak was entirely devoted throughout his life.

Perhaps the most enduring fact about Korczak is that when the Nazis occupied Poland in 1939 and forced all the Jews to live in ghettos, he never abandoned the two hundred children in his care. The diary he wrote in the final months of his life, when the orphanage had been moved into the Warsaw ghetto, is poignant proof of his total dedication to them. Despite extreme conditions in the overcrowded ghetto, where starvation and typhoid were a constant threat and people were dying in the streets, Korczak refused to yield to the Nazi determination to deprive the Jews of their humanity, and continued to organize every possible sort of intellectual and spiritual provision for the children, such as concerts, plays, talks, and discussions of philosophy.

An eye-witness account by the pianist Władysław Szpilman describes the tragic final procession of Korczak and the orphans across the ghetto to the Umschlagplatz, from where the transports left for the death camps: "He told the orphans they should be happy, because they were going to the countryside.... When I ran into them on Gęsia Street they were walking along, singing in chorus, beaming . . . and Korczak was carrying two of the smallest, also smiling, in his arms, and telling them something amusing." "He was true to his convictions to the very end of his life," says Michalak, "when along with the children in his care, he died in the gas chamber at Treblinka concentration camp." It happened in early August 1942.

Korczak the writer

Korczak left behind a large written legacy including books on education – the most famous of which is *How to Love a Child* (1918) – stories, plays, essays, letters, and of course novels and stories for children. The best known is *King Matt the First* (1922), the story of an orphaned prince who inherits his father's throne at a very young age. Despite the efforts of his ministers and other adults to prevent him from being more than just a figurehead or to save his country from war, King Matt boldly runs away to fight at the front and wins the love and admiration of his people. But when he tries to reform the country according to principles of fairness and generosity, letting the children run everything while the adults go back to school, his utopian experiments end in disaster. At the end of the story he loses a second war, and is forced into exile on a desert island. In a series of exciting episodes that make entertaining reading, Matt goes through recognizable stages of development, rebelling against the adults to gain his independence, learning how to be an adult himself, and forging an identity through relationships with others and some difficult experiences.

King Matt the First ends sadly, and so does its sequel, *King Matt on the Desert Island*. Korczak's children's books do not hide the realities of life from their readers, but often confront them with the sort of problems that life presents, including unfair treatment from adults, the hardships of poverty, and the demands of working for a living. *Kaytek the Wizard* is a fine example of how Korczak's novels for children were not only designed to entertain, but also to educate.

The sources of inspiration for *Kaytek the Wizard*

Kaytek the Wizard aimed to be the answer to every child's dream of freeing him or herself from the endless control of adults, and then shaping the world to his or her own designs. From the very start Korczak based the book on suggestions made by children with lively imaginations about how they would behave if they had magical powers. For instance, he had come across educational methods at a school for "morally neglected" delinquent boys, where the students were asked what they would do if they were invisible. "If I was invisible I'd play tricks on policemen," said one boy, "I'd take his gun and kick him." "I'd go to the movies for free," said another. But a different boy said: "If I was invisible I'd help everyone . . . I wouldn't play tricks or make people sad."

Their replies are recognizable in the behavior of Kaytek, who sometimes uses his magic powers to do people favors, and sometimes to cause willful mischief. Like them, Kaytek is a troubled boy, a little rascal who can't conform and please the grown-ups, however hard he tries. As the psychologist characterizes him in Chapter Eleven, "he is not evil, but he loses his temper very easily. When he does something bad, he's sorry, but he refuses to take the blame . . . everything quickly bores him . . . . He's impatient, he lacks discipline, and he's a prankster – those are his shortcomings. He has a good heart – that is his virtue."

Kaytek probably owes some of his character to one of Korczak's favorite children, a boy called Adaś Piekołek. At the orphanage, Adaś came to symbolize the type of troubled child who was highly intelligent but naughty and wayward. Like Adaś, Kaytek is restless and bored, but also full of natural curiosity, fascinated by mysterious and unusual discoveries. Like

Adaś, Kaytek is from an impoverished background. Kaytek's father has problems finding work, and the boy knows what it is like to go without. Thus Kaytek is a hero with whom Korczak's original readers could identify.

"Every child should be able to find a book that is close to his heart," said Korczak. But he also believed that literature should give guidance. Just as King Matt finds out that being king involves huge responsibility and that his decisions can backfire on him, so Kaytek discovers that his powers have limits and that misusing his magic spells can do harm and cause sorrow. He also learns that good intentions can be misunderstood: when he tries to make the world a better place, his efforts are met with suspicion and then physical attack. "Korczak wants to give children rights, to put them in charge of themselves and the world," writes literary scholar Hanna Kirchner, "but at the same time he implies that first there must be a tough lesson in self-discipline."

Besides including ideas from the children's own imaginations, *Kaytek the Wizard* also features many allusions to their favorite adventure and fantasy stories, as well as to popular culture of the day including movies, comics, and the tabloid press. Kaytek's parents read him Ali Baba and Little Red Riding Hood, and he also refers to traditional Polish legends about Madey the robber chief and Boruta the devil, for instance. There are plenty of familiar images from fairy tales, such as the Cap of Invisibility and the seven-league boots. There are also scenes and characters that parody the contemporary world, for example the session of the League of Nations, the scenes on the ocean liner, and characters such as the spiritualist, and the astronomer who talks about aliens.

Some phrases in the book sound extremely politically incorrect to the modern ear, but would not have been considered unusual when the book was written, such as pejorative references to black people as cannibals or apes, and to Jews as inferiors. Wishing to remain faithful to Korczak's original text, the publishers have chosen to leave these phrases as they were written.

One of the biggest targets for Korczak's satire in this book is Hollywood. Korczak often took the children in his care to the cinema, and on the way home they had lively but serious discussions about the cowboy and other adventure movies they had seen. He wrote about the value of well-chosen movies as a source of knowledge and experience for children. There is evidence to imply that he hoped *Kaytek the Wizard* would be made into a movie. However, he was not a fan of the then new Disney movies, and criticized the studio for showing children terrifying images. Kaytek's experiences of Hollywood, where he is treated like a prisoner, illustrate Korczak's generally critical view of Hollywood as a place that exploited its talented child stars.

How *Kaytek* was written

The story took several years to form in Korczak's imagination, and clearly underwent change while it was being written. As becomes obvious in Chapter Eighteen when the author addresses the readers directly, Korczak consulted the orphanage children throughout the creative process. The memoirs of a colleague named Czesław Hakke confirm this: "For many evenings . . . the Dear Doctor invited the children after supper to read the next chapter of his book. I was a witness to some of these meetings between the author and his future readers. After reading an extract, they started to discuss if it was all right, or if something needed to be changed. Generally the children accepted Korczak's exploits, but there were also critical voices, and conclusions that some events should be 'corrected.' Sometimes Korczak justified a particular situation, saying it had to be like this and not different, and sometimes he agreed and made a relevant note."

The book was originally published in episodes in a children's newspaper. The fact that the chapters most obviously written in consultation with the orphanage children are incomplete implies that the text may already have been at proof stage when it was discussed with them, so there was no opportunity for major rewriting. However, when the entire story was published as a book it retained the original text, so perhaps Korczak wanted the children's contribution to be evident. Unfortunately no information has survived to tell us about Kaytek's adventures in the original draft which the children found so terrifying that they asked Korczak to remove them. We shall also never know if the story ever had an ending.

Kaytek the Wizard in English

Although this is the first translation of *Kaytek the Wizard* into English, a number of Korczak's books have appeared in English and other languages. *Kaytek* has previously been published in German, Spanish, Hebrew, and most recently French.

In the Polish original, Kaytek's name is "Kajtuś," the diminutive of the name Kajetan, which is the Polish equivalent of the Roman name Caietanus, which still exists in Italian as Gaetano. As this name only exists in English as the very esoteric Cajetan, it was hard to select a suitable name for him in this translation that English-language readers could recognize. After experimenting with various options based on alliteration and other Polish saints' names, I followed the French translators' example and chose another diminutive of Kajetan, "Kajtek," with the spelling changed to the more manageable "Kaytek." In fact the hero is called Antek (short for Antoni), but is nicknamed "Kajtuś" by a passing soldier in Chapter II. The soldier calls the child "Kajtuś" because in the era when the book was written, the name was used as a general form of address for any little boy, but regrettably, I could find no better way to convey this nuance in translation.

The language of Korczak's writing is very rich, ranging from lively, realistic dialogue to poetic, dream-like descriptions. Kaytek's speech would have sounded perfectly natural to his original readers, including slang phrases that were current in the early 1930s. I have aimed to make the translation accessible to modern readers but without introducing anachronisms. I have also kept all the Polish features of the story, including the Warsaw settings, cultural, and historical references. This has meant adding some footnotes which may look a little academic, but which I hope the readers will find helpful.

I would like to thank Joanna Olczak-Ronikier for letting me read her biography of Janusz Korczak in manuscript, and to acknowledge my debt of gratitude to the French translators Malinka Zanger and Yvette Métral, whose translation, *Kaytek le Magicién*, was very helpful to me.

–Antonia Lloyd-Jones, London, April 2011

References

Eva Hoffman, *My Hero: Janusz Korczak*, "The Guardian," London, 9 April 2011.

Hanna Kirchner (ed), *Janusz Korczak – pisarz, wychowawca, myśliciel* ("Janusz Korczak – writer, educator and thinker"), Instytut Badań Literackich PAN, Warsaw, 1997.

Janusz Korczak, *Dzieła* ("Collected Works"), Vol. XII, Oficyna Wydawnicza Latona, Warsaw 1998, introduction entitled *Geneza utworu* ("The Genesis of the Work") by Józefa Bartnicka.

Janusz Korczak, *King Matt the First*, translated by Richard Lourie, Farrar, Straus & Giroux, New York, 1986.

Ivan Michałak, *2012 Rokiem Korczaka?* ("Will 2012 be Korczak Year?"), Polish Book Institute website, 10 February 2011.

Joanna Olczak-Ronikier, *Korczak: Próba biografii* ("Korczak, An Attempt at a Biography"), Wydawnictwo W.A.B., Warsaw, May 2011.